"I want to report a missing child."

Lena took a long, quavering breath. "Kimberly Lee Portillo, six years old, last seen at Jefferson Elementary School about four this afternoon."

"Your name, please."

And so she went through the whole rigmarole, the endless red tape, the questions.

"I'm sending a patrol car to your house, ma'am. If you have a recent picture of the missing child, it will be helpful."

The missing child. "Yes," she said faintly, "I have one."

She wasn't aware she was still holding the phone until her mother took it out of her hand. Gloria hugged her and said carefully, "Call Mike, honey."

Somewhere inside Lena a flame of anger ignited. She welcomed it, a relief from the dread, a momentary respite from her suffering. "No," she said with finality. "Never."

ABOUT THE AUTHOR

Lynn Erickson is the nom de plume of neighbors Carla Peltonen and Molly Swanton. Their writing partnership has been a long and successful one, stemming from common interests, extensive travel and insatiable curiosity. Now they live in Aspen, Colorado, with their families, a setting they put to good use in many of their books.

Books by Lynn Erickson

Don't miss any of our special offers. Write to us at the following address for information on our newest releases.

Harlequin Reader Service
U.S.: 3010 Walden Ave., P.O. Box 1325, Buffalo, NY 14269
Canadian: P.O. Box 609, Fort Erie, Ont. L2A 5X3

CHILD OF MINE
Lynn Erickson

Harlequin Books

TORONTO • NEW YORK • LONDON
AMSTERDAM • PARIS • SYDNEY • HAMBURG
STOCKHOLM • ATHENS • TOKYO • MILAN
MADRID • WARSAW • BUDAPEST • AUCKLAND

ISBN 0-373-70782-7

CHILD OF MINE

CHILD OF MINE

CHAPTER ONE

LENA PORTILLO RAN a tight ship at Al's Auto Body. She was secretary, mother, slave driver and psychologist all in one. In her cluttered office in front of the cavernous garage on Canoga Avenue in Canoga Park, California, she managed every facet of Al's business—everything except the actual repairs.

Al must have known he had a treasure; in the five years Lena had worked for him, he'd seen more profits and had more peace of mind than he'd ever had before. He paid her pretty darn well, too—for a *female,* he loved to joke. Lena's last raise made her salary thirty-two thousand dollars a year, more than she ever could have imagined, but increasingly less than she needed. Like everyone else, she guessed.

Lena hung up the phone and glanced at the grimy schoolroom clock on the wall. Four o'clock. Her mother, Gloria, would have picked Kimmy up at school by now. *Thank heavens for Mom,* Lena thought. She couldn't imagine how she'd hold down this job without Gloria's help.

Lena punched the last key to finish the weekly payroll, then pushed print, and the printer in the corner started whirring and spitting out payroll checks. Al's five employees, not to mention Lena, were waiting for them. They all lived paycheck to paycheck, working hard, raising families. Ordinary people.

Lena knew her co-workers well, and their wives and children. Their wives were mostly in the same boat as Lena was—working, harried, with never enough hours in the day, never enough money, just making ends meet, worried all the time.

She was just reaching for the phone to call Gloria and talk to Kimmy when it rang again. She picked it up and wedged it between her ear and shoulder. "Al's Auto Body," she said while tearing the paychecks apart, ready to hand out to the men.

"Is my car done?" asked a female voice. "The Mercedes?"

"Um, which one? Is this Mrs. Fairhaven?"

"No, no. I'm Lucy Hubbard. The blue 350SL."

"Oh, Mrs. Hubbard." Lena got up and looked through the window into the shop. "Just a second, let me check."

She put the woman on hold and pressed the intercom button. "Harry," she said, "is the blue Mercedes done?"

Harry's voice came back, tinny. "Nope. Waiting for the paint. Monday."

Back to the phone. "Mrs. Hubbard, your car will be ready Tuesday morning." She *always* gave the guys extra time.

"Tuesday? But I need it this weekend."

"I'm sorry, Mrs. Hubbard, but the paint color is a very unusual one," she improvised, "and we've had to order it from the manufacturer. You wouldn't want your car to have the wrong paint on one fender."

"Oh, God," the woman said petulantly. "I *need* it."

She probably had five other cars in her oversize garage, Lena thought, glancing at the woman's address on the invoice. Beverly Hills.

"It'll be ready first thing Tuesday morning. I think I told you Wednesday originally, Mrs. Hubbard, so this is actually early. I'm really sorry if we've inconvenienced you."

"Oh, all right. Are you sure it'll be ready Tuesday?"

"Absolutely."

"I'll send Rufio to pick it up."

"Fine, Mrs. Hubbard. Should we bill you?"

"Send it to my husband's office. Do you have that address?"

"Let's see." Lena checked the work order. "Yes, I have it. Thanks, Mrs. Hubbard."

She put the phone down and shook her head. These women—and men—with so much money that a two-thousand-dollar dented fender was no more serious to them than a broken fingernail. And the Hubbards' insurance would cover most of it anyway. Lena, of course, had to send her own bills to the insurance company. Someone, she supposed, took care of all Mrs. Hubbard's problems.

She reached for the phone again and dialed Gloria's number. She did this every day, an afternoon ritual, to talk to her daughter and reassure her mother she'd be there by five-thirty to pick Kimmy up so Gloria could get to her job as hostess at a popular steak house. She wished she could be at home all day for her six-year-old daughter, a regular *Leave It To Beaver* mother, but things didn't always work out the way you wanted them to. She had sure learned *that* the hard way.

Gloria's phone rang, once, twice, three, four times. Lena glanced at the clock again—four-fifteen—and a tiny stab of anxiety tickled her belly. Gloria was *always* home by now. And sometimes Kimmy would pick up the phone herself, her piping little voice, always excited, recounting to her mother the day's events. "And, Mommy, Mrs. Sherby let me *hold* the frog, and I got to read... There was a hard word, Mommy, but I sounded it out, and Tommy Daniels wanted to trade lunches, but I wouldn't, and..."

Kimmy. Kimberly Lee Portillo. With her big dark eyes and brown hair she could easily be Lena's natural daughter, but she wasn't. She was adopted, abandoned by her birth mother, a crack baby, a tiny screaming bundle left at a church six years ago. The minister had called the Los Angeles police, and a squad car had been sent to investigate. The two young cops on the call had been shocked, horrified, and they'd taken the infant to the nearest hospital.

Lena filed some invoices, stacked orders to go out tomorrow morning. Four thirty-five. She'd wait five minutes, then call Gloria again. Five minutes, she was thinking when one of the workers opened the door, came in and plunked himself down in the folding chair in front of her desk. He smelled of grease and paint thinner and was wiping his hands on an old rag.

"What now, Ken?" Lena asked, eyeing him.

"It's Stephanie. Got a minute?"

"God, Ken," she began, sighing. His wild relationship with his girlfriend was driving everyone nuts. And he never stopped asking for advice.

"She says last night was it. We had this fight, see, right after dinner at—"

"You want my opinion?" Lena broke in. "End it. Find some nice quiet woman. Stephanie's a neat lady, but you two mix like oil and water. It's never going to improve, either. Now, that'll be a hundred dollars for my services. Get out of here and let me finish the payroll, will you?"

Ken stood up reluctantly, pouting. "Hey, Lena," he

said, pausing, "what if, I mean, what if you and me went to that new rib place over on—"

"No way," she said, cutting him off. "I don't date fellow workers. In fact, I don't date, period."

"But it's not like—"

"Outta here, Ken. Shoo. I have work to finish."

The truth was that all the single men at work had hit on her over the years. At thirty-one, Lena was perhaps more attractive than she had been in her youth. There was a confidence and maturity in her bearing; she was tall, with shiny dark hair that she usually pulled back in a ponytail, a wide mouth with a deep indentation in her upper lip, a vaguely Indian look to her eyes and nose, and cheekbones from a Spanish ancestor's liaison with an Aztec.

After Ken finally left, she reached for the phone again, but it rang in her hand. She snatched it up. "Al's Auto Body."

"Lena?"

"Yes... Mom, is that you?" Her mother's voice sounded strange, tense.

"Did I forget... I mean, is Kimmy there with you? Did you pick her up?"

"No, Mom, I would have told you..." A hand of steel suddenly closed around her heart and tightened. "You mean Kimmy wasn't at school?"

"Oh, God," Gloria said. "No, no, she wasn't there. I asked her friends, every kid on the playground. I'm in the school office right now, Lena, and we can't find her!"

Lena closed her eyes, horrible scenarios racing through her head. Then she told herself to calm down. She put a hand to her forehead. "Mom, listen, she probably went home with one of her friends."

"She *never* goes home with anyone. You know that. She waits for me," Gloria said, distraught.

"Well, maybe she did today. Maybe she went...oh, I don't know, to the pet shop near the school. She loves the kittens."

"Lena, she wouldn't do that."

"Maybe one of her friends' mothers gave her a ride somewhere. To McDonalds' for a snack." Her mind whirled feverishly, thinking up safe venues for her child. "Or the library. Story hour. Or..."

"Lena, what should I do?" Gloria was near tears.

"I'll call her friends, Mom. I'm sure she's at someone's house."

"I'll stay here in case she shows up. The principal is very upset."

"I can imagine."

Gloria's voice was hesitant. "Should we call...the police?"

Lena's stomach clenched. "No!"

"But, honey..."

"I'm sure she'll turn up any second. I'll call her friends. Don't call the police, Mom." The police—that would make it official somehow that Kimmy was really missing, and she couldn't accept that. Not yet. This was all a big mistake. It had to be.

With difficulty, she dragged her mind back to her mother's voice.

"Will you phone me here if you find out anything? I'm half out of my mind. I'm calling in to the restaurant now. There's no way I could go to work. I'll be here. The number's—"

"I know it, Mom. I'll call you as soon as I can."

"Oh, God, I hope Kimmy's okay. There're such sick

people around these days. The poor innocent baby. Oh, Lena…"

"Mom, please, she's fine. She's got to be fine. We'll find her."

When Lena hung up she noticed that her hands were shaking, her mouth was dry, her heart was racing. Kimmy, her baby. Gone?

Oh, I'll punish her when she shows up, Lena thought. *I'll paddle her backside. I'll ground her till she's twenty-one! I'll…*

What if someone really had taken Kimmy? Some crazy, demented child molester. You read about it every day. What if she'd been kidnapped? That was ridiculous, absurd. Lena wasn't rich enough to pay a ransom. She had nothing of value. She wasn't famous.

She had to calm herself and think of the names of Kimmy's friends, look up the numbers in the phone book. All cute little first graders. Benjamin Halloran, the boy Kimmy had a crush on. Ally Samson, her best friend. Mary Lue Shelton, Marty Figlio and that girl who'd had the birthday party last week. Ally's mother would know.

Her fingers shook, hit the wrong numbers on the phone, and she had to start over. Ally's mother had no idea where Kimmy was.

"When I picked Ally up she was at the school playing," Margy Samson said. "That was about, oh, just before four o'clock."

"And she was okay?" Lena asked.

"Sure, she was playing ball with another girl. I didn't even notice, you know. Oh, I wish I'd stayed there or something.…"

"Why would you do that? I bet she's just gone off somewhere. Oh, is she going to get it when I find her."

"Let me know, will you?" Ally's mother said. "Call me when you find her. Please."

Benjamin Halloran's mother didn't know anything, either—Ben had walked home. She asked him if he'd seen Kimmy, but he only shrugged, or so his mother told Lena.

A couple of numbers didn't answer, so Lena left messages. When she finally hung up, she knew nothing more than when she'd started: no one knew where Kimmy was.

She phoned the school, spoke to the principal, listened to her mother's frightened voice, and decided she couldn't stay at work another second. Where was her daughter? Was she okay? Had she wandered off or forgotten the time? Had she walked home by herself? Lena called home, in case Kimmy was there, but no one answered.

She took a deep breath and went out into the garage. She found Al working on a red Porsche, his skinny frame bent double as he polished the hood with a heavy machine. She had to tap him on the arm before he noticed her. He straightened, as always a stub of a swollen cigar butt held in his mouth. He switched the stub from one side of his mouth to the other, took off his protective glasses and earplugs and fixed his sharp blue eyes on Lena.

"Listen, Al, I've got to leave early today. Kimmy... Well, a little problem's come up. I have to get to her school. I put the phone on the machine and the checks are on my desk."

"Sure, go ahead. She's okay, your kid?"

"Oh, fine, yes," she replied vaguely.

"See you tomorrow morning," Al said. "Have a nice evening."

Have a nice evening. The words rang in her mind as

she headed for the parking lot. It was a beautiful, warm October day in Southern California, but Lena didn't notice. She got into her car blindly, her pride and joy, her one indulgence: a sleek black 1968 Pontiac GTO convertible. She'd had Al and the guys in the shop working on it little by little over the past five years, whenever she had some extra money, and it was restored to perfection now.

Today she didn't notice it, though, didn't pay the least bit of attention to its burnished gleam, the throaty roar of its engine or the smooth shifting of its four-on-the-floor gears as she drove toward Kimmy's school in Woodland Hills.

She told herself over and over that her daughter would show up. It was only a silly mistake, a little glitch in the usual routine. Kimmy had been missing for less than an hour—they'd find her any minute, and Lena would scold her daughter and maybe cry a little, then they'd all have a good laugh together and Gloria could go to work after all.

For goodness' sake, Lena had taught Kimmy never to talk to strangers, never to get into a car with anyone she didn't know. She knew about dialing 911, and she knew she should wait in the playground outside of her school until her grandmother picked her up. She'd been told and told those things, and she was a sweet, endearingly solemn, very responsible little girl.

Nothing could have happened to her. She'd probably be at school when Lena drove up. Sure she would.

Could you feel more responsible for an adopted child than a natural child? Lena wondered. She couldn't know what was in other people's heads, but she knew how she felt. Kimmy had gotten off to such a dismal start, abandoned, sick from her birth mother's drug habit, that Lena had an almost compulsive urge to make everything perfect in her child's life. One of the young policemen who'd originally found her had felt responsible, too; he'd gotten emotionally involved, checking on the baby every day, keeping track of her when she went to Social Services. He had a soft heart, the big, blond Los Angeles cop, even though he looked tough. Lena knew all about his soft heart—she'd been married to him then.

They'd decided to adopt the darling baby girl, and when the adoption agency finally located the birth mother, the woman had signed the papers relinquishing her rights so fast it made everyone's head spin. Signed the papers and disappeared.

Lena and her husband—Mike Quinn—had proudly brought the baby home. It was an occasion that had been covered by the papers. Sometimes Lena looked through her photo album and saw the grainy newspaper picture of her and Mike, so happy, so hopeful. Gloria was there, too, grinning. A grandmother at last.

Well, Lena was still a mother and Gloria was a grandmother, but the man in the picture hadn't been a father for five years now.

She pulled up in front of the school, shut the car off, drew a deep breath and went inside. Surely by now they'd found Kimmy. She'd be sitting in the office, contrite, with some excuse.

But she wasn't there. Gloria was waiting, looking slighter than usual, as if she'd shrunk since Kimmy had gone missing. Her usually neat hair, dark and glossy and pulled back into a bun, had strands falling around her face. Her small features were pinched, her olive skin sallow. Miss Trenholm, the principal, was with her, looking just as upset despite her usual professional calm.

"You haven't found her," Lena said.

"Oh, honey, I'm so worried!" Gloria cried.

"I'm so sorry about this, Mrs. Portillo," Miss Trenholm said. "I feel responsible. I don't know what could have happened."

Lena didn't correct the principal's misuse of her name. She wasn't Mrs. Portillo, as there was no Mr. Portillo—it was her mother's maiden name. People called her that all the time, and she didn't care, as long as no one ever called her Mrs. Quinn again. "I'm sure it wasn't your fault, Miss Trenholm."

"It *is* early in the school year, and first grade *is* a big step up from kindergarten," the principal said. "We've had several episodes over the years, and I assure you we've always found the children safe and sound."

"Do you have any suggestions as to what to do next?" Lena asked. "I've called all her friends."

Miss Trenholm hesitated. "Is there a…a person you're in a relationship with? Sometimes it happens that…"

"No," Lena said firmly, "there's no one."

"An ex-husband?"

Lena almost laughed. She shook her head. No, *he* wouldn't be interested enough to bother snatching Kimmy. And besides, he didn't even know where they lived.

"It's been nearly an hour and a half," Miss Trenholm said, checking the wall clock. "We'll need to call the police. There are procedures—"

"What if a child molester took her?" Gloria burst out.

"*Mom.*"

"Oh, God," Gloria sobbed.

"She's fine. I know she's *fine,*" Lena said, but her throat ached, and she was suddenly terribly afraid. Her knees went weak and she sat down too quickly on an office chair. "Kimmy," she whispered.

"I think," Miss Trenholm said, "that we should call the police now and then you go home and wait."

Lena looked up quickly. "You really think...?"

"Yes, honey," Gloria said. "Call the police."

"Oh, my God," Lena said. "You both think something's happened to Kimmy."

"No, no, it's just a precaution," Miss Trenholm assured her.

Lena felt nausea rise in her chest and she could hardly breathe. It couldn't be happening, not to Kimmy, not to her precious little girl. She turned away.

"Let's go home," Gloria said. "We'll call the police from your house. I'll do it if you want."

Lena looked up again. "What if she comes back here? What...?"

"I'll be right here to watch for her." Miss Trenholm hesitated. "And then, of course, they'll send cars around to check the area."

They. The police.

Somehow Lena got out of the school and followed Gloria's car to her own house. The small stucco bungalow on the narrow lot, lined up on the street with others so similar. But it was *her* house; she'd bought it and fixed it up, and she paid the mortgage every month with a fiercely possessive satisfaction. She drove her car into the driveway. Gloria parked at the curb, and they both got out and stood there on the postage-stamp lawn in the gathering dusk and looked at each other.

"Come on," Gloria finally said. "Let's go in and make that call."

It was, oddly, as if they had switched roles—Gloria calm and in control now, while Lena could hardly move, her limbs leaden, her head thick, her heart beating so hard it sapped all the energy from the rest of her body. And her mind kept repeating the mantra: Kimmy, come back. Kimmy, be safe.

Gloria unlocked the door with her key. She lived in her own place a couple of miles away, but they were at each other's homes as often as at their own. She flicked the lights on.

"Do you want me to call or do you...?" Gloria began.

"Wait!" Lena said. "The answering machine. Maybe there's a message... Maybe..." She found the strength to move to her machine. Yes, the red light was blinking. She pushed the play button and waited, her breath trapped in her chest. Oh, there were messages, all right, four of them. The dentist's office, a friend who wanted to go bowling, a credit card company, a wrong number.

Lena sank onto the couch and put her head in her hands. Then she heard Gloria pick the phone up and start punching numbers.

Tiredly Lena lifted her head. "No, Mom, let me. It's my daughter."

Slowly Gloria held the phone out. Her eyes met Lena's with sadness and fear and understanding. "Okay, honey," she said.

The phone rang in Lena's ear. What was she going to say? Would they really do something to help find her daughter? It rang again, and Lena straightened her shoulders.

"Woodland Hills Police," said a bored masculine voice.

Lena took a long, quavering breath. "I want to report a—" she cleared her throat "—a missing child. Kimberly Lee Portillo, six years old, last seen at Jefferson Elementary School about four this afternoon."

"Your name, please."

And so she went through the whole rigmarole, the endless red tape, the questions.

"I'm sending a patrol car to your house, ma'am," the officer said at last. "It should be there soon. If you have a recent picture of the missing child, it will be helpful."

The missing child. "Yes," she said faintly, "I have one."

"You sit tight, ma'am. They'll be there soon."

"Okay, thanks," she said automatically, and she wasn't aware she was still holding the phone until her mother took it out of her hand.

Gloria hugged her tightly, then held her at arm's length and said carefully, "Call Mike, honey."

Somewhere inside Lena a flame of anger ignited and flickered. She welcomed it, a relief from the dread, a momentary respite from her suffering. "No," Lena said with finality. "Never."

CHAPTER TWO

THE WOODLAND HILLS police arrived twenty minutes later, two uniformed officers, an older one with a mustache and a younger one with fair hair and a nice face.

Lena let them in, and they stood, hats in hands, and introduced themselves: officers Krubsak and Mullin. They were polite and soft-spoken, and they were probably sympathetic, maybe had kids of their own, but Lena knew from being married to a cop what they were thinking. She knew all about the inside jokes, the foul things cops said, the black humor that kept them from going nuts when they saw the violence people could inflict upon one another. Oh, sure, she could just imagine what they'd say to each other when they left her house: "Probably got the kid locked up in the basement. Nah, hacked to pieces. Maybe some boyfriend got his hands on her. Hell, it's almost always the family." Cops saw those things and joked about them to stay sane.

And now it was Lena they'd joke about. And Kimmy. She couldn't bear it.

But she had to. She had to ask them to sit down, had to answer their questions and try to be calm because she needed their help. She had to sit there, her hands between her thighs to keep them from shaking, and watch them take out their notepads, and steel herself for their questions.

Gloria told them of her arrival at Jefferson Elementary.

"And it was your habit to pick Kimberly up after school?" Krubsak asked.

"Yes, unless she was going to a friend's house, but I always knew that ahead of time. She always waited for me. If it rained, I got there earlier."

"I called all her friends." Lena said wearily. "They last saw her at the playground just before four o'clock."

Mullin spoke up. "Would she have wandered off or gone with someone without telling you?"

Both women shook their heads emphatically.

"We'll need to go to her school and talk to the children, but we can't do that until tomorrow," Krubsak said.

"I can tell you some of their names, and I'm sure the principal will give you a list. She was very upset," Lena told him.

"Doesn't look good, does it?" Krubsak said. "For the school, I mean."

"It wasn't her fault," Lena protested.

"How do you know, Mrs. Portillo? We have to check out everything."

Mrs. Portillo again. "I'm *Miss* Portillo," she said. "I'm not married." Defiantly.

"Is there an ex-husband?" Mullin asked.

"I'm a single parent," Lena said firmly, ignoring the look Gloria flashed her.

"What about Kimberly's father?"

"Actually," Lena said, hating to have to explain it all, "my daughter is adopted. Her father was unknown."

"What about the real mother, then?" Krubsak asked. "We've had cases like that, you know, where the real mother wants the kid back."

"Not *this* real mother," Lena said. "She was a drug addict and she abandoned Kimmy. When they found her she couldn't sign the relinquishment papers fast enough.

Then she disappeared. Believe me, she never wanted the baby and she still doesn't—that is, if she's even alive.''

"Still, we should check her out.''

"I can't remember her name. I'd have to look in the adoption papers.''

"Well, you might want to do that and let us know, Miss Portillo.''

"Okay, sure, but what are you going to do about finding my daughter?''

"We've got patrol cars out looking. We'll get her picture faxed to everyone. You do have a picture?''

Lena went to the bookshelf behind the couch and picked up Kimmy's school picture from last year, slid the photograph out of the frame, held it, studied it for a moment—the wide smile with a front tooth missing, the big brown eyes, the soft tendrils of brown hair. Oh, God, Kimmy.

"Do you have a boyfriend?'' Mullin asked.

"What?'' She looked up, the picture in her hand. "A boyfriend. No. I don't have time. Are you kidding?''

"Sometimes it's a guy you're having a relationship with who takes a kid. Jealous or possessive. Whatever.'' Krubsak shrugged.

"No, there are no men in my life. I haven't even had a date in a year,'' Lena said, handing the photo to him.

"And your mother.'' He turned to Gloria. "Mrs. Torres, there's no one you can think of who would take your granddaughter?''

"No,'' she answered.

"An ex-husband, a boyfriend?''

Gloria gave a short laugh. "You flatter me, young man. I'm a widow, and I don't have *boyfriends* at my age.''

"Sorry, but you know what I mean.''

"No, there's nobody I'm having a relationship with."

"Enemies?" Mullin asked. "Someone who has a grudge against you, something like that?"

"God, no," Lena said.

"Okay, this is what we'll do," he went on. "We'll put a tap on your phone first thing. Anyone who calls, the number will automatically show up at the station. That is, of course, if there is a phone call."

"You mean for ransom?" Lena asked.

"Yeah."

"But what if it's not a kidnapping for ransom? What if it's someone..." Her voice trembled.

"We'll have patrols out all over the neighborhood. We'll start a door-to-door search around the school, then widen out. There'll be an APB out on her with the picture."

"Excuse me," Gloria put in. "Is there someone, some division, that specializes in this kind of crime? Should you call someone else in? The FBI?"

"The FBI can only be called in if we're sure it's a kidnapping," Krubsak said, "and then only after twenty-four hours."

Lena asked a question she knew was stupid, but the words came tumbling out of her mouth. "Do you think it's a child molester?"

"Well, now, ma'am, it's too soon to jump to conclusions, and there's nothing pointing to that at this time. Your daughter is most likely lost, probably somewhere not far away."

"I hope so," Lena whispered, "Oh, God, I hope so."

The phone tap was set up, and Krubsak spoke to his precinct on the phone, organizing the door-to-door search.

"I'm leaving Officer Mullin here until morning," he said. "Just in case."

"Just in case what?" Lena asked.

"It's procedure, ma'am. I'll take this picture down to the station, and we'll get it out. We're part of the new TRAK system—we can send it all over the country if we need to. Don't worry, we'll find your daughter."

At nine o'clock he left them with Officer Mullin. There hadn't been a phone call, not one, although Lena listened and waited minute after long minute.

"Try to get some sleep, honey," Gloria finally said.

"Oh, sure," Lena replied.

"I know."

"Can *you* sleep?"

"Probably not."

"You could go home," Lena said. "Maybe you'd sleep better there."

"Oh, sure," Gloria said, echoing her daughter's tone.

"I haven't eaten. Have you?"

"No." Gloria sighed.

"I can't."

"Neither can I."

"Where is she?" Lena asked. "Where is she?"

Gloria hugged her, and they stood like that for a long time.

THE PHONE RANG at seven in the morning, jerking Lena out of a fitful doze. She rushed into the living room to answer it, glanced wildly around for Officer Mullin, saw him nod at her. She picked the phone up.

"Hello?" She could barely recognize her own voice.

"Mullin, please," said a man's voice.

Lena stood there, her heart racing, her mind not quite comprehending who was on the phone.

"It's for you," she finally said, holding the receiver out, and he came over and took it from her.

Lena hadn't even bothered to undress the night before—she still wore jeans and a short-sleeved red blouse. She'd barely slept a wink, and now as she sank onto the sofa, she felt the weight of unending dread settle on her again. She listened to Mullin's conversation, but it wasn't news—they hadn't found Kimmy. Apparently it was only someone telling him who would relieve him.

"What is it?" asked Gloria from the hallway.

"Nothing, Mom. It's nothing."

"Oh, I thought..."

"I know."

"Did you sleep?"

"No, did you?"

Gloria didn't bother answering. She looked awful, her hair a mess, her face drawn, shadows under her eyes. Lena guessed she herself looked just as bad.

"All right," Gloria said. "They'll find her today. I know they will." She tried to smile. "I'm going to make some breakfast now. You have to eat, honey. And go take a shower, change your clothes. Go on now."

"Oh, Mom, I won't feel better until I've got Kimmy back."

"You have to stay healthy, keep up your strength. Do what I say."

Listlessly Lena took a shower and changed her clothes. She couldn't bear to look at herself in the mirror, because when she did she saw the black terror in her eyes, and it frightened her. She pulled her hair up in a careless twist and secured it with a clip.

When she emerged from her bedroom Gloria was feeding a tired-looking officer Mullin a plate of eggs and toast. She put one in front of her daughter, too, but Lena couldn't do more than sip some coffee and nibble a corner of toast.

Another policeman drove up and Mullin left, taking the police car back to his station. The new officer was heavy and dark haired. Fontaine, his name tag read.

"Is there any news?" Lena asked desperately.

"Nothing that I know of," Officer Fontaine said. "The door-to-door search broke off last night and will be resumed shortly. So far nothing's turned up."

After breakfast Lena decided she had to do something. The waiting was destroying her; she felt as if every nerve in her body was raw, twanging with agony. She was so used to being busy, working every minute of the day, that she couldn't just sit, tired as she was.

She drove around the neighborhood first, the convertible top down so Kimmy could see her. Several patrol cars were in evidence, some cruising, one parked, its occupants at the door of a house. The police were trying to help, Lena told herself, but it seemed so hopeless. If Kimmy had been in the neighborhood, she'd have come home, wouldn't she? Or perhaps the police were asking people if they'd seen anything suspicious. What? Some evil maniac stalking her daughter? Oh, God.

She saw the road ahead through a film of tears. Was Kimmy okay? Was she tired, cold, hungry? She got so hungry in the morning.

Lena reached the school, and there were police cars there, too. Children played on swings and jungle gyms in the school yard. She heard their high-pitched yells and stopped her car to watch. Kimmy should be there with them, with her friends, yelling and running and giggling, falling maybe and scraping a knee, bravely holding back tears.

It didn't seem right to Lena that life went on as usual

for these kids and their parents, that they could still run and laugh and play when her life was turned upside down and terror was her constant companion. She could barely recall what it felt like not to be afraid. She drove around the school, on every street that surrounded the school, block after block, searching the lawns and houses and stores and alleys and gas stations she passed, looking for her daughter single-mindedly, irrationally, compulsively.

She forgot to eat, felt sickness gnawing in her belly but ignored it. She drove and drove, and once she got lost and had to retrace her route, only to find herself on Ventura Boulevard again. She stopped several times to call home in case there was news, but there wasn't.

"Any news?" Lena asked wearily when she finally got home.

Gloria merely shook her head. "But the press found out somehow. We've had a few calls. Officer Fontaine handled them."

He nodded. "We can hold them off for only so long, you know. But if they get into a frenzy, we'll try to shield you from it."

"Thank you," Lena said. *Oh, God, the news media.*

The evening passed with agonizing slowness. There were a few phone calls, one from Miss Trenholm, another from Ally's mother, two more from local TV stations. Gloria fielded the calls—Lena sat, head in her hands, or paced like a caged tigress.

After trying to eat some of the food Gloria prepared for supper, Lena got up and went into the backyard. She wanted to scream, she wanted to weep and tear her hair, but none of those things would do Kimmy any good.

She heard the screen door slam, and her mother came out.

"You can't go on like this," Gloria said. "For God's

sake, call Mike. He'll get the whole LAPD in on the search. Lena, honey, he may not have been the best husband, but he was a damn good cop. He'll find Kimmy, you know. Call him, Lena.''

"You think he's magic, Mom? You think he can wave a magic wand and poof, she'll be home?''

"No, no, but he can help. If they know one of their own is in danger, the police will try harder. You know that.''

"Did it ever occur to you that he might not be interested in helping me?''

"No," Gloria said firmly.

"I haven't seen or heard from him in five years. I have sole custody of Kimmy. I refused any contact after the divorce, no visitation rights, no child support, nothing. He was an alcoholic who'd hit bottom, a danger to himself and everyone around him, and I cut him out of my life. Now you think I should go begging to him?'' She shook her head.

"Please, Lena, I know he'll help.''

"He probably drank himself to death by now." *No, not Mike.*

"He's not your father, Lena, if that's what this is all about," Gloria said quietly. "And he hasn't drunk himself to death.''

Lena gave her a sharp look. "How do you know?''

"I know," Gloria said, holding her daughter's gaze.

"No," Lena whispered, and she made a slashing motion with her hand, dismissing the subject, and went inside.

Her feet took her to her daughter's room, where she stood, staring unseeing into space. Then she sat on Kimmy's bed, smoothed the pink-and-blue plaid coverlet, patted the stuffed dog that lay on the pillow. She pulled

Kimmy's tattered old blanket out from under the pillow and held it to her face, closing her eyes, drawing in her child's scent, and then she cried, hot tears soaking into the blanket, her body shaking, her mind reeling, lost, unable to think.

Where was Kimmy? Where was she?

THE KID WAS no problem at all. She lay curled up on the back seat of the old station wagon and dozed most of the time. Jane Cramm kept turning around and looking at her.

"It's too damn hot," Danny Hayden said.

"Do you want me to open my window some more?" Jane asked.

"Nah, the dust blows in."

"We'll be out of the desert soon, Danny," she said. She hated it when Danny got irritated, and she tried very hard not to rub him the wrong way.

Fortuitously, Danny seemed to forget about his discomfort. He even craned his neck to take a quick look at the kid. "She's cute, ain't she?" he asked in a pleasant voice.

Jane turned again and studied the child. "She's real cute. I can't believe I even had a kid that cute, you know, Danny?"

"You're all right," he replied.

Jane couldn't help smiling. Sometimes Danny was nice to her—as long as she didn't do something dumb to aggravate him. That's why she'd gone along with this caper—it'd been all his idea. But, Jane had to admit, she'd been real curious to see the child she'd given up for adoption; well, at least she had been once Danny planted the idea in her head. "I'm sure glad you said I could keep her, Danny."

He snorted, and Jane wasn't sure how to interpret that.

Sometimes Danny did things she couldn't figure out. She wasn't sure he'd meant what he said about her keeping Kimberly. You couldn't always believe him. Jane had a disquieting idea about why Danny had wanted the girl in the first place, but she tried not to think about it.

"Maybe we don't have to give her any more pills, huh?" Jane asked. They'd been feeding her Valium ever since they'd picked her up at the school yesterday. "She's awful good."

"That's *why* she's awful good," he said with heavy sarcasm. "Listen, the one thing we don't need is a screaming kid. Someone would notice. Or she could try to run away. Just do what I say." He shook his head in disgust and swore under his breath.

Dutifully, Jane said nothing. She fiddled with the radio knob, finally getting a station from Phoenix, Arizona, even though they were hundreds of miles north of Phoenix, heading east toward Flagstaff on Interstate 40. Around them the dry-as-dust desert was fading into dusk, the sky ahead blue-black, the sun's glow on the horizon behind them.

"I'm hungry," Danny said.

"Okay. You want to pick up some burgers or something?"

"Out here?"

"Well, I guess we could find a store, you know, a gas station store. I'll get us something. And she needs to eat, too. Kids need to eat a lot, you know, because they're growing. And milk, she needs to drink milk."

"Yeah, yeah, keep an eye out for someplace to stop."

Jane turned and knelt on the seat, leaning over to look at Kimmy. She was so pretty, with long, dark, shiny hair and huge brown eyes with long lashes and skin so smooth and creamy and untouched it made Jane's heart ache. Had she ever looked like this? She used to be pretty as a child; she recalled her mother saying so, and her aunt. She'd never known her own father, and she didn't know who Kimberly's father was, either. He must have been good-looking, though.

She'd gotten pregnant seven years ago, and she'd known right off she couldn't take care of a baby. To tell the truth, she hadn't minded being pregnant, because men had kind of liked the way she looked, but a baby? No way. She'd never regretted giving the baby up until Danny had started working on her, and now she wasn't sure whether the desire to keep Kimberly was hers or Danny's.

She put her hand on the little girl's head and stroked her hair back. "Wake up, Kimmy," she said softly. "Are you hungry? Want something to eat?"

The girl opened her eyes with effort; they were clouded and dull from the Valium.

"I want my mommy," she said plaintively.

I am your mommy, Jane wanted to say. "We're going to stop soon and get something to eat, okay?"

"I want to go home," Kimmy said.

"Want some ice cream?" Jane asked hopefully.

"I want my mommy," the child repeated, her eyes beseeching and scared.

Jane didn't know what to do. She was supposed to keep the kid quiet, but no matter what she said, Kimmy cried or asked for her mommy. Jane hadn't known a little kid could be so stubborn.

"You can't see your mother right now. We're going on a trip," Jane said. "Remember? I told you..."

"I want to go home."

Sighing, Jane turned around to face the darkening highway. Flagstaff Mountain loomed, barely visible in the dusk. It would be cooler in the mountains, she thought, and Danny wouldn't get irritated at the heat. The old station wagon had no air-conditioning, but it was big and comfortable, and Danny liked it.

She pulled down the visor and studied her face in the dusty mirror on the back of it. She tried very hard to see any resemblance between her face and her daughter's, but she couldn't. Maybe she'd looked like Kimmy once, but that must have been a long time ago. Now, at thirty-two, Jane was painfully thin, her dark hair dull and scraggly, her skin coarse, and she was missing a tooth.

She put her fingers on her cheek and met her own brown eyes in the mirror. It was so dark now that she could barely see herself, and she could imagine that there was something in her face that still resembled the pretty little girl she'd once been. An unaccountable sadness filled her, and she saw in her mind's eye the years behind her stretching back and back; she had a vague inkling that it had not, perhaps, been inevitable that she'd ended up here, in this car, with this man, driving through the desert with a child in the back seat.

"What the hell're you doing?" Danny demanded.

She sat straight up, snapped the visor back into place. "Nothing, honey, honest," she said, avoiding his eyes.

"I want my mommy," the child wailed.

CHAPTER THREE

MIKE QUINN BLEW a sharp blast on his whistle, then let it drop on its chain against his sweatshirt. "Front and center!" he yelled to the gangly black kids. "Get over here!"

All seven boys sauntered over to the sideline on the basketball court.

Mike put his hands on his hips and shook his head in disgust. "Marvin," he said, "how many times I gotta tell you? Follow the shot. You hear that? *Follow the shot.*"

Marvin shrugged wide, bony shoulders. "Sure, man, no prob." Then he grinned. "But when you gonna show me the money?"

Everyone laughed. Everyone but Mike. "Real funny, kid," he said. "But losers never see the bucks. Sure, they see the color of a welfare check once a month, but that's it. You wanna see the money? The real stuff? Then you work for it. You work till you ache all over. And for starters—and this goes for all you guys—you get those hands up and follow your shots in. You pay attention. To the ball. You never take your eyes off the board. You let the other guy get the rebounds and you're a loser, man, a big loser. Because that dude's going to get noticed. *He's* gonna make it to college. And then someday some scout'll spot him and make him an offer. The pros. The big time. The money. You guys get the picture?"

A few nods, a couple of "Yeah, mans."

"Okay, then." Mike clapped his hands. "Get on the court and run the drill. Marvin, you take the first shot and—"

"Follow the ball," Marvin finished for him. "Follow the ball," he began to chant, jabbing playfully at another player as he took to the court.

Mike watched the boys. They were quite a crew. All were from South Central Los Angeles, and all were on some sort of probation, either from school or from a judge. Two of the seventeen-year-olds were former gang members—one had been tossed out of school for pulling a switchblade on a math teacher. Two others had been serious addicts, still had track marks showing on their arms and behind their knees. They were clean now, or so Mike believed. For how long? No one knew.

They were all essentially troublemakers; that was fact. But Mike worked them out hard. Three nights a week. And at least on those nights he knew they'd stay clean. When he sent them home at nine they were too darn tired to do much except eat and sleep. Still, he worried about them. Sometimes at work one of their faces would pop into his mind and he'd think, *Is Billy going to make it? Or is he going to end up on the coroner's slab before his eighteenth birthday?*

With Mike on the court doing footwork drills alongside the team, they worked hard all evening. They were an odd-looking group, three of the boys under six feet in height, the others all taller than Mike's six-two. Whereas all the boys were still youthfully thin and gangly, Mike, at thirty-six, was built substantially. A big man. Lean but large boned, with Irish-pale skin, dark-blond hair that flopped to one side and a good, solid face that was somehow handsome despite that slightly askew prizefighter's nose. For his size and his age he still moved well, keeping pace with the kids, never showing them any weakness.

Shortly before nine Mike whistled them over to the sideline. "Okay," he said, "good job. I saw lots of hands and arms in the air out there. You fellas work that hard tomorrow night and we'll beat the pants off the Westenders."

"Man, they are like already dead, dude," Ray intoned.

"Meat, they are meat," Marvin put in.

"You got it," Mike said, and he joined them in a round of high fives. "Now, keep clean till then. Think you *ladies* can handle that?"

Billy snorted. "Easy as pie, bro."

"Okay, then, go on home and get some rest. I'll see you all tomorrow."

"Ta ta, man," Ray said, and they all headed toward the locker room in the old neighborhood gymnasium. Mike hung out shooting baskets until the boys cleared the gym entirely, then he switched off the court lights, checked the locker room and left, crossing the cracked asphalt parking lot to his car.

It was a bad neighborhood, right in the heart of L.A.'s notorious South Central District. Some of the guys at work swore they'd have to be paid big bucks to get anywhere near the area, especially after dark. But Mike Quinn wasn't that concerned. As he often told Joe Carbone, his friend and mentor at police headquarters, "I have a better chance of getting killed on the freeway."

And Mike liked the kids. Liked coaching them and talking to them and simply being there if one of them needed an ear. He knew their brothers and sisters and parents, too. Knew where they were coming from. The hopes and dreams and the despair. Especially the despair. He'd been there.

He unlocked his car, got in and pulled out of the lot, driving toward Manchester Avenue as he tuned the radio to a talk show. Tonight's subject was apparently teenage daughters stealing their mothers' boyfriends. There was a lot of anger in the voice coming over the air, a shriek and the click of the phone. The talk show host took another call.

Mike turned north onto the 405 freeway and then west on 10, which took him straight into the Santa Monica beach district. Home. It sounded pretty good, but in reality his apartment was in one of those funky, two-blocks-off-the-beach old houses. Probably built in the late 1940s. The landlady was in her sixties. She'd renovated the place several years ago, and it now contained four small apartments. The building itself was painted salmon, with white trim at the doors and windows. The roof leaked, and the whole place stuck out like a sore thumb on the block.

The rent was nevertheless high—it was after all, the beach. Mike's apartment—two rooms and a bath—was at the rear of the house, stuffy in the summer and too cool and damp in the winter. But when the breeze was from the ocean, he could smell the salt in the air. And he heard the seagulls from dawn till dusk. The inflated rent was worth every cent.

When he was inside he eyed the shower, but that could wait. Right now he was starved. He pressed the button on his answering machine and went to the fridge, where he pulled open the door and peered inside. Ah, he thought, last night's leftover sub sandwich.

The machine spoke in the background. "Hey, Mike, Joe here. Nice job at that liquor store yesterday. You're catching on. Oh, and by the way, stop by my office first thing Monday. They want you over in Bakersfield to conduct a two-day training program. You're getting famous. See ya.'' *Click.*

There were a couple of other messages. One from a bank—soliciting—another from his mother, reminding him about the upcoming Halloween party at his brother's. The big, loud Quinn family at its best. Or worst.

Joe's message, though, was good news. Joe had taken Mike under his wing when Mike's life had been swirling straight down the drain. He'd lost his family. Damn near lost his job. He'd certainly lost his will to live. Mike sat on a stool at the Formica counter in his kitchen and munched the sandwich, gulping orange juice straight from the bottle in between bites, and his mind went back to that nightmare time.

Sure, he'd always liked a drink or two. His family drank—the men did, at least. A beer with supper, a few at the bars with buddies. And hey, cops drank like fish, so it had been easy to fall into the pattern. He'd told himself it was to "let down."

He'd loved the male bonding thing that came with his job; his partner back in the days when he'd been a young patrol cop in the San Fernando Valley area had been Jeff Davidoff. They'd been as close as brothers, closer. Davidoff drank only vodka, because he was Russian, and they'd always laughed like maniacs when he told someone that. God, they'd had good times. And they'd done good work, too, routine traffic stuff, domestic disputes, a few convenience-store robberies. Two tall young cops, Mike blond, Jeff dark. They'd perfected their swaggers and that slow, intimidating way of taking off their mirrored sunglasses when they stopped a speeder.

Jeff had been best man at Mike's wedding, and he'd hung out a lot at the Quinns' first small apartment. He'd adored Lena and offered to baby-sit Kimmy when they adopted her.

Life had been good. Mike had his wife, a new baby, a job he loved, a partner he trusted with his life.

Then fate had intervened. He remembered the day with absolute clarity. It had been in August, an inferno in the Los Angeles basin, the Santa Ana winds kicking up dust, driving people crazy. The air-conditioning in the patrol cruiser had been broken, of course. He and Jeff were bitching and sweltering and drinking cold sodas when the call came over the radio: officers under fire, suspected bank robbery.

They'd raced to the scene, siren wailing, as excited as kids. "Action!" Jeff had yelled exuberantly, driving like a madman.

The bank robbers were shooting it out with the police. They'd had machine guns, for God's sake. One officer had already been hit, the others were cowering behind their cars, and the bad guys were holed up in the bank, shooting out of the front door.

It had been a scene from hell with a pitiless sun baking the cops in their dark uniforms. Jeff and Mike were kneeling behind the open door of their cruiser, waiting for a clear shot, when Jeff told Mike he was going to get behind a concrete planter closer to the door. "Cover me, partner," he'd said, like in the old cowboy movies, and then he ran, crouched low, zigzagging, Mike laying down covering fire, but a stray bullet from one of the robbers' guns tore through Jeff's lungs and blew a hole out the other side.

He died there in Mike's arms, his blood leaking onto the sizzling concrete, and the last thing he said was, "Tell my mother...tell her...tell her..." And then he was gone.

Mike made something up to tell Mrs. Davidoff, and

that was the last coherent thing he did for a month. He started drinking seriously then, coming home late, hungover in the mornings, sick as a dog, then drinking again to wash the memory from his soul.

Lena had tried talking to him, and so had his own mother. The guys at work hinted around. But Mike couldn't stop. If a day went by without booze, he shook and remembered Jeff's blood all over him, the way life had gone out of his eyes. He'd think of the funeral, the formal policeman's goodbye, with uniforms, a gun salute. Davidoff's parents and his sister. It hurt too much, and he couldn't handle it.

He was offered counseling at work, routine in cases like his, but he declined it. To talk about the event would be to relive it, and he couldn't face that—better to forget, to drown his memories.

It got worse and worse. He used up all his sick days. Lena cried a lot. His friends gave him a wide berth. He was either drunk or hungover or angry for months, but he could live with those feelings.

And then there was that final night with his family, with his beautiful young wife and his darling year-old baby girl. He and Lena had fought—he never recalled over what—and he'd had a few shots of vodka, which he'd started drinking when Davidoff died, and he'd felt so low, so sick, so utterly used up and worthless. In a moment of rare clarity he knew that Lena hated him, Kimmy was afraid of him, he wasn't doing his job anymore, and he knew he was unable to continue that way for another hour or minute or second.

That's when he'd gotten his police-issued .38 Special and cried and held it to his head, while Lena begged him to put it down, sobbed and stood in front of the baby's door, then called his father to come and get him.

Larry had come, taken the gun and led Mike away, out of the house, and Lena had told him never to come back, she couldn't go through this again.

He'd passed out in his dad's car on the way to his parents' house, and when he'd woken up the next day, he knew he had to change or die.

Well, he'd tried to die and failed, so change was the next step. Of course, it had been too late to save his marriage. Lena had disappeared, divorced him, taken a new name, and he didn't have the heart or right to fight her over anything. It was over.

Joe Carbone, a sober alcoholic Mike knew only casually from headquarters, had helped him pick up the pieces of his shattered life. Five years ago now. Joe had helped others, too, but he and Mike had become particularly close. And it was Joe who'd helped Mike get his present position with LAPD's prestigious Hostage Negotiations Team, which Joe headed.

Now Mike was making a name for himself within the police community. Not just in California, but in neighboring states, as well. He'd had a couple of breaks, he admitted. His first one had come shortly after being transferred to Hostage Negotiations; Mike had worked a situation in which a computer analyst had lost his job, been drinking heavily and had ultimately taken his ex-wife and children hostage. The man had been armed to the teeth.

Mike had gotten him to talk on the phone, and after four hours the man had surrendered. Mike knew he never would have been able to talk the guy down if he himself hadn't had some real-life experience with booze and guns and despair. It turned out the computer analyst was of some local renown, and the media made a big deal about it.

That had been two years ago. The next break in Mike's

career had come on the heels of the first, only this time it was a disgruntled postal worker holding a group of twenty fellow workers hostage with an automatic weapon. This dude had been sober, but the hopelessness was there just the same. It had taken two days to wear the man down, and Mike had been the one he wanted to talk to. The media coverage was impressive, and people on the street—a few, anyway—had recognized Mike's face.

It felt good to really help. Just as it felt good to work with his basketball group and the eight-year-old boy Mike saw on weekends as an Adopt-a-Buddy in L.A. It gave Mike's life purpose and direction. His one big regret was that he'd lost his own family on the route to self-discovery.

He finished the leftover sandwich and showered, then telephoned Jenn, Jennifer Hilty, a divorcée with two small children whom Mike had met several months ago. She was a down-to-earth woman, thirty-six—his age—who owned and operated an aerobics studio in Santa Monica. She had the body to prove it, too.

"Hope it's not too late to call," Mike said, stretching out on his couch, "but I wanted to see if you're free for lunch tomorrow. Can't do dinner—I've got that basketball game."

"Mmm, lunch," she said, hesitating, teasing. "Let me check my calendar."

"If it's a nice day, we could eat on the pier," Mike said. "Take the kids along."

"Bob's got the kids tomorrow. His weekend, you know." Bob was her ex. "So I'm free. I've got a nine-thirty class, but then I'm off till Monday."

"So it's yes?"

"Of course. But maybe we should just get takeout or something, eat at my place. And then who knows?"

Mike knew exactly what she meant. "Sounds good."

"Just good?"

"Sounds great," he said, and after he'd hung up he thought about that. Sex with Jennifer was as good as it got.

But then Mike frowned. That wasn't entirely true. With Lena it had been perfect.

Mike sat up and wiped the frown from his face. "Water under the bridge," he said out loud. He rose and turned off the lights and was heading toward the bedroom, when the phone rang. "Damn," he muttered, hoping it wasn't work.

It wasn't. But Mike couldn't have been more surprised when he realized who it was.

"Gloria," the woman said. "Mike, it's Gloria Torres."

He sat down in the darkened room, collecting himself. Lena's *mother*.

It all came rushing back, the checks and Christmas and birthday cards he'd sent to Kimmy through Gloria—all returned unopened. The calls he'd made to her, trying to locate Lena and the baby—Lena had changed her name, moved, done a real good job of disappearing. And all Gloria had ever said to him was, "You know I can't talk to you, Mike. I'll just tell you they're okay." Then she'd hang up.

But Mike was a cop. He'd pulled a couple of strings and found out Lena had taken her mother's maiden name, Portillo, and he'd located her only a few miles away in Woodland Hills. He'd kept tabs on her. Still did. But he'd never contacted her. Oh, he'd found out where Lena worked, where she lived, but he'd never invade her space, not after he'd put her through that living nightmare.

"Mike?"

"Ah, yeah, Gloria, I'm here," he said, rubbing his cheek absently.

"I...Mike, I need to see you."

Her voice sounded strange. "What is it?" Mike asked, the hair on his arms raising.

"It's...it's Kimmy."

He was struck numb for a long moment. "Gloria... Oh, God, don't tell me..."

"No, no, Mike, it's not what you're thinking. I mean, I just need to see you. There's a problem. I can't talk now."

"What the hell kind of a problem can there be with a six-year-old?" Mike demanded.

"Can you meet me in front of my house in thirty minutes?" she asked.

"Gloria."

"Please, Mike, not on the phone. Please. I... We need your help. Thirty minutes?"

And all he could say was of course he'd be there, and Gloria hung up.

WHEN GLORIA HUNG UP the bedroom telephone, she had a sudden sweeping moment of panic. She never should have called him. *Never.* But then the panic subsided, replaced again by common sense. If Lena were thinking rationally, she'd realize how much greater their chances were of finding Kimmy with the whole LAPD on the search. And only Mike could accomplish that. Not only was Mike a cop, but so was his father, his uncle and even his first cousin. All cops. Mike could call in the troops in a way no civilian ever could.

Gloria rose from the side of Lena's bed just as her daughter walked into the room.

"Who was that on the phone?" Lena asked wearily.

"Ah, work. I had to check in at work. I'm afraid I've got to run over there for a few minutes," she lied.

"At this hour?"

"They, ah, can't find the time-clock key or something," Gloria said, but already Lena was someplace else, sagging onto the side of the bed, her face in her hands.

"Oh, Mom," she said, her voice breaking. "I just don't understand any of this. Who would take her? *Why?* I don't have a dime to my name. And if it's some sicko... Oh, my God, we'll never get her back. Never."

Gloria eased down next to her daughter and gently brought her head to her breast, stroking her long brown hair. "We'll get her back, honey, I swear to God we will."

"You can't *know* that, Mom," Lena sobbed.

"It's a gut feeling. I have a gut feeling she's okay."

Lena's head came up. "Are you sure? I mean..."

"Shh," Gloria said, smiling, "shh. You know my intuition's always been pretty darn good. And I do have a feeling, sweetie. Now, try to lie down and close your eyes. You're exhausted. There's nothing you can do right now, and you need to rest. Please, honey."

Lena did lie down on top of her bedspread, an arm flung over her eyes, her chest rising and falling unevenly. Gloria touched her reassuringly, then rose.

"I'll only be a few minutes," she said quietly. "The policeman's in the living room, and he'll get you if there's a call. Try to sleep."

She left the bedroom reluctantly, wanting to be with her child every moment of this terrible ordeal. But more than ever she was convinced that Mike Quinn had to be brought in. If they were ever going to see Kimmy again, they needed all the help they could muster. Despite everything, Mike was a good man deep down where it counted. Surely Lena, if she ever allowed herself to think about it, knew this.

She told the policeman monitoring the phone the same lie, even though she knew her call to Mike had been taped. Whoever was monitoring incoming and outgoing calls at police headquarters must have been wondering. It didn't matter anymore. When they checked the number Gloria had called, they'd know it was Mike. Sooner or later the truth about Kimmy's adopted father was going to surface whether Lena wanted it to or not.

Gloria drove the short distance to her house gripping the steering wheel. She didn't know what to expect when she met with Mike. Lord, it had been five years. She had seen his picture once in the newspaper, and she'd been surprised and happy for him. Still, she didn't know whether he'd be glad to see her, angry or just plain distraught, as she and Lena were.

Hostage Negotiations, Gloria thought, that's the department the article had said he worked with. She remembered mentioning it to Lena, who hadn't had the time to read a paper in years, but her daughter had only put her hands stubbornly over her ears, cutting Gloria off. Now Gloria turned the corner onto her street and wondered how Mike held it together with his drinking. Maybe he'd cut down. Maybe he didn't even touch the stuff anymore. It didn't matter. So long as he could call in the troops, nothing mattered.

When she pulled up to the curb in front of her house she saw him in her headlights. He was standing next to his car, his hands jammed in the pockets of a leather jacket. Gloria got out, steeled herself against a surge of guilt and walked over to him. He looked the same. He was still a handsome man, tall and fair, that imperfect face set off with blue eyes that seemed to reach deep inside a person. Mike Quinn. Gloria realized instantly that she still liked him.

He nodded soberly. "Gloria," he said. "You're looking well."

She gave him a weary smile and they shook hands. Then, before she could say a thing, he asked her in a grave voice what on earth was going on.

"It's Kimberly, Mike. She's...missing."

He let out a quick breath. "What do you mean 'missing'?"

"I went to get her at school yesterday, like I always do, and she wasn't there."

Mike let it sink in and then he swore softly under his breath, still digesting the news. "And you and Lena have no idea, none whatsoever, where she is?"

Gloria shook her head slowly and leaned back against his car. She told him everything then, how they'd gone to the principal, phoned Kimmy's friends, checked everywhere they could imagine. And then they'd called the police.

"They spent all day today questioning people," she said. "Everyone. The teachers, the kids, even the mailman who delivers around the time I was to pick up Kimmy."

Mike listened quietly, but Gloria could see the stricken expression on his face. He asked some questions of his own, but nothing Gloria and Lena hadn't been asked a dozen times already.

"So you're saying that Kimmy disappeared from a relatively busy playground and no one saw a damn thing?" he finally asked.

"So far it looks that way."

"The cops are monitoring Lena's phone, I assume?"
Gloria nodded.

"And Lena?"

"She's in pretty bad shape, Mike. She's exhausted and
frightened to death. I don't even know if she can think
straight right now. I don't know that I can. I only know
that you've got the connections to call in the troops.
Surely your father and your uncle can call in markers,
Mike, get us some real help. I never would have dumped
this on you, but we're desperate."

Mike studied her face for a moment, then said, "Does
Lena know you called me?"

Gloria shook her head. "You know how it is, Mike."

"Yeah, sure," he said, and she could hear bitterness
creeping into his voice. "But she can't keep me out anymore. Kimmy's my legal daughter. Lena knows that.
Dammit," he said. "She should have called me immediately. I'll head over there right now."

But Gloria grabbed his arm. "No, Mike, no! You'll
make it worse. Lena's about to break. Just do what you
can from the sidelines. *Please,* Mike, I'm begging you."

He studied her again, searching her face, and then finally, mercifully, he nodded. "All right," he said softly,
"all right, Gloria, we'll do it your way for now. I'll go
home and get on the phone right away." He turned to
leave, then he hesitated. With his back to Gloria, he
asked, "Does she really still hate me that much?"

Gloria bit her lower lip and then she sighed. "Yes,"
she said. "Yes, I'm afraid she does, Mike."

CHAPTER FOUR

THE FOLLOWING MORNING the Woodland Hills police decided to call in the FBI; they'd come to the conclusion that this was no simple case of a lost child.

Lena knew full well that the local police distrusted the feds and hated to call them in. She remembered so clearly how Mike and his partner Jeff would make fun of the ineffective, bungling "fibbies," and she certainly wasn't looking forward to their presence in her life.

Nevertheless, FBI Special Agent Alan Sabin came to interview her that morning. He was a small, wiry man with a sharp nose too big for his face, a square bony jaw and a horizontal slash for a mouth. He gave no hint of what he was thinking or feeling. He asked her and Gloria all the same questions, over and over, and recorded the whole interview on tape.

There had been no phone call, no ransom demand. If Special Agent Sabin thought that was odd, he gave no sign of it, nor could Lena glean any insight into whether he felt the lack of a demand was good or bad.

No wonder Mike hated the FBI, she thought. And as if having the FBI and the LAPD in her face wasn't enough, the news media were beginning to smell a good story. No longer were they just phoning the house, tying up the line, but they were beginning to camp out on the street—first one news van and then another and another, all poking mikes and cameras in everyone's face: the FBI agent's, the cops', Gloria's. It was becoming a circus. Lena wanted to scream at them all: Stop asking useless questions and *do* something!

The police were on the case. She knew that. They even had bloodhounds searching the area around the school. The handler had come for a piece of Kimmy's clothing so his dogs could get her scent. Lena had given him a T-shirt of her daughter's, and then she'd wept when she saw it in a strange man's hand.

After lunch, which Gloria fixed but Lena only picked at, she decided she had to pull herself together and get things organized for Al, even though it was Saturday and the shop was closed. Of course Al had forbidden her to come to work until she knew her daughter was safe, but she ignored his threats. She was going out of her mind sitting around the house. Gloria promised to stay there and call her instantly if she heard anything. But when she arrived outside the garage door and went into the cold, dim place, she burst into tears again.

She called home the second she got into the office.

"Nothing," Gloria said. "They're taking our guard dog away after today." The "guard dog" referred to the policemen who stayed at her house.

"What does that mean, Mom? That they're giving up?" Panic exploded inside her.

"No, no. It just means that they don't think there'll be a call or anyone coming to the house."

"If there's no call, then someone's taken her. God knows where. Or maybe they didn't take her far. They just..." She could never put into words the worst-case scenario. She couldn't say it, but she thought about it constantly.

"Shush," Gloria said. "Don't you even think that!"

"I can't help but think it, Mom," she said wearily.

She put a hand on her forehead. "Mom, what about all the reporters out front? The police aren't going to leave us alone to deal with them, are they?"

"No, no, honey," Gloria said. "There'll be a patrol car stationed here. It's just that they don't have the manpower to monitor the phone from inside. Everything will be okay."

"Sure," Lena said.

It took her all afternoon to get organized. She was so distracted she worked much more slowly than usual and had to check and recheck her figures.

Al came in about three. He walked into the office in his usual outfit—jeans and a T-shirt—chewing on his cigar stub. "I knew you were here," he said. "I spoke to your mother."

"I've got everything just about done," she said.

"I told you not to come in," he growled around the cigar.

"I don't care what you told me."

"You think this place won't run without you?"

"Frankly, no, I don't."

"Ah, hell, you're probably right."

"I'll leave in a little while," she said, rubbing her eyes with her thumb and forefingers. "It's hard. I can't think."

"I never had any kids," Al said, "but I can imagine."

"No, you can't," she said tiredly.

"No, I guess not. Listen, Lena, the guys all offer their support. If they can do anything, or if I can, just let us know, okay?"

"Thanks, Al. If there's anything, I'll tell you." She felt only a dull sort of gratitude, as if there was nothing left inside her but despair.

She showed Al a few of the more important details. "You can call me," she told him. "I'll be home."

Before he left he gave Lena a hug, a warm, fatherly hug, even taking the noxious butt out of his mouth when he did it. "We all care about you and Kimmy," he said. "We care a lot, Lena. You're like family, you and the guys. And don't worry about money. However long it takes, you'll get paid the same as if you were here."

She wished she could make a grand gesture and tell Al not to pay her while she was gone, but she couldn't. She needed her paycheck—her mortgage was due soon. So she just said, "Thanks, Al, thanks a lot," then her mind wandered elsewhere and she hardly heard him leave.

After turning on the computer, she started entering figures on the spreadsheets, trying to get everything up-to-date. All the while she tapped on the keys, her mind kept trying to escape the confines of the office, worrying, scared, wondering *why, why?* And *who?* Where *was* she?

Then she couldn't help remembering Gloria's advice: call Mike. Was she being too stubborn? Was this the time to back down on the promise she'd made herself five years ago? Could Mike really help? If he could, shouldn't she try every path, every possibility, however remote or uncomfortable or ridiculous?

She knew she was stubborn, but she'd always considered it a positive attribute. She reached her goals, she persevered, she didn't let anyone ride roughshod over her. Yet was her stubbornness jeopardizing her daughter now?

Call Mike. What if she did and he made things worse with his drinking and his fits of temper and black spells of depression? What if the whole awful, sick ordeal started all over again? And what if his parents and that self-righteous sister of his tried to get custody of Kimmy, as they'd threatened during the divorce?

A judge might say Lena was an unfit mother for allowing her child to get kidnapped from the school playground. A judge could say anything and take her child away. But, of course, none of that mattered right now, because Kimmy was already gone.

What should she do? The question gnawed at her, and she stared into space, thinking, weighing her options.

To see Mike again... She envisioned him, something she hadn't let herself do for a very long time. Tall and fair, deep-set blue eyes, a slightly off-center nose, a powerful chin. Endearingly homely. She'd loved him so much once, when she'd been young and naive. She'd always dreamed of a man like Mike Quinn who'd sweep her off her feet. And he had.

His drinking hadn't mattered at first, because they were young and everyone they knew partied and drank. She should have known after her own father had died of alcoholism, but she hadn't. Dumb, dumb.

Oh, how she'd loved Mike. And how he'd been destroyed by his partner's death and his descent into violence and depression. That one night had finally put an end to their marriage; she could never trust him again after that.

Could she trust him now?

She turned off the computer, wrote a few last notes for Al and stood, looking around the office. She had to go home now, home to that gaggle of reporters out front and her mother's unspoken fear and the waiting, the endless, terrible waiting. Her heart ached for her child, and she hoped, prayed, that Kimmy wasn't cold or hungry or lost or in pain. She prayed Kimmy wasn't suffering. The thought flew into her head unbidden that perhaps Kimmy wasn't suffering at all anymore, but she shut it off; it was unthinkable.

She turned off the lights in the office and walked through the dim, empty garage. It was quiet, too quiet, this Saturday afternoon—her footsteps echoed hollowly in her ears. She locked the outside door and went to her car. The sun was warm on her back; the sky was blue. Somewhere a dog barked, and a bird flew from a tree branch beyond the empty parking lot. She felt irrationally as if the beautiful weather was an insult, a slap in the face when her existence was pure hell. It should be cold and gray and raining.

She opened her car door and got in, rolling down the window. The car was hot inside after sitting all afternoon in the sun. She was about to insert the key in the ignition, when the passenger door opened, startling her. The door opened wider and a man slid in next to her. Shocked, she stared into Mike Quinn's eyes.

"Mike," she rasped, her hand at her throat.

"Sorry if I scared you," he said, watching her, studying her, feasting his eyes on her for the first time in five years. "But I thought this was the best way. You still don't lock your car, do you?"

For a very long moment she stared back at him in stunned silence, and then she whispered, "Mike?"

"Yeah, it's me."

Her face was pale and drawn, and she looked worn and tired, thinner than he remembered. But beautiful, still beautiful, maybe more so. Maturity had given her a grace and a confidence that were new, and his chest tightened to see her so afraid.

"How did you," she stammered, "how did you know where I was?"

He searched her face, trying to test the waters. Was her temper still as fiery as it had been? "I knew" was all he said.

"But…"

"Lena, I knew, that's all."

"Why are you here? Don't tell me you… Oh, God, my mother told you." She stared at him, her chin trembling. "You know, then."

"Yes, she told me. Don't be angry with her. She did what she thought was right."

"Oh, for God's sake, Mike, she's treating me like a child, and you're no better. Playing a ridiculous cloak-and-dagger game like this." She was angry, her dark eyes smoldering.

"Sorry," he repeated, "but I can help, Lena. There's no time for fighting between us—we need to find Kimmy."

"Oh, God."

She put her face in her hands, and her shoulders shook. He wanted so badly to touch her and comfort her, but he knew he couldn't; he'd forfeited any right to do that long ago. There could only be the business at hand between them.

"Lena, I can help," he repeated. "I checked out the case with the Woodland Hills department. I have some ideas.…"

"What ideas?"

"Let's get you home, Lena. No sense sitting here in the car."

"Don't you patronize me, Mike!" she flared. "I've been taking care of myself and my daughter just fine without you…until…until…"

"I know," he said. "I only meant…" He paused. What had he expected—that she'd fall into his arms, that the past five years would be erased? "Lena," he said quietly, "let me help you on this. Forget the past. It's Kimmy who matters now."

He saw tears fill her eyes, and she bowed her head.

He followed her home in his own car. He'd never let her know that he'd occasionally driven by her house just to see where she lived, to see that she was okay. Of course he'd never parked in front of it or gone inside. He'd wanted to, so many times. He'd wanted to pick up the phone and call her; sometimes the temptation was so strong it hurt. But he hadn't, because he knew Lena's pride and stubbornness, and he respected her need to sever all ties with him. He figured it was better for her, and that was the important thing. How ironic that it had taken a tragedy to allow him back into Lena's life.

Gloria's face lit up when she saw him come into the house. "Thank God," she breathed.

"You should have told me, Mom," Lena said.

"You wouldn't have listened."

There was a policeman on duty outside the house, and he came in to investigate the visitor. "And you are?" he asked.

Mike took out his wallet and flipped it open, showing his badge. "Quinn, Metropolitan Area. I'm a...friend of Lena's. She's asked me to help."

"Hey, aren't you the one...didn't I see you on TV?"

"Maybe," Mike said.

"Glad to meet you." The cop shook hands with Mike. "My shift's over soon. It's good to know someone's here inside with the ladies, because the press out there are getting real antsy."

"Yeah, I know. I've been in touch with your captain."

"Are you taking over the case?"

"No, I'm just here to help," Mike said. He knew better than to step on toes. Nothing got cops more worked up than someone encroaching on their turf.

Gloria made coffee and the three of them sat around

the kitchen table. Mike couldn't help noticing the familiar items that Lena had kept from their marriage: some furniture, the teakettle, the cups Gloria poured coffee into. So familiar, yet so totally strange. Sometimes, for a split second, it was as if the intervening years had not existed, but then he'd become aware of the unfamiliar kitchen, the worry on Lena's face, and the time they'd been apart stretched into an unbridgeable gulf.

"Tell me," Lena said, "tell me what's going on, Mike. Is there something the police haven't mentioned? Are there any leads, any suspects, anything?"

He shook his head. "Nothing. They're not holding anything back, Lena."

"You know the FBI's on the case now?" she asked.

He nodded.

"Can they help?"

He shrugged. He didn't want to alarm her, but he had little faith that the FBI could find Kimmy—she wasn't anyone famous, after all. They'd only go through the motions.

"What could have happened to her?" Lena cried. "Why can't anyone find her?"

Gloria put a hand on Lena's arm. "It's only been two days, honey."

"Oh, God," Lena sobbed, putting her face in her hands, "it's been a lifetime."

Mike hated witnessing her suffering. He wanted, once again, to touch her, to hold her. His hands remembered the feel of her, and they itched to reach out and... He erased the thought.

She looked up at him. "How can you help? What can you do?"

"I've spoken to Pop and Uncle Ted. They'll take a

few days off and help out with the investigation. And Scott, you remember my cousin Scott?"

"Of course I remember him."

"He'll help, too. They're trying to get off-duty guys to volunteer to canvas the neighborhood. *Someone* had to see something. The more men to saturate the area the better."

"But the Woodland Hills police have already done that," Lena whispered, hopelessness filling her voice.

"It has to be done again," he said. "And if there are no witnesses, we'll go back and do it once more. Show her picture, the works. Sometimes people don't remember what they saw—their memories have to be jogged." He hesitated. "There's something else we can do. You can go on TV, Lena, and plead for Kimmy's return."

"Oh, no… Oh, Mike, I…"

He put up a hand. "I know how hard it'll be, but if the kidnapper is watching—and the local stations will play and replay the tape—you might be able to humanize the situation in his eyes, gain sympathy. And don't forget," he went on, "someone else might recognize Kimmy from her picture. It's happened before. Look how well those national TV shows work, you know, like *America's Most Wanted.* It's worth a shot."

Lena was listening, her eyes closed, her hands still white and shaky.

"Anyway," Mike said, "I'll handle it. Don't even worry about it. In the meantime we'll start requestioning people, anyone who could possibly have seen anything."

"And you think you'll find something new?" Gloria asked.

"Listen, Kimmy didn't vanish without a trace. We know where she was last and when it was. That's good—that's real good. We start from there."

"The playground at the school. Four o'clock Thursday afternoon," Gloria said.

"Yeah. One of the kids, I figure. One of her friends had to see something. She was there surrounded by kids when she was taken." He saw Lena flinch, and he felt the pain as if it were his own.

"Taken," Lena whispered. "You think, you *know* she was taken. How do you know? Tell me, Mike."

"It's the only logical conclusion. If she hadn't been taken, we would have found her by now. The bloodhounds couldn't pick up a scent. They milled around the school yard, went as far as the sidewalk, and that was it. So she didn't walk away or wander off or go on foot with anybody. It had to be a vehicle right there at the curb. Someone got her into a car."

"But she's been told a million times never to get into a car with a stranger," Lena protested.

"She's a little girl. Think about it. All a person would have to do is grab her arm and pull her, or even pick her up bodily. She had to be moved only a few feet. Five seconds maybe."

"Why? Why, Mike? What did they hope to gain?"

"I don't know," he said. Then, grimly, he added, "Not yet. But I will."

Lena had let her coffee go cold. She got up and poured it into the sink, then leaned on the counter. Mike met Gloria's gaze across the table, and he saw her pain, her helplessness.

He got up and went to Lena. He put a hand on her shoulder and felt her skin jump under his touch. "Listen," he said softly. "We'll find her. I swear to you."

She turned to face him, and he saw the flash of hope in her eyes, but then she backed away, her face clouding over, and he knew two things: he'd been too close to her, physically too near, and it frightened her. He also knew she didn't trust him. But then, she didn't know he'd quit drinking, did she?

She poured herself another cup of coffee, deliberately turning her back on him, then went to sit down at the table.

"I don't drink anymore," he said in the heavy silence. "In case you were wondering."

Lena looked up, a wry twist to her mouth. "That's nice," she said with pointed sarcasm.

She didn't believe him. Of course not. Why should she? He'd promised her before, and it had lasted—how long?—a day or two, maybe a week once. Nor was there anything he could say to convince her. Not Lena.

"I think that's wonderful," Gloria said. "I'm glad for you, Mike."

"Thank you," he said, noticing that Lena's mind was already elsewhere. He dropped the subject, sat down at the table and sipped some of his lukewarm coffee. Lena's head was bent over her cup, her hands gripping it, white-knuckled. She said something he didn't catch, then she looked up and repeated the question.

"What's the usual outcome in a case like this?" she asked. "Be honest, Mike. In your experience, what happens when there's no ransom demand?"

He was tempted to lie. But she'd know—Lena had always been able to tell when he was lying. He tried to frame his answer carefully. "Every case is different," he said. "There's no hard-and-fast answer."

"Come on, Mike, cut the bull," she said with a vestige of her former spunk.

"It usually means someone has kidnapped the child to...well, because they have a fetish. They're compulsive. They're sick."

"And what happens to these kids, Mike? Do you find them? Do you get them back?"

"There's every possibility that Kimmy will be found," he said in his professional voice.

But Lena pushed herself up from the table, leaned forward on her arms, her face white, her voice shaking. "Dead or alive, Mike? Dead or alive?"

"*Lena,*" her mother said.

"We'll find her, Lena," he said. "We'll find her, I swear."

She stayed there, still leaning forward, her eyes black holes of anguish in her white face. He could see the fine texture of her skin and the way a few dark tendrils of curling hair fell over her forehead. She took a deep breath, obviously trying to steel herself in front of him, wanting to hide her loss of control, but on the edge, held together only by a desperate effort of will. God, he had loved this woman.

She straightened up and caught his gaze and held it. "Find her, Mike," she whispered. "For the love of God, find my...find Kimmy."

"THIS WILL BE your room, Kimmy," Jane said as she pushed open the door to a bedroom at the back of the run-down adobe house. "It needs cleaning up, I guess, but we left in a hurry, see, to come and get you. It's not bad, is it? And you'll like Santa Fe."

The little girl—*my little girl,* Jane had to remind herself—was pretty dragged out from the trip and the pills. But she'd come around. Kids were real tough that way, or so Marie Carlin, who had the house next door, always said.

She switched on the overhead light and led Kimmy in and thought that it was good she'd talked to Marie because, really, Jane didn't know squat about kids, and Marie had five little round ones who all looked healthy. Yeah, Marie could come in handy.

"I want to go home." Kimberly's voice broke into her musings. "I want to go home to my mommy."

Jane felt her nerves rub against her skin. Kimmy was okay for a kid, except when she whined like this. At first she'd supposed the kid was going to be upset and cry and all that. But it had been days, all the way from California to New Mexico, and she was still griping. She and Danny had fed her, let her go to the bathroom, made her real comfortable in the back seat. They'd been friendly. You'd think the kid would quit whining.

It was then that Jane realized she was losing it. She needed a fix. "You wait right here, see?" she said to Kimmy. "I gotta do something and I'll be right back."

"Don't lock me in! Please!" Kimmy cried suddenly, but Jane had already closed the door and twisted the dead bolt Danny had put on it.

She went into the bathroom and lifted the lid of the toilet's water tank. Taped inside was a bag of crack cocaine and a syringe. Just seeing it had a calming effect on her, and within five minutes she was in the kitchen heating up a can of soup for Kimmy, the rush of well-being welcome and familiar.

When the soup was ready she went back to Kimmy, who was lying on the single bed on a pile of Danny's old jeans and T-shirts.

"Hey," Jane said, "it's okay, kid—Kimmy, I mean. Here. Here's something to eat. You'll feel better. Come on, now. Take a sip. I heated it for you myself."

Kimmy finally ate a little, and then Jane made her swallow half a sleeping pill. "Take the vitamin pill," she urged, handing her a plastic glass full of water. "Be good and take it.'' Then she waited in the room for Kimmy to settle down, and as she sat on an old stuffed chair in the corner, watching the flesh of her flesh, she thought again with surprise what a pretty child she'd had. Pretty, and smart, too. She wondered what Danny's plans were. He and his friends wouldn't really want to use this child for a movie the way they had that last girl, the one who had just disappeared one day. Surely Danny wouldn't do that to Jane's own blood.

I'll talk to him, she thought, emboldened by the drugs flowing in her veins. *I'll make him see that she's too young for that kind of stuff.* That other girl had been older.

But by the time Danny got home from visiting his buddies at the roadhouse, Jane's high was wearing off, replaced by the dulling effects of a couple of shots of tequila.

Danny, too, was drunk. ''Spaghetti again?'' he thundered. ''That all you know how to cook?'' Then he swore, sticking his face close to hers. ''You're no good for nothin','' he said. ''Can't even make your own sauce. Gotta buy that jar stuff.''

Jane cowered against the sink. ''Danny, please,'' she whimpered. ''We just got here a couple of hours ago. I didn't have time.''

He swore at her again, then finally backed off, eyeing her. ''That brat go to bed all right?''

''Yes, Danny.''

''You feed her something?''

''She ate. Sure she did.''

''I don't want her all scrawny like you.''

''No, Danny, she'll be fine.''

Danny scowled at her more fiercely. ''You are scrawny.''

"I..."

"Let's see how scrawny you are," he sneered, and he moved toward Jane again, his eyes darkening, moist.

She let him have his way, leading her into the bedroom, pulling off her sweatshirt and jeans, mounting her. Sometime during the act Kimmy awakened and Jane could hear her crying through the paper-thin walls. She closed her mind to it and tried to concentrate on Danny's movements. It was real hard, though, because something in the kid's plaintive sobbing reminded Jane of something from her own distant past. She'd been a kid, too. A real little kid. She'd been crying. And there'd been a man on top of her then, just like now.

CHAPTER FIVE

LENA FINALLY GOT some sleep on Saturday night, but only with the help of two glasses of wine. She slept fully clothed on Kimmy's bed, awoke, cried against her child's pillow and slept fitfully again. On Sunday morning it rained, a gray, misty rain that reached inside her and chilled her soul.

She showered, fought tears when she looked at Kimmy's shampoo on the shelf, then dressed in jeans and a clean white blouse with a dark green cardigan on top to keep warm.

By now it was only seven-thirty. She knew Mike wouldn't be there till nine or so, because that's what he'd told her last night before he'd left, something about having to make the end of a basketball game and he'd be out late. So when the knock came at Lena's front door shortly after eight, she was surprised and then relieved. Maybe it was Mike with some news.

It wasn't Mike at her door. Instead it was his older sister.

"Colleen?" Lena said, holding the door open, trying to fit her mind around the reality of the woman's presence. It had been years....

"Oh, my poor darling," Colleen said before Lena could collect her thoughts. "I had to come over right away. I just heard this morning. Not an hour ago. Oh, you poor, poor dear."

"Come in," Lena said, meeting Colleen's falsely sympathetic smile with one of her own. "This is quite a surprise."

"It's not too early...?"

"No, no, I've already had a half a pot of coffee. Would you like a cup?"

They'd never been friends. And as Lena led Mike's sister into the kitchen, she couldn't help remembering what Colleen had said on the morning of Lena and Mike's wedding: "We've never had a Mexican in the family. If you really cared about my brother, you'd live with him. There's no reason to get married. No reason at all. If you think this will better your station in life, think again."

Essentially Colleen had called her a gold-digging Mexican tart. Forget that Mike was hardly rich—quite the opposite, in fact. Never mind that Lena's family had been American citizens for longer than the Quinns. And forget that Mike had pursued *her*. Because, as Lena had pointed out to Colleen, it was none of her goddamned business.

After the wedding day she and Colleen had barely been polite. Lena might have considered a truce, although she felt then, as she did now, that Colleen owed her an apology. But Colleen wasn't here today for that. And as Lena grudgingly poured her a cup of coffee, she suspected that Colleen, single career woman extraordinaire, had come only to gloat.

Bitch, Lena thought as she handed her ex-sister-in-law the cup and saucer.

"You must be so upset," Colleen was saying. "I can't imagine."

"Mmm," Lena said. "Even if you did have a child, Colleen, it would still be hard to explain what a crisis like this does to you." It came out nastily, and instantly

Lena regretted her words. "That was low," she said. "I'm sorry. But I'm all grown up now, Colleen, and I try to deal in the truth. I don't think we were ever friends. And I can't believe you've come over here after all this time to offer your sympathy or your friendship."

Colleen stared at her for a moment and then finally nodded. "Well, you certainly have grown up," she said levelly.

"Yes, I have. I've had to."

"Then you won't mind if I tell you I've come here as an adult myself."

"Go on," Lena said cautiously.

"In a nutshell," Colleen said, "Mike is finally over you. He's met someone, a supernice lady with two small children. They're very much in love. They're talking about marriage, and I only came over here to warn you to—"

"Oh, please," Lena said, cutting her off, throwing a hand in the air, "give me a break. I'm not interested in Mike, and I'm sure he's not interested in me. What I care about...what *we* care about is the child we adopted six years ago. Did that ever occur to you, Colleen? Do you give a damn about Kimmy at all?"

"Well, of course I—" But she was interrupted by the sound of a key in the front door lock.

"It's my mother," Lena said. "I think this conversation is at an end anyway. I get your message, and you can rest easy. I'm not interested in your brother."

Colleen rose and put her cup and saucer in the sink, then turned to her just as Gloria appeared in the kitchen doorway with a bag of groceries. "I'm glad we had this talk," she said, and then she nodded at Gloria. "Mrs. Torres."

"Hello, Colleen," Gloria said. "It's been a long time."

"Yes. Nice to see you again." Then she turned to Lena. "I'll see myself out."

"Fine," Lena said coolly. "Do that."

When Colleen was gone, Gloria looked at her daughter, let out a long breath and said, "Phew. Want to tell me what *that* was about?"

But Lena only shook her head.

As promised, Mike arrived a couple of minutes after nine. And he had a surprise for her, something she hadn't at all been prepared for.

He'd come with a news team.

Lena stared incredulously at the lights and cameras being hauled into her living room, then she grabbed Mike's arm. "I...I can't do this! I can't go on TV and beg...."

He drew her into the kitchen. "I brought them this morning so you wouldn't have time to agonize over it. I knew if I told you, you'd go haywire. Let's just get it over with," he said.

She bit her lower lip. "I can't go on TV. I'll...I'll lose it, Mike."

"The idea *is* to lose it," he said in a calm voice. "I've arranged for the tape to air on all the local channels. You'll only have to do this once. I'll be right here with you. It'll take two, three minutes and it'll be all over."

"Oh, God," she whispered.

"I know," he said. "I know. Just think of Kimmy. Someone out there may have seen her. You need to do this."

She stood there shaking, her mind whirling. What was she going to say? And she knew she'd cry. She'd break down and spill her guts and her deepest, darkest fears to the whole world.

"Ready," said a voice from the living room.

Lena could see the bright lighting and a female reporter—she recognized the face—sitting right on her couch, waiting.

"The reporter will guide you through a couple of questions. It'll be easy," Mike was saying. "Then the camera will pan on your face and you'll ask whoever took Kimmy to return her. When they edit the tape, they'll keep flashing Kimmy's picture with a 1-800 number below. It's all taken care of."

"Mr. Quinn, we're ready," said the well-modulated voice again.

The reporter signaled the cameraman, a red light went on and the woman put a grim expression on her face. "Miss Portillo," she began, "can you tell us when and how your daughter, Kimberly, disappeared?"

Lena went on autopilot. She said something like, "We call her 'Kimmy,'" and after that she barely remembered what she said, other than, "If anyone has seen my daughter, please, let the police know. She had on blue jeans with pink hearts on the knees, a T-shirt and tennis shoes and a blue windbreaker. She has long brown hair and brown eyes."

All she could think of was to stay in control, to keep her dignity, to speak clearly, but the lights were shining in her eyes and the reporter was asking more questions, and she supposed she answered them. The only thing she could really remember afterward was that she looked directly at the camera and begged, yes, begged, the kidnapper to return her child. "Please, please, whoever has my little girl, please let her go." And then, in case Kimmy ever saw this, she said, "Kimmy, sweetheart, we're here waiting for you and trying to find you. We love you.''

And then it was over, and the crew cleared out of Lena's house and it seemed as if she gradually reoccupied her own body.

"You were wonderful," Gloria said, "absolutely wonderful."

All Lena could say to Mike was, "Thank God you didn't warn me."

Later, when she'd gotten her breath back, Mike brought them up to speed on the investigation. "I've already been by the Woodland Hills police station," he said. "Nothing new to report. I did get the full student list, though, and I'm going to work on it until something gives."

Lena took a calming breath and looked at him. "The police already interviewed all the kids in the playground that day," she said, hugging herself.

"So I do it again. And again if I have to. And right now Pop and Uncle Ted are out with several of the guys from L.A. Metropolitan talking to teachers and the janitor and the bus drivers. *Again*."

"Something'll turn up," Gloria said, stacking the coffee cups and a few dishes in the dishwasher. "I know it will."

"I wonder," Mike said then, "I wonder if I could see Kimmy's room."

She nodded, understanding. After all, he'd been the caring man who'd taken the abandoned infant girl to the hospital in the first place, the man who'd stopped by every day to see how the little crack baby was doing. And it had been Mike who'd first suggested they talk to Social Services about adoption. They'd been planning a family soon anyway. But that had been before Jeff Davidoff's tragic death and Mike's descent into hell.

Lena shook herself mentally. "Sure," she said. "Down the hall to the right. I'll, ah, show you."

It hurt to see him standing in Kimmy's bedroom. Lena leaned a shoulder against the doorjamb and watched him as he eyed the room, the pink skirted dressing table, the dollhouse Gloria had given Kimmy for Christmas, the white toy chest with the painted lambs on it, the collection of stuffed animals on the windowsill. There was even the little brown fur rabbit Mike had given Kimmy as an infant.

He touched it. "I remember this," he said quietly.

Lena felt a flood of emotions then, each vying for ascendancy. There was resentment—Mike here, invading the special privacy of their lives again. Mike, the man who'd put a loaded gun to his head when his year-old daughter was sleeping only a few yards away. Yes, Lena resented Mike's presence. She resented needing his badge to pull the strings she couldn't. All these years she'd made it on her own, she and Kimmy, and now here he was in charge of their lives. She felt a surge of bitterness toward him and a peculiar kind of jealousy.

Mike stood in Kimmy's room, an invader, an alien, and Lena wanted suddenly to scream at him, *Look at what you did! If you hadn't been such a rotten drunk, my child, our child, would still be here in this room!* She said nothing. What good would it have done? And it really wasn't Mike's fault. It wasn't Gloria's fault or her own, either. She had to stop searching for someone to blame.

After a time the jealousy and resentment settled, and her heart actually began to soften toward the man who'd never gotten to know the child he'd chosen as his daughter, the man who'd sadly thrown everything away because of alcohol and a selfish sort of depression inherent in his work.

He looked awfully big and out of place in this little girl's domain, a giant among the dolls and fur animals. He'd opened a pop-up picture book and was smiling, then he caught Lena's eyes. "I missed a lot, didn't I?" he asked.

Out in the living room Mike picked up his leather jacket from the arm of the couch. "Half the kids I need to see will probably be at Sunday school or out to breakfast, but I'm going to give it a shot. If I hear anything, anything at all, I'll—"

"I'm going with you," Lena said.

Mike stopped short. "No way."

"I know these kids. I know most of their mothers. I can talk to them."

"And I can't?"

She sighed. "Right. You're working with Hostage Negotiations—I guess I knew that. But these are kids, Mike. They *know* me. You might intimidate—"

"Give me a little credit, Lena," he said.

"I can't sit here and do nothing," she blurted out. "Let me help. Let me at least tag along. Please."

"Haven't you been through enough already today? I don't think—"

"For my sake, Mike," she cut in. "I'm going stark raving nuts with this waiting."

Mike studied her for another moment, and Gloria said, "I'll man the telephone here, just in case."

And then he relented. "All right, okay. But you just sit and listen."

"Of course," Lena said, grabbing her purse. "I'll

drive, though—I mean, if it's okay? I know where a lot of these kids live and…''

"Sure," he said. "Whatever. You always did like to be behind the wheel.''

Lena ignored his subtle jab. She was relieved just to be going along. Anything to keep busy. She'd steel herself against Mike's sudden control of her life; she'd do whatever she had to. *Just stay focused,* she told herself. *Forget Mike, forget who he is. Who he was.*

It wasn't a large school district, and Lena knew the streets fairly well. She drove her souped-up GTO smoothly as Mike read off the names on the list, beginning with *A*.

"Will Abbott," Mike said. "You know the kid?''

"Vaguely. I think his father's an insurance agent. Maybe he's a real-estate agent.

"They're on Keokuk Avenue."

"Okay," Lena said.

The Abbotts were all still in their pajamas and robes when Mike and Lena knocked on their door. Mike introduced himself, flipping his badge, and then introduced Lena. Will Abbott's father recognized Lena and asked them in immediately, mentioning that a policeman had already telephoned. "That was yesterday," he said.

The family was sick over Kimmy's disappearance. Will's mother hugged Lena and got teary eyed.

Mike chatted with the six-year-old in a friendly, quiet manner and then got down to business. "You know Kimmy, don't you?" he asked.

"She's in my class," Will replied, fiddling with the TV remote control before his father took it away.

"And you were in the playground area after school the day she disappeared."

"Uh-huh."

"Were you playing with Kimmy?"

"Nah." He made a face.

"You don't play with the girls, do you?" Mike asked in a conspiratorial tone.

"Nah." Another face.

"I didn't either in first grade," Mike put in. "So tell me, were the girls playing with a soccer ball?"

"I...I think so."

"I only ask because my notes say that Ben Halloran thought the girls were tossing the ball around just before the school buses left. Does that sound right?"

"They always play with the soccer ball," Will said.

"Do you know which girls?"

Will screwed up his face, thinking. "I think it's Mary Lou and maybe Ally. And Marcia."

"And Kimmy?"

"Uh-huh."

"Will," Mike said in a very quiet, attention-getting voice, "did you see a stranger on the playground that day?"

Will shook his head.

"Maybe the stranger was outside the fence," Mike went on. "Maybe standing there or in a car."

"I don't know," Will said.

"There are so many parents who wait in cars," Will's father said. "You know, picking their kids up."

Mike turned to him briefly. "Something like eighteen or more that afternoon. Including Kimmy's grandmother."

"The girls get in trouble a lot," Will chimed in.

"How's that?" Mike asked.

Will shrugged. "They throw the ball into the street. Mrs. Martini says they can't play with it if they do it on purpose."

"Mrs. Martini? She was one of the playground monitors?"

"Uh-huh. She's my teacher."

Lena looked expectantly at Mike, but he shook his head. "She wasn't on the playground that day."

Then Will's mother spoke. "The kids are supposed to go straight to the buses or to private cars. They don't always, though. Tomorrow," she said, "a few of us are going to talk to Miss Trenholm about some after-school supervision on the playground. I think after Kimmy's... Well you understand."

"Of course," Mike said.

When they were back in Lena's car she checked the time. "My God," she said, "that took half an hour. If each interview takes that long, Mike, it'll be days more...."

"I know," he said gravely, "I know."

Before noon they'd talked to three more children. Getting anything out of a six- or seven-year-old was like pulling teeth. The only facts they had were that Kimmy, Ally, Mary Lou and a girl called Marcia had been tossing a soccer ball around. One of the children they interviewed corroborated Will's story about the girls frequently getting into trouble for throwing the ball over the fence into the street.

At a fast-food place where Lena and Mike stopped for a bite to eat, Lena pressed for interviews with Ally and Mary Lou. "I realize the police have already talked to them both a couple of times, but I think we should—"

Mike nodded. "We will. I just want to talk to a couple more kids first. If I can get one thing, one new viewpoint on what went on that afternoon in the playground—"

"We *know* what went on."

"No, Lena, we don't. All we know is that the kids

remember the usual routine. I'd like just one small break, something new to put in front of the girls before we talk to them. As it stands now, they've been asked the same questions and they've given the same answers. I want something, anything, to jar their memories.''

Lena picked at her French fries and sighed. "I understand. But what if there isn't anything? What if both girls were gone by the time Kimmy disappeared?''

"Gloria was at the school on time. The buses hadn't even left yet. But Kimmy was gone. Believe me, something out of the ordinary happened, and someone had to see it. The trouble with kids is that their memories are short and they tend to recall only the mundane occurrences in their daily lives. That or something special,'' he added, "like a birthday party or a trip to Disneyland. You know.''

"You're good with the kids,'' Lena admitted.

"Right,'' he said, skeptical.

She looked up. "No, you are. I'm surprised.''

Mike made a grunting noise, dismissing her words. He went back to his food, and that was when Lena remembered his sister's visit, the news about Mike remarrying. The woman, according to Colleen, had children. A ready-made family for Mike. She wondered how he was really handling the booze. She'd heard what he'd said, but then she'd heard it all before. Her father had been a pro at denial. And so was Mike. Oh, she knew all about drunks who weren't drinking. It was only a matter of time before—

"Ready to go?'' Mike said, breaking into her train of thought.

"Ah, sure,'' Lena said.

They went to two more houses that afternoon. One family wasn't home; the other family was, but the little girl was sick with a cold and not up to an interview. She'd been picked up at school early the day of Kimmy's disappearance, so the interview would have been a waste of time anyway.

Exhaustion caught up with Lena as they left the last house. She felt that now-familiar sinking sensation and pulled over to the curb, letting her forehead rest on the steering wheel. "Oh, God" was all she said.

Mike was very quiet for several minutes, and then he turned toward her, resting an arm on the back of her seat. It had begun to rain again, a monotonous drizzle oozing from a leaden sky. The wipers swished on the glass.

"Lena," he finally said, "you've held up like a trooper so far. Try not to let go now. Something *is* going to give. It always does."

"If Kimmy were... Oh, Mike, wouldn't I know it, *feel* it, if something awful had happened?"

"I think you would," he said. "Sure, you'd know."

"Liar."

He laughed softly. "Hey," he said, "where's that free spirit I pulled over for speeding? What was it—eight years ago now?"

Lena groaned, remembering. It had been a blazing hot summer day, the Santa Ana winds whipping down into the greater Los Angeles basin like breath from hell. She'd just had the rebuilt engine put into the car, and the top was down. She'd been speeding all right, doing ninety-three in a fifty-five zone, and Mike had rushed up behind her in his patrol car, lights flashing, siren wailing. When she'd pulled over and Mike had sauntered up to the car, ticket pad in hand, she'd slowly removed her sunglasses and taken the offensive.

"Officer," she'd said, "I realize I was going a little

over the speed limit, but I'm trying out a rebuilt engine, and you can't tell a thing at fifty-five.''

"Uh-huh," he'd replied, his eyes hidden behind mirrored sunglasses. But he was big and fair and intimidating as hell in his spit-and-polish uniform.

"See this invoice?" She'd pulled the bill for the engine out of her purse. "Eight hundred and ninety-six dollars. Would you pay it before checking out the car?"

"License and registration, please, ma'am," he'd intoned.

And that had set her off. "You can't ticket me!"

"License and registration," he'd repeated, "and your proof of insurance."

"I'll...I'll lose my license!"

"So you've had previous tickets?" he'd asked, deadpan.

"What do *you* think?" she'd snapped back, and that had been the beginning of their relationship.

Mike had indeed ticketed her. But then he'd shown up in traffic court and allowed that Miss Torres might not have been going all that fast, his radar had been on the fritz that whole day, etc., etc. And after court he'd walked up to her and asked her out.

"You've got a lot of nerve," she'd said, "but I suppose I owe you one."

"How about going out with me, then?"

"This is extortion or something."

"Uh-huh," he'd said. "Either have dinner with me or I'll tail you everywhere you go."

"You're not even that cute," she'd said.

"Dinner, Miss Torres?"

"All right, dinner. But it'll cost you a week's salary."

In the end, Lena hadn't been able to do that to Mike. They'd gone to a cheap but good Italian place that was Lena's favorite. Six months later they'd been married.

"Remember?" Mike was saying now. "I clocked you at ninety-five on the freeway."

"It was ninety-three. Don't exaggerate."

He smiled. "Okay, I'll concede the point. I just want to see some of that old spark. You can get through this, Lena. If you hang tough, you'll make it."

"I'm trying," she said. "I really am."

The next family on the list was the Samsons. Ally Samson was Kimmy's best friend; she was also one of the last children who'd played with Kimmy in the school yard. Her mother had already told Lena that Kimmy had been there when she'd picked Ally up. She'd repeated this to the police, and Ally had been interviewed several times.

"Oh, Mike," Lena said, "what if she can't tell us anything else?"

"We'll see," was all Mike said.

The Samsons weren't home. According to a neighbor who was mowing his lawn, they had gone camping.

They had no more luck at the Meacham house. Then they drove to Mary Lou Shelton's and found the little girl just arriving home from spending the weekend with her father and his new family. Mrs. Shelton was very sympathetic, hugging Lena, sitting Mary Lou down and telling her to pay very close attention to the questions the nice man was going to ask.

Mary Lou sat on a footstool and looked at Lena. "Is Kimmy going to be at school tomorrow?"

Lena felt the hot burn of tears press behind her eyes. "If we find her, sure. She wouldn't want to miss school."

"Good," Mary Lou announced.

She was a precocious child who was better than most her age at recalling details. "I never left the playground," she told the group, "because Mrs. Martini gets real mad if we do. She said she'd take the ball away, too. So I never, ever throw it in the road.''

"That's good," Mike said, "but didn't one of you throw the ball—by accident, of course—into the street that day?''

Mary Lou sighed and looked at her multicolored fingernails. "Marcia did, by accident.''

"I see," Mike said. "And did Marcia get the ball?''

"Kimmy did.''

"Oh," Lena said.

"That first time," Mary Lou added.

"So someone accidentally threw the ball into the street a second time?" Mike asked.

"I think it was Marcia again." Mary Lou gave another sign. "But that time Kimmy told her not to be a brat and to get it herself.''

"So Marcia went into the street," Mike said. "And then what happened?''

"Nothing. She got the ball and that's when Mommy honked the horn for me.''

"Where was Kimmy then?''

"Waiting for Marcia at the fence. She was calling, 'Hurry up! My grandma's going to be here soon.'''

"And what did Marcia do then?''

"She had the ball. I remember she ran past me with the ball.''

"Why do you remember that?" Mike asked.

"Because she bumped me and she looked like she was mad or something.''

"At you?''

Mary Lou shook her head. "I don't think so. But she looked mad.''

They left the Sheltons' shortly after that, and Lena wondered at Mike's silence. "What was all that stuff about? You know, about the ball? Are you thinking one

of the girls might have seen something in the street?"
she asked, steering around a corner.

"I'm not thinking anything," Mike said.

But Lena knew that look of concentration. "Tell me.
I'm not one of the kids, Mike."

"It's probably nothing," he said. "But I am wondering just what it was that made Marcia look so angry."

"Mike, little girls are like that. They have very complicated social relationships. Someone's always mad at someone else. It probably doesn't mean a thing."

"Complicated relationships," he repeated. "I'll try to remember that."

It was almost six that Sunday evening when they returned to Lena's house. Gloria came out to meet them and had very little news. "That FBI man was back this afternoon. Asking questions. He wants you to call him tomorrow. And several of the parents from school called to touch base, but other than that, zilch. I was hoping," Gloria said, "well, you know."

And then Lena walked Mike to his car. "A wasted day," she said, hugging her cardigan around her. "Another wasted day."

"Maybe not," Mike said, opening his door. "Remember the TV interview will be played over and over."

She tried a weak smile. "I want to thank you, Mike," she said.

"For what?"

"For all you're doing. You and the other guys. Really."

"Hey," he said, getting into his car and rolling down the window, "I'm Kimmy's father. No matter what you believe, I'll always be there for her." Then he added, "For both of you."

But Lena didn't have the courage to believe him.

CHAPTER SIX

A COLD SHOT of adrenaline awakened Mike at four-thirty on Monday morning. *Jennifer.* Holy cow, he realized he'd had a lunch date with Jennifer on Saturday!

Well, he couldn't telephone her at this ungodly hour. Still, he was wide-awake now, his mind working.

He got up and made coffee, showered and tried to listen to the twenty-four-hour news channel, but it was impossible to focus on anything but the desperate plight of his daughter.

Of course he'd have to go into headquarters this morning and talk to Joe Carbone. He'd need time off. How much? It was hard to say. They might get a break in Kimmy's case today. Or maybe tomorrow. Or maybe a month from now. The terrible truth was that too often missing children were never found. He himself was gut sick—but Lena. He couldn't begin to imagine what this was doing to her. The idea of never knowing Kimmy's fate was inconceivable.

At eight he phoned Lena, explaining there wasn't much they could do till after school was out. In the meantime he'd clear his desk at work.

"You're taking a leave?" she asked.

"Yeah," he said. "I'm due some vacation time. I'll also touch base with my father and Uncle Ted again, just in case. But as of last night, there was nothing new on their ends. They've been working the school-employee angle—bus drivers, teachers, janitor. Dad canvassed the immediate school neighborhood again yesterday. So far no dice.''

"Oh, Mike," she said, her voice trembling, "it's been four days. I'm starting to think…''

"Don't," he said tightly. "Don't start making up scenarios.''

"I can't help it.''

"Just wipe your mind clean. I'll be by at three-thirty to pick you up. Meanwhile I'll try to reach some of the parents we missed yesterday, set up appointments. This may take all evening.''

"That's fine," she said. "I'll get Mom to sit by the phone.''

"Lena," he said, "the chances of Kimmy's abductor calling after all this time are slim to none.''

"It's not just that. Kimmy knows our home number. She also knows 911. There's always a chance, well, that she could somehow get to a phone, you know.''

"She could," Mike agreed.

"She's very resourceful.''

"She gets that from you," he said.

Shortly after talking to Lena, Mike drove the few blocks to Jennifer's house. He would have telephoned her, but after forgetting their date, he figured his explanation had better be in person.

Jennifer had just gotten her kids off to school when he pulled up in front of her two-story, mission-style house. He parked his used beige Volvo behind her shiny new BMW. Their houses were only a mile apart. It might as well have been a million.

When she answered the doorbell, she was already in a leotard, tights and a light sweater, ready for work at her studio. A very attractive green-eyed woman with pale skin and long, curling auburn hair. She gave him a cool look and did not invite him in.

"Is my calendar wrong?" she asked.

Mike blew out a breath. "Something happened, Jennifer. If I could come in for a minute...?"

"I can't believe this," she said. "There's no reason on earth why I should let you into my house."

Jennifer was an independent nineties woman who didn't go in for games. She didn't have to. First off, her ex had left her and the kids pretty well-heeled, but second, she was one of those extremely good-looking women who took excellent care of herself. From the male attention Jennifer always drew, Mike imagined she could have all the dates she wanted. She and Mike had met through his sister, Colleen, and Jennifer had flirted with him. He figured she was one of those women who were drawn to the element of danger that was ever present in a cop's life.

He cocked his head and looked at her standing in her doorway, barring his way. Yeah, Jennifer would ditch him in a second if she wanted. "It's my daughter," he said. "You remember I told you about her? Kimberly. She's missing."

Jennifer's face fell. "Missing?"

"It happened on Thursday. Right from the playground at school."

"My God," she said, opening the door to him, "I had no idea. That must be what the message from Colleen was about. Oh, Mike."

He sat in her well-appointed off-white living room and told her all about it—everything that he knew, anyway, which was tantamount to nothing.

"Oh, Mike," she said, "you must be going out of your mind."

"I am. But it's worse on her mother. After all, I haven't seen Kimmy since she was a year old."

Jennifer nodded solemnly. "I know," she said, "and I've always thought the woman was, well, selfish not to let you help out, at least financially. Children need both parents."

Mike had explained to Jennifer about his partner's death and his drinking and about how Lena had severed all ties, even taken her mother's maiden name to hide from him. Jennifer never seemed to quite fathom it. Of course, he'd left out the part about putting the loaded gun to his head in a drunken fit of depression over Jeff's death.

"So it was this woman, Gloria, who was supposed to pick your daughter up at school?" Jennifer was asking.

"Gloria, yes," he said. "She's Kimmy's grandmother. Evidently she was on time, but Kimmy had already disappeared."

Jennifer closed her eyes for a moment, then sighed. "It's a shame, a real crime," she said, "that Lena wasn't at the school to pick up her own child."

Mike stared at her, frowning. That was the first real bitchy thing he'd heard her say since they'd started seeing each other. He was taken aback and he was disappointed. But then he thought about her statement and realized that her reaction was probably normal.

The only thing he said in defense of Lena was, "Kimmy's mother has to work long hours. She's lucky she's got Gloria to baby-sit."

Mike left the house by nine-fifteen, explaining that he didn't know when he'd be over again but that he'd keep her informed.

"How does it look for Kimmy?" Jennifer asked at the door.

He shook his head. "To be honest, not good. When something doesn't break in the first twenty-four hours, the odds get worse."

"Well, good luck," she said, and they kissed, a brush of their lips. Jennifer put a hand on his cheek. "Call me," she said.

At the LAPD Metropolitan Area headquarters, where Mike was stationed, everyone was surprised to see him walk in. Joe came striding out of his glass-enclosed office and confronted him.

"What in hell are you doing here, Quinn?" Joe asked, hands on hips.

"Don't start on me," Mike said, "I'm only here to dump my paperwork on one of the other guys."

"Already done." Joe folded his arms over his chest. "Now, I want you out of here for as long as it takes."

"Hey, Mike!" one of the other team members called from across the room. "I got your basketball kids all taken care of. Monday, Wednesday and Fridays. Right?"

Mike lifted a hand and gave him a nod of thanks. One less thing to worry about. He made a mental note to call Jay's mother. Jay was the kid he worked with in the Adopt-a-Buddy program. Maybe, though, by next weekend they'd have Kimmy home. *God willing*, he thought.

"I'd get out of here before the fibbies come back if I were you," Joe said then. "They've been a big pain in the butt around here all weekend. Especially that Special Agent Sabin. He's a real ass. And I sure don't like some of the questions they've been asking the guys."

"I can just imagine," Mike said, knowing the FBI would be looking into his background. His and Lena's. The parents were often the number one suspects in a case where a child disappeared and no ransom was being sought.

He frowned. "I suppose they want to question me."

Joe shrugged. "If they can't find you, they can't question you. Am I wrong?"

Mike nodded. "What about that class you wanted me to hold in Bakersfield? Do you think Raddo could handle..."

"Already done," Joe said. "Now, take off. And for God's sake, call me every day. And if anything breaks..."

"I'll let you know," Mike said.

"We're all praying for her," Joe said, "you know that."

"Thanks. I think we're going to need all the help we can get."

After leaving headquarters in downtown L.A., Mike drove to his dad's precinct in the Hollenbeck Area. Both his dad and uncle had been stationed there for their entire careers. Mike's father, Larry, was a homicide detective who could have retired ten years ago but figured he'd go bananas at home. Uncle Ted was also a detective, but with vice. His son, Scott—Mike's first cousin—was a patrolman. He was sort of a lazy kid who always took the least path of resistance. Riding around in a patrol car and responding to 911 calls suited him just fine.

Everyone at the Hollenbeck station knew Mike. They'd all heard about his daughter, too.

"Anything, anything at all we can do to help, just ask," he was told a dozen times as he wended his way through a clutter of desks to his dad's cubbyhole.

Larry Quinn looked up from a stack of paperwork. "Hey, kid," he said, rising, shaking his son's hand, "any news?"

"Not a damn thing," Mike said, and he sat down across from father.

Larry Quinn was a big man, too, taller than Mike by an inch, and he outweighed his son by twenty pounds. Not fat, but big boned. If his hair had been darker, he could have stood in for John Wayne.

"I've got a couple of printouts here from the national data bank on known child molesters in the area," Larry told him, and he handed Mike the sheets. "It's pretty recent. Ted's working the angle that our perp's a weirdo. He's out doing some checking on the streets right now."

Mike nodded. He didn't have to say how much he appreciated all the support—his family knew it without having to hear it.

"Now me," Larry said, "I've been thinking that maybe we could take a new tack here. What if someone, say a parent who'd recently lost a child, decided to remedy the situation? It's happened before. A grief-stricken mother just snaps one day. She sees a kid, a nice-looking kid around the age of her own, and she takes her. Just up and snatches her."

Mike let out a breath. "I don't know, Pop. Cases like that are few and far between."

"Could happen, though. This afternoon, soon as I clear some of this damn paperwork off my desk, I thought I'd get in touch with the county coroner's, try to get a list of kids, girls, around Kimmy's age who've died recently." Then Larry Quinn tapped his pen on a stack of files. "I still think we oughta try to find out where the birth mother is."

"I agree," Mike said. "The trouble is, she's not in any of the data banks. Doesn't have a driver's license, not registered to vote anywhere, zip. No one's heard or seen a thing since we found her and she signed the adoption papers six years ago. Chances are, the way she was using, she's dead by now."

"You've checked with Social Services and the adoption courts, you know, to see if anyone was trying to get info on Kimmy's whereabouts?"

"Woodland Hills cops did it first thing," Mike replied. "FBI checked some more. And keep in mind that Lena's been using her mother's maiden name. I just don't think that Jane Cramm, if she's even alive, could have traced Kimmy. Hell, I'm a cop. It took me a few weeks of pulling strings to find them."

"Yeah," Larry said, "I remember." Then he frowned. "I just hope there's nothing we're overlooking."

"So do I," Mike said. "So do I, Dad."

Mike arrived at Lena's a few minutes before three-thirty that afternoon and found her cleaning out the storage closet off of the kitchen.

"Staying busy," she said, giving him a weak smile. "I'll go change. Give me a minute?"

"Sure," he said, hands in his jean pockets.

"There's coffee made."

"I'll get a cup."

Mike poured himself some coffee, then wandered into the living room. He remembered most of the furniture, though Lena had had the couch recovered. He stood by the built-in bookshelves and stared at the many photos Lena had there. Pictures of her and Kimmy. Of course there were none of him. Idly he wondered if she'd thrown them away.

He noticed, though, that even if there were no mementos of his life with Lena, there were no photos of any other man, either. Did Lena have someone? Surely if there was a man in her life, he'd be present during this crisis. He could ask her. But then he realized he'd sooner burn in hell. Besides, he had a life of his own now. He had a woman, too, a good woman. They'd even spoken about marriage. Not planned anything. But both had mentioned not being entirely against remarriage.

Lena appeared in black jeans and a bright teal-colored cotton top, sleeves pushed up. She'd combed her long brown hair out of the ponytail she'd been wearing, and it fell softly against her shoulders. Mike stared at her for a moment too long before asking if she wanted to take his car or hers.

"Mine," she said, shrugging. "I know the streets."

She walked out to the road ahead of him, shoulder bag swinging against a full hip. God, how he remembered those hips. When they'd been married, he'd wanted to punch out more than a few guys for leering at that perfect fullness.

He got in the passenger side, slammed the door and told himself to forget it.

"Where to first?" she asked, sliding the gearshift into reverse, turning her head to back out.

"We'll go by the Samsons'. Ally Samson's. I talked to her mother this morning. She said she'd meet us at four."

"Oh, I hope Ally can help us. I know the police have talked to her before, but…"

He heard the desperation and hopelessness in her voice. And he felt it, too. There was no other way, however, to conduct an investigation. You simply had to go over and over what little you had and pray for a break.

Ally's mother was apologetic for going on the camping weekend. "If I'd known you needed to talk to us again, I would have stayed right here." Margy Samson showed them in, giving Lena a comforting hug. "Just tell me what we can do. Anything."

Mike started carefully, as always, with Ally, whom Kimmy had known and played with since preschool. He recalled Lena telling him he was good with kids. He didn't know about that. He was okay with adults, gentle and authoritative when it came to negotiating for a hostage's life. But kids? Truthfully, he was never sure how to handle them. Some were shy. Some forthright. Some were just downright obnoxious. He wondered what Kimmy was like. He wondered a lot about that. And he was beginning to wonder if he'd ever find out. It had been four full days without a single clue.

Ally was outgoing and very sweet. He imagined she'd be a sensitive young lady someday soon, the kind of friend who'd be close for a lifetime.

The interview went well, although they learned nothing new, except for the fact that it had been Mary Lou who'd first thrown the ball over the fence into the street. "Mary Lou calls Mrs. Martini a poop-face," Ally announced.

"Mmm," Mike said. "Is that because she disciplines you girls for playing in the street?"

"Uh-huh," Ally said. "Mary Lou and Marcia once had to go to Miss Trenholm's office."

Lena spoke up then. During all the interviews she'd sat in on, this was one of the few times she'd shown her frustration.

"For God's sake, Mike, we know all this," she said, leaving her chair, hugging herself as she walked to the front window and stared out.

He could see the quake in her shoulders, and he knew she was barely keeping in control. He met Margy's eyes for a moment.

To Lena, he said, "Just a couple more questions, all right?"

She didn't answer.

"Okay, Ally, so Marcia came back then, with the

ball," Mike said, "and Marcia bumped into Mary Lou. Like she was angry."

"She wasn't mad at Mary Lou," Ally stated positively.

"Oh?" Mike said.

Ally shook her head. "She was mad at those mean people."

Mike felt every nerve in his body tense. He noticed that Ally's mother had straightened in her seat and that Lena had spun around and was staring wide-eyed at Ally.

Mike took it very, very carefully. "You mean the people who were on the sidewalk?" he asked.

She shook her head, and that was when Lena took a step toward her. Mike put up a warning hand. He smiled at Ally. "So these mean people who made Marcia mad weren't on the sidewalk. Do you remember where they were?"

"In the car," she said without hesitation.

He couldn't believe it. He'd talked to how many kids? And until this moment not a single one had recalled anything like this.

"Okay," Mike said calmly, "Marcia was mad at the people in the car. Do you know why, Ally?"

Ally shook her head. "I think the mean man said something."

"And this was what—when Marcia got the ball?"

"Uh-huh."

"But you didn't hear what the man said?"

"No, my mommy was there for me."

"I see," Mike said, signaling both women in the room to keep their cool. "So tell me, Ally, was the man driving? Was he behind the steering wheel?"

"I don't know." She looked at her mother, who gave her an encouraging smile and a little nod.

"Ally," Mike said, getting her attention again, "was the other person a man, too?"

"I don't know."

"That's okay. I was only wondering because you said the mean people, so I thought maybe you saw another person."

Ally shook her head and then tears filled her eyes. "Did that man take Kimmy away?" she blurted out.

"We don't know," Mike said.

The interview went downhill from there. Mike ended the questioning when it was obvious they weren't going to learn another thing from Ally. Not today. But he knew that a police psychologist—one who dealt primarily with children—might have to be called in to do another interview.

At the door, Margy Samson said, "Do you want me to keep asking her?"

But Mike told her emphatically that he didn't want the Samsons to mention it. "The last thing we need Ally to do is make something up to please us. Okay?"

"Sure, I understand," she said.

In the car, Lena was clearly out of her mind with frustration. "Let me talk to her again," she begged. "Please, Mike, we both know Ally must have seen more. She knows me—she'll be relaxed. Mike, you've got to let me...."

He put a hand on her shoulder then, and surprisingly Lena burst into tears. He wanted so much to draw her close, to comfort her, but he knew she'd never allow it. Instead he kept his hand there, very gently, and let her cry herself dry.

Several minutes later she sniffed and raised her head. "Oh, God," she said, "what if it's the same story with

Marcia? What if she *does* remember these people and they have nothing whatsoever to do with Kimmy?"

Mike finally took his hand away. "Hey," he said, "why don't we just take this one step at a time? Let's go on over to the Meachams' and see what we can learn. Okay? You up to driving or do you want to—"

Lena gathered herself quickly. "I'm fine. I really am. I'm sorry I lost it."

"Don't be. If no one was watching," he said, "I'd do the same thing."

She shot him a look. "You're such a terrible liar, Mike Quinn," she said, and then she put on big round sunglasses and pulled out into traffic. He sat back, comfortable with her driving, and felt relief. The old spunky Lena was back. For now.

The Meachams lived in a more modest neighborhood of Woodland Hills in an old duplex, a wood-framed house that had seen better days. Lena didn't know them at all because Marcia was new to Jefferson Elementary School. Mike was slightly taken aback when a man in a wheelchair came to the door. Marcia's father.

"Nancy's still at work," he told Mike and Lena, "and me? I'm pretty much home, as you can see. Full government disability."

Mike nodded, then Gary Meacham called to his daughter, who appeared from the back of the house. "Marcia," he said, "these folks are here about your friend Kimmy. They want to ask you a few questions."

Marcia was a pretty little girl, though Mike could see the hint of deviltry behind her blue eyes. It wasn't hard at all to believe the playground monitor, Mrs. Martini, would have her hands full with this youngster.

As usual, Mike went slowly with the child, trying to gain her trust and put her at ease. Finally he began with the questions about the soccer ball and how it ended up in the street. "So you accidentally threw the ball over the fence," he said. But Marcia was quick to say that it had been Mary Lou who'd done it.

"Oh, I see," Mike said. "Sorry, I don't have my notes with me. Now, let's see. It was you, though, who offered to leave the playground and get the ball."

"Kimmy got it the first time," Marcia said, just to keep things straight.

"Right," Mike agreed. "But the second time's the one I'd like to talk about."

"Okay," she said.

"Was there anyone out on the street near the playground, Marcia?" he asked, hating to lead her on but needing to push. Time was growing short. "Someone in a car?"

She screwed up her face and thought. "Uh-huh."

Mike wanted to smile. This was corroboration. "Did you see the man in the car? Did he say anything to you?"

"He was mean."

Gary Meacham raised his brows. Obviously he'd been present when his child was first interviewed and nothing had been said about a man in a car.

Mike met his eyes reassuringly for a moment and then went on. "Okay, Marcia, let's see. Do you remember what this man said to you?"

"He said, 'Scram. Go away, kid.'"

"Why did he say that?"

She shrugged and looked at her feet. "The ball was kinda by his tire."

"Oh. But you got it anyway. Did he scare you, Marcia?"

"Sorta."

"And you got mad."

She nodded. "I didn't do anything bad."

"Of course you didn't," Mike said. "So tell me, did this man get out of his car or anything?"

She shook her head. "He leaned out."

"Of the window?"

She nodded.

"And what did the other person in the car do?"

"She just was sitting there."

"I see," Mike said. *She.* He met Lena's eyes calmly. Inside, however, his heart was beginning to pound. "Okay, so this woman didn't say anything to you. How about the other people in the car?"

"There wasn't anyone else."

"Oh. Okay. I was wondering, Marcia," he said smoothly, "did these people in the car look like anyone you know, or maybe like someone on TV?"

She seemed to think about that, then shook her head.

"Were they old?"

She didn't know. She did remember that they both had long hair about the color of daddy's.

"Light brown," Mike said.

"Uh-huh," she replied.

"Okay," Mike said, "about the car these people were in. Do you remember what it looked like, Marcia? Like its color, or if it was big or small?"

She screwed her face up and thought. "It had wood," she said.

"Wood?"

"Uh-huh. On its side."

"Wood paneling?" Lena suggested.

Marcia gazed back at her, not understanding.

"I mean," Lena said, "did the car have wood on its sides? One of those station wagons with wood sides?"

"It was like Jodi Pratt's car, only different," Marcia said.

"A Wagoneer. The Pratts have a wood-sided Wagoneer," Gary Meacham said.

"Only different," Marcia insisted. "It was old. The wood was coming off."

"An old wood-sided station wagon," Lena said. "Ford and Chrysler made them since the sixties. It was fake wood, either painted or a wood-grain kind of stick-on paper. I know 'cause we had one in the shop a few years back and Al had to repair the thing."

Mike smiled at Marcia. "Is that what it was, Marcia? A station wagon? You know what a station wagon is?"

"Like Janie Caudill's car," Gary Meacham prompted.

"Uh-huh," Marcia said, "only it was old and there was wood."

"You're a very smart young lady," Mike said, "and you've helped us a lot, Marcia." And then Mike couldn't help asking, albeit jokingly, "I don't suppose you got the license plate number, young lady?"

To everyone's utter shock, Marcia sat up very straight and said, "Daddy has the same one."

It was a long moment before anyone could speak. Finally, Mike said, "Come again?"

"My collection. Holy Toledo! She's talking about my license plate collection," Gary said, and he spun his wheelchair around and headed toward the back of the house. "Are you all just going to sit there?" he called.

He led them into a spare bedroom that was used as a den. TV, stereo, books and pictures and family memorabilia everywhere. On one wall there were dozens of old license plates.

Marcia studied the wall. After only a few moments she pointed up. "That one."

"Which one?" Lena cried.

"That one. The red one."

They looked up. Near the ceiling was a distinctive bright red-and-yellow plate: New Mexico.

Mike and Lena had an identical thought: how many old wood-paneled station wagons could there possibly be in a sparsely populated state such as New Mexico?

No one said a word, however, until Mike breathed, "Well, O-K-A-Y," and then everyone spoke at once.

FOR A SHORT AND WIRY man, Danny Hayden was very strong. He grabbed Jane by the hair and yanked her head back until she cried out.

"I'm goddamned sick and tired of your bitching," he grated out. "Now, stuff this pill down the kid's throat and get her ready."

"Please," Jane whimpered, but he only tugged harder on her hair.

"Get her the hell ready!" he said fiercely. "This job's worth two big ones, and I ain't lettin' her off the hook. Now, get in there."

It was useless to argue with Danny, and Jane did what she was told. When she unlocked the door to Kimmy's back room the child was huddled in a far corner, staring blankly at the old black-and-white TV they'd put in there to keep her quiet.

"Here," Jane said, holding a glass of milk in one hand, the tranquilizer in the other. "Come here and drink this."

Of course Kimmy didn't realize she was being drugged on a regular basis. Tranquilizers in the day, sleeping pills at night. Jane had told the kid she had to take her vitamins. What did a kid know, anyway?

Drugging her didn't bother Jane. But what Danny was

planning did. She'd argued against it ever since they'd first snatched the little girl, but he was unrelenting. They needed the money, and that was all there was to it.

He'd bought Kimmy a new T-shirt for what he called "tonight's party." It was a pretty, rainbow-colored shirt, and after Kimmy took the pill, Jane showed it to her.

"Do you like it?" she asked.

Kimmy just stared at her, in one of her brat moods.

"You sure are spoiled," Jane said.

"When can I go home?" Kimmy asked abruptly, looking up at Jane with big brown eyes.

"Soon," Jane said. "If you're good."

"When?" Kimmy persisted.

And Jane realized the kid didn't believe her. "I don't know when," she said, exasperated. "When Danny says, I guess."

"I don't like him," Kimmy said, pouting.

"You better do what he says," Jane warned, "or he'll get mad." Unconsciously she put a hand on her head where he'd yanked her hair.

Kimmy's own hair was tangled, and Jane tried to brush it out, but she kept hitting snarls, and Kimmy cried out every time she did.

"Mommy does it better," the kid whined.

"She's had more practice," Jane replied, losing patience.

"She puts conditioner on my hair so it doesn't tangle."

"Conditioner," Jane repeated. "Big deal."

"And sometimes she makes French braids."

"What the heck are French braids?"

"They're fancy and they're real hard, but Mommy does it for me, like when there's a party!"

Jane grabbed her shoulders. "Will you just shut up about your mommy? I'm your goddamned mommy."

Kimmy's lower lip began to tremble, and Jane realized she was going to cry. Danny would be furious.

"Shush," she said in a gentler tone. "Hey, don't you like you're new shirt?"

"It's okay," Kimmy said.

Jane sighed. "Now, you have to go with Danny tonight. You have to do whatever he says and be real, real good. Or else."

"I don't want to."

"You have to, Kimmy. Do you understand?"

"What for?"

"You just have to go, that's all." Jane tried to smile. Boy, this stuff with kids was hard. She'd thought you told them what to do and they did it. But it turned out that they had minds of their own, and they were smart and they talked back and argued. And they recognized a lie when they heard one. At least Kimmy did. How did mothers manage the little brats?

She took the child's hand and led her into the kitchen, where Danny was eating a bowl of cereal for dinner.

He looked at the kid and smiled, as if to disarm her. "Hi, there, Kimmy," he said with false joviality. "We're going to see some friends of mine."

Kimmy said nothing, but Jane could feel the child's little hand tighten in her own.

"So, you all ready?" he asked.

"Wait. Let me get her jacket," Jane said. It was cool in October in Santa Fe, eight thousand feet high in the mountains of New Mexico. It sure wasn't California.

Jane went back to Kimmy's room, got the jacket and helped her put it on. The child was obviously used to a grown-up doing this—she knew right when to put her arms up for the sleeves.

"Let's go." Danny was getting impatient.

"Be good," Jane warned once again, and then Danny took the child's hand and led her toward the front door.

Jane stood there and watched them go, watched Kimmy turn her head to look back at her beseechingly. Those big brown eyes. And Jane knew that when she'd been young, she'd felt that exact same way—scared, lonely, confused. *Poor kid,* she thought, and she wasn't sure whether she was thinking about Kimmy or herself.

She sighed when she heard the station wagon start up. She guessed Danny knew what he was doing. No one was going to hurt the kid. It was only a movie. Kimmy would be so drugged out she wouldn't remember a thing anyway. And they needed the money.

And today Danny had said they only wanted to *see* the kid. Well, when they saw how pretty she was they'd want her. Sure they would.

It would be okay, Jane told herself. And once this job was over, they'd be like a real family, the three of them. It'd be nice, she mused, to have something of her own for a change.

Her own kid, her very own.

CHAPTER SEVEN

IT WAS AFTER eight o'clock when Lena pulled into her driveway and turned her car off. She sat there for a minute, head bowed.

"You okay?" Mike finally asked.

"No," she said simply.

"But we've got a lead."

"Maybe." She shook her head. "Maybe it's nothing, some kid's father in the car who was in a bad mood."

"Listen to me, Lena," Mike said quietly. "I've got a hunch."

"Oh, great. A *hunch*."

"Okay, a hunch is a wild guess. What I have is intuition, and that comes from experience. A cop's intuition. This is a solid lead. That man and woman took Kimmy. They went to her school and waited and took her."

She turned her face to him in the darkness. "But why? Why Kimmy?"

"We don't know that yet. Either they took a random kid or they were really after Kimmy. It doesn't matter at this point. We'll find her." He hesitated. "Lena, do you believe me?"

"I don't know," she whispered. "I want to, but I'm so scared."

He put his big hand on hers where it rested in her lap. "Trust me," he said, and she felt the warmth of his hand,

and it frightened her how easily she remembered his touch.

"I can't, Mike," she said. "I can't risk it." She was afraid to move; his hand still imprisoned hers. "I can't risk Kimmy." Didn't he know how she felt? He'd let her down so many times. That's what drunks did best—they let people down. The closer the person, the more they got let down. She couldn't let it happen to her again.

"Come on," he finally said. "Let's go in, get something to eat. And I'm going to call Pop. He needs to know about the car."

Lena heard him on the phone. He sounded so hopeful telling his father the news. She wished she felt the same way, but the lead seemed so nebulous.

Gloria heard the phone conversation, too. "Oh, my God," she said, "you've found the people who took her?"

"Not quite yet, but it's a good lead," Mike said.

"Thank heavens! Oh, I know you'll get her back now."

"It's not that easy, Mom." Lena said. "They could be anywhere."

"Mike'll find them," Gloria replied. "Now, come on and eat. I made tamales."

Lena ate, so distracted she couldn't tell if the terrible, empty ache in the pit of her stomach was hunger or fear.

"What now?" Gloria asked over her prize tamales.

"We search the records for a wood-paneled station wagon with New Mexico plates. They should have them at the state motor vehicle department. Unless the plates or car are stolen or not registered. But neither of those cases is likely. No one'd steal such an old car, and there aren't many vehicles around that aren't registered at all." Mike paused. "Pop's coming over here soon. He's bringing Uncle Ted and Scott. We're going to make plans. Hope you don't mind. I thought it'd be easier.''

Lena looked up abruptly. ''They are?''

''Don't worry, we won't bother you. Just go to bed, get some rest.''

''I don't think so,'' she said. ''I think I'd better sit in on your war council.''

He shrugged.

''She's my *child*, Mike.''

He studied her from under sandy brows. ''She's mine, too,'' he said.

The Quinn men arrived as Gloria and Lena were doing the dishes. They crowded in the door, filling Lena's small living room, three big blond men, tall and broad. Four of them counting Mike. She hadn't seen them in five years, and she noticed that Scott had put on a lot of weight sitting in his patrol car.

They were very subdued as they greeted her and Gloria. ''Long time no see. Sorry about the circumstances. We'll get her back for you, Lena. Looking good, Gloria. Yeah, I put on a few pounds.''

They took up the couch and the armchair, and Mike brought two kitchen chairs in, one for Lena and the other for her mother.

''Okay,'' Mike's father said, ''so we know a few things now.'' He reiterated the facts, then looked at Mike. ''Right, Son?''

Mike nodded.

''The question is, who would come all the way from New Mexico to get one child? Did they have a reason or did they pick just any kid? If we knew the reason, we'd find 'em quick, but we don't, so we have to work backward, trace the vehicle. We're damn lucky it's not a common type of car, and we're damn lucky New Mexico has a relatively small population.''

Uncle Ted spoke up. ''We've got a two-pronged attack here. We trace the vehicle. We're also in the process of tracing this woman, Jane Cramm, Kimmy's biological mother.''

''You don't really think...?'' Lena put in.

''Hey.'' Ted turned to her. ''We can't rule out the possibility. It seems to be a real trendy thing to do these days. Hell, fathers and mothers kidnap kids from each other. Biological parents get kids back from adoptive parents through the courts, even years later. Damn courts just hand them back. Maybe this woman, Cramm, maybe she's nuts enough to have done it.''

''But she disappeared,'' Lena said. ''It's been six years.''

''Crazier things can happen,'' Ted said. ''The FBI is trying to trace her, but they'll only have federal records. If she's never filed an income tax form, for example, they may not have her.''

Lena sat there trying to listen, but in her head images whirled: two dreadful creatures in a run-down ancient station wagon, with Kimmy in the back, tied up, crying, scared to death, hungry, thirsty, not understanding why her mother didn't come and rescue her. She gave a short sob and became abruptly aware of Mike watching her, his brows drawn. Judging her. She felt hot all over, then cold, and she had to look away, pretend she didn't feel Mike's eyes on her, his gaze like a hundred tiny feet walking on her flesh. She despised her own weakness and hated even more for Mike to see it; she wanted no chinks in her armor where Mike Quinn was concerned.

She was so weary, so exhausted, and now all these men were crowding her house, familiar men out of a past she'd tried to forget, to erase. It was as if her life were turned back on itself and the past five years of hard work and independence had never existed.

"So, we have to trace this Jane Cramm. Do you have an address or a description, a Social Security number?" Scott was asking.

"I never saw her," Lena said. "I think they found her in a shelter, and she signed the papers, but we never met."

"No description, then," Larry said.

"She was in her twenties," Mike said. "I remember that. So maybe she'd be around thirty."

"Or she overdosed and died. Six years is a long time in an addict's life," Lena said.

"It's a possibility." Ted nodded.

"The thing is," Mike said then, "someone has to do the nitty-gritty work, the footwork. In New Mexico. Hell, before that. On the route there. Someone has to cover that ground and ask questions." He looked around at the circle of men. "I'm going to do it. I've taken a leave and I'll do it myself. Frankly I don't trust the feds to do it right. I don't trust *anyone* else to do it right."

Lena heard his words, but it was his tone that impressed her: serious resolve. She felt an unwanted stirring of admiration. This was not the man she remembered. Or was it all a big act? Would he go home tonight and hit the beer and whiskey chasers and forget his resolve by morning?

"Okay," Ted was saying, "you do New Mexico. I know a guy in Albuquerque, a detective there name of Hidalgo, John Hidalgo. Helluva good man. I'll call him and arrange things."

"I can only guess at the route they took back to New Mexico, if that's where they went. I looked at a map earlier. Interstate 40 is the easiest way to get there. Now, I realize they could be heading to the southern part of the state, but the population centers are on 40, so I have to go with it. And 40 goes straight to Albuquerque, where I need to end up anyway.''

''Sounds good,'' Uncle Ted said.

''If these people in the station wagon left a trail, I'll find it,'' Mike said grimly.

Lena hadn't voiced an opinion until now, and frankly she was skeptical about Mike's hunch. These people could be totally innocent, parents or relatives who'd been at school to pick up a child. Or if they were the ones who'd taken Kimmy they might not have gone back to New Mexico. Maybe they lived in California and simply drove a car with out-of-state plates. Maybe they'd gone to Mexico or Canada. The thing was, Mike really *could* be onto a lead. And they had absolutely nothing else to go on. She'd be damned if she was going to sit here in this house frantic with worry when she could be doing something.

She took a breath and blurted out her thoughts. ''I'm going with Mike.''

The four big men turned leonine heads and stared at her.

''I'm going,'' she said.

Mike shook his head. ''Lena, this is police work. Sorry.''

''Not official police work,'' she said stubbornly.

''Lena,'' Larry said. ''I know you're upset, but you can't do Kimmy any good by going with Mike.''

''I need to get close to her,'' she said. ''She needs her mother.''

''I may be dead wrong about where she is,'' Mike protested. ''I may...''

"You had a *hunch*," she reminded him. "And what else do we have?"

"Lena," Ted began.

"You can't..." Scott said simultaneously.

"I'm going," she repeated.

Gloria tried, too. "Lena, maybe..."

"No way, Lena," Mike said.

She shut up then, realizing not one of them would listen to her, but her mind worked incessantly, chewing away at the problem. She had to go with Mike.

"So I leave in the morning," Mike was saying. "I'll keep in close touch. You have the number of my cell phone. Any information you get, you call me. Anything."

The Quinn men nodded, rose and said they'd be going. They repeated their assurances to Lena, but she wasn't listening.

"Don't worry," Ted said, "Mike'll find her. Get some sleep."

Mike left last. He stood in the doorway for a moment, eyeing Lena. "Take it easy," he said. "I'll find her."

"Thanks, Mike," Lena said mildly. "You're leaving in the morning? For New Mexico, I mean?"

"Yeah, early. I've got to go home and get some shut-eye."

"You'll call me?" she forced herself to say.

"Absolutely."

"Okay," she said. "Good luck."

Then he was gone and she closed the door behind him and turned to see Gloria glaring at her, her hands on her hips.

"Okay, Lena," Gloria demanded, "now you just tell me what you have in mind."

LENA'S ALARM woke her at five-thirty. It was still dark out, and she felt heavy and almost as tired as when she'd dropped into bed last night. She hadn't slept well, tossing and dreaming of Kimmy, waking, dozing. God, she hadn't slept well in days, running on fear and adrenaline and desperation. She moved quietly so as not to awaken her mother, who would only try once again to talk her out of what she was going to do.

She threw a few things in an overnight bag, a jacket for cool weather, underwear, blouses, a pair of pajamas. Then, unable to help herself, she got the blanket from under Kimmy's pillow and her favorite teddy bear and threw them in, too.

The house was quiet, only the hum from the refrigerator audible. Outside, the sky was brightening, a faint mother-of-pearl glow behind the coastal range. She tiptoed out, leaving the door still locked behind her. No note. Gloria knew where she was going.

She started her car and backed it out of the driveway, headed down the street toward the Valley Freeway. She'd pried Mike's address out of Gloria, and she hadn't even bothered to tell her mother how sneaky and underhanded she thought Gloria had been to secretly keep in touch with Mike all these years.

The streets were empty at this hour; even the freeway was practically deserted. She made good time, racing through the dawning city, her lights cutting swaths ahead of her.

Mike couldn't have left already, could he? She couldn't have missed him. Turning south on the 405, she blasted through the just-awakening suburbs toward Santa Monica. It wasn't hard to find his address, just off the beach. His building was painted a ghastly color of salmon that glowed in the dimness of the early hour.

Lena breathed a sign of relief as she pulled up behind

Mike's Volvo, which was parked in front of the building. He hadn't left yet. She'd considered going right up to his apartment door and knocking, but she'd decided it would be better to ambush him at the last minute, when he wouldn't have as much time to argue with her.

She turned her car off and sat there, waiting. It was six-fifteen; she'd made excellent time. So far so good. But the hard part was yet to come. What would Mike do when he saw her? Would he be hungover and have one of his temper tantrums? She had no choice—she *had* to convince him to take her along. She'd follow him all the way to Albuquerque if she had to. If...*when* they found Kimmy, she had to be there.

She didn't have long to wait; at 6:35 Mike emerged from the shadows of the building. He was carrying a duffel bag and digging in his pocket for his car keys. It was such a familiar mannerism of his that she was instantly transported back in time; she could have been still married to him, waiting for him in the car, watching the way he moved, hunching up his shoulders that certain way. Despite her nervousness, she couldn't help noticing that he'd lost some weight since she'd last seen him. He looked lean and fit, and he'd even shaved, which surprised Lena. In the old days, he'd have been unshaved, puffy, irritable. Maybe he was taking this thing more seriously than she thought—maybe it had shaken him up so badly his mind was only on finding Kimmy. Well, Lena thought, good.

He tossed his duffel bag into the back seat, started to get behind the wheel, and that was when Lena got out and went up to the driver's side of his car.

"Mike," she said.

He stopped short in the process of putting his key in the ignition. He froze.

"Mike," she repeated.

"What in hell?" he said.

"I have to go with you."

"Lena, don't start. We've been over this. I thought you understood."

"All I understand is that I have to find my little girl. I have to be there when you find her. My God, Mike, she doesn't even know you. She'll be traumatized already, and then, for more strangers to take her... Don't you see, Mike? I have to be there."

He got out of his car. "Lena, I understand your concerns, and they're valid, but the minute she's found, I'll call you. You can talk to her."

Lena shook her head. "It's not the same."

"I don't even know if she's *in* New Mexico. It may be a wild-goose chase."

"I know, but it's better than sitting home losing my mind. Mom will be there if Kimmy is found in this area. I have to do this, Mike." She didn't want to beg, but she had to convince him somehow.

"You can't, Lena. You know that. I can't take you along on police business."

"But, Mike..." she began, and then she saw him focus on something behind her, and he frowned. Lena whirled around, but there wasn't anything except a blue BMW driving down his street; she turned back to him, ready to start arguing her case again, but he wasn't paying any attention to her.

"What...?" Lena muttered as Mike walked right past her.

The blue car had stopped at the curb, and Mike was approaching the driver's door. *It must be someone he knows,* she thought when a woman got out of the BMW and stood with the car door between her and Mike. Lena heard her say, "'Morning, darling, I thought I'd run by and see you off."

She was very attractive, whoever she was—the girl-friend Colleen had told her about, Lena supposed. She had an impression of auburn hair pulled back into a po-nytail, clear, pale skin, a sweatshirt that read The Work-out, but all she felt was impatience, the need to convince Mike and get on the road.

"Oh," the woman said, glancing at Lena. "I...is this...?"

Mike looked uncomfortable. "Jennifer, this is Lena. Lena, Jennifer."

Lena nodded brusquely; Jennifer smiled unconvincingly.

"I have to go now," Mike said.

"I know. I just wanted to say good luck," Jennifer said.

Lena stood there, the pale morning light beginning to illuminate the scene—Mike, Jennifer, Lena herself, an awkward threesome. And she wasn't sure what to do next; she only felt an irrational anger and a terrible impatience.

"Mike," Lena started.

"Lena, listen, you can't go with me." He seemed embarrassed, as if he didn't like airing dirty laundry in front of his lady friend.

"You can't stop me from following you," she said, not caring.

Jennifer looked from one to the other, surprised. "She can't mean... Lena, you aren't planning on going with him?"

"Excuse me, but I don't think this is any of your business," Lena said coldly.

"Lena," Mike said.

"I'm sorry—really I am. It's so awful about your daughter. I mean, Mike told me," Jennifer said, "but you can't go with him."

"Watch me," Lena said, tight-lipped.

"Lena, go home. Wait there. I'll call you. The second I know anything," Mike promised.

"No."

"Oh, please listen to Mike," Jennifer said. The fake pity, the possessiveness in her tone, grated on Lena's nerves. She turned to the woman and said fiercely, "It's not your child."

Jennifer drew back.

"Look, this is ridiculous," Mike said. "Lena, go home. If you try to follow me, I'll call in the LAPD. I'll put out an APB on you, and they'll stop you."

"I'll get there some other way, then," Lena said in a hard voice. "I'll show up in Albuquerque. You can't stop me. Kimmy's my child!"

"Oh, for God's sake," Mike said. "Jennifer, I'm sorry about this. I've really got to get on the road now...."

"Don't you apologize for me," Lena snapped.

"I'm leaving now."

He gave Jennifer a kiss, then closed her car door for her, leaning down and saying something to her through the window that Lena couldn't hear. Then, calmly, he watched her drive off, got into his own car and started it up.

Lena felt her heart drop into her stomach. He was leaving without her; he wouldn't listen. She stood there for a minute, defeated, and then, as Mike pulled out from the curb, she ran to her own car and got in, turned the key in the ignition, jammed it into first gear and took off down the quiet street after him.

She followed him for one block, then two. He kept

looking in his rearview mirror. He went another block, past apartment buildings and houses and a few shops. He was heading for the freeway; she knew exactly what route he'd take out of L.A.—Interstate 15 to 40. She'd follow him all the way if she had to, and to hell with what he or his girlfriend thought.

At the stoplight three blocks from Mike's apartment, he jammed on his brakes and came striding back to her car, angry.

"Dammit, Lena, go home!" he rasped.

"No," she said calmly.

The light changed. He got back into his car and drove away. She followed. Then she saw him jam on his brakes again and pull over. She stopped behind him. What now? A frisson of fear rippled through her. Was he angry enough to do something to her? Did he still have that awful temper?

He got out of his car again and came back to her. Leaning down, he said, "You mean this, don't you? Dammit, Lena..."

"Yes, I mean it."

He straightened and swore and then leaned down again. "Okay, okay. Goddammit, you can come."

"Thank you, Mike," she said, her heart pounding like a drum. *Be nice,* she told herself. *You won.*

"Let's go back to my place, leave your car there," he said, resigned.

"We'll leave *your* car there," she said. "Mine's faster, and Kimmy may see it and recognize it and..."

"I can't argue anymore. You win, Lena. Fine, we'll take your car. What the hell."

In five minutes she'd followed him back to his place, he'd parked and thrown his duffel bag into her car. Then he stood there, looking down at her in the driver's seat.

"Move over," he said.

"What?"

"Move over. I'm driving."

She was about to retort, but she clamped her mouth shut and slid over. Without a word he got in, adjusted the seat and put the car in gear. Neither of them said a word; the tension in the car could have been cut with a knife. He drove fast—skillfully, she had to admit—and she held her tongue so as not to antagonize him any further.

Silence except for the rushing wind and the hum of tires on the road. Then they were turning onto the freeway, and Lena took a breath, feeling as if she'd been holding it all morning. The commuter traffic heading into the city began to get heavy, and the sun backlit the buildings and the coastal range ahead of them.

Kimmy, Lena thought. *Sweetie, I'm coming to get you. Hang in there, baby.*

Mike drove, his muteness accusatory, but Lena didn't care anymore—she was on her way to finding her daughter.

"Admit it," she finally said, breaking the silence. "Admit it, Mike. I'm right to come. You wouldn't even recognize Kimmy."

"And whose fault is that?" he shot back.

And then Lena shut her mouth and turned her head away to watch the scenery flashing by, every second, every minute, possibly bringing her closer to her daughter.

She hoped. Oh, God, how she hoped.

CHAPTER EIGHT

THE TENSION in the car was unbearable, and finally Lena couldn't stand it anymore. She could afford to be the first one to give in now—she'd won the main battle, hadn't she? *Be mature,* she told herself. *Be reasonable.*

So she opened the glove compartment and found a road atlas. She studied it, rehearsing in her head the amiable tone of voice she'd use.

"I'm sure you're right," she began. "Someone from New Mexico would take Interstate 40. Ten is too far south. It makes sense."

Mike said nothing.

Later, as they followed the mountainous route on the edge of the Mojave Desert, she tried again, forcing herself to be pleasant. "I just wish we could be sure, you know, that we're on the right track."

"It's the only shot we've got right now," he said, pulling into the passing lane.

"I know, I know," she said. "I only wish, well...I've been doing a lot of hoping and praying. It doesn't seem as if Kimmy disappeared only five days ago. It seems like forever. I can't even remember what life was like before this happened."

"Mmm," he said.

Oh, she knew how ticked off he was. But really, what had he expected her to do? Sit at home frantic with worry while he was on the chase?

Two hundred miles along the route, outside of Needles on the Arizona border, Mike pulled into a truck stop to gas up. "This damn car of yours," he said under his breath. "What's it get—eight miles to the gallon?"

"Well, ten or better on the open highway," she said defensively.

"Great. It's a real economy model. I don't know why you've kept it all these years."

She opened her door. "You used to like it," she said.

While Mike filled the car, Lena went inside to use the rest room. When she was done, she showed Kimmy's picture to the cashier, explaining that the child was her daughter and that she'd been kidnapped.

The cashier was very friendly but of no help. "Jeez, lady, I didn't work on Thursday, and I never work nights," she said.

"Well, thanks anyway," Lena replied just as Mike was coming in to pay for the gas.

Outside again, he said, "No luck, huh?"

"I didn't think there would be."

"And just what is that supposed to mean?"

Hopelessness and fear overcame her, and her attempts to be mature and polite evaporated like steam in cold air. She stopped short and confronted him. "Do you know what the odds are that those people in the station wagon took Kimmy? Or how about the odds on them driving to New Mexico just because a car has New Mexico plates? But better than *that*," she said, "what are the odds that they gassed up here? There're hundreds of stops, and these places must have ten different cashiers to cover all the shifts."

They stood there under the hot desert sun, and he glared at her. "You got a better idea? If so, let's hear it."

Lena stared back defiantly.

"Police work is ninety-nine percent drudgery. You check dozens of possibilities to maybe get one small break. Hell, you're the one who begged to come along. Now is not the time to wallow in your doubts, lady. If you don't like it, I'll be glad to stick you on a bus home."

"Over my dead body," she said, and she turned on her heel.

"Just hold on a minute," she heard Mike say, and she stopped short, her back to him.

"Dammit, Lena, we can do this the hard way or we can do it the easy way, but we've sure as hell got to do it. It's your choice."

She stood there silently.

"I've been trying to give you a lot of room, but don't push me too far. I don't want to be stuck with you any more than you want to be stuck with me," he said harshly.

She whirled on him. "You don't have to remind me of that."

"Then act like you remember it," he said.

He walked to the car and got in, and there was nothing Lena could do but follow him.

Mike stopped often to flash Kimmy's picture that day. He pulled into two places in Kingman, Arizona, and every little dusty stop along the barren highway. Luckily, Lena thought, the turnoffs were few and far between in this isolated region of the desert Southwest.

They did very little talking. Even at their late lunch Lena had nothing to say to him. They were on a desperate quest, but that didn't mean they had to be friends; he was right about that. She'd tried to be civil, but obviously he wasn't going to cool off about her insistence on coming along.

She looked up from the grilled-cheese sandwich she was nibbling at and glared at him. Maybe he wasn't mad about her coming along. Maybe he was just hungover. She knew those sour moods of his. He could have left her house last night and gone to a bar, one of those cop hangouts he'd always loved so dearly. Sure he'd said he wasn't drinking anymore. But then, how many times in their marriage had he quit?

She studied him. His blue eyes were clear, but eyedrops could solve that. And maybe he'd showered off the alcoholic stench. It didn't mean a thing that he looked healthy. Her father had looked pretty darn chipper right up till the end.

It all came back in a sick rush—the nights Mike had come stumbling in drunk, sometimes passing out on the couch, waking with the hangover from hell. Never stopped him, though. She'd still loved him, idiot that she'd been. Loved him right up until he'd put that gun to his head. Then she'd turned her heart to stone.

She wondered how his lady friend, Jennifer, put up with it. They didn't live together, so maybe she hadn't gotten a full dose of his mood swings, the alcoholic bitterness and fits of depression. Colleen had said they were going to be married. Jennifer would get the full picture then. You bet she would, and no matter how much she loved Mike, she'd never be able to tolerate the binges.

Lena pictured the woman. Very pretty and very well groomed. She took care of herself: hair, skin, nails, clothes. This Jennifer was no slouch. How had they met? Lena wondered, but she shut off the question and erased from her mind the image of them kissing. It was none of her damn business.

They'd been taking shifts driving. It was Mike's turn again, and after they ate, he slid in behind the wheel.

Lena looked at him as he turned onto the on-ramp of the interstate. Five years, she mused. She hadn't seen this man in five long years, and yet he seemed to have barely changed. He still wore his dark-blond hair longish and there were no wrinkles on his face. He had a tan. When they'd been married, Mike had gotten little sun. She supposed he was outside a lot now with his new assignment.

She glanced at him. "What, exactly, is Hostage Negotiations?"

"Just what it sounds like."

"Come on, Mike, you can do better than that."

He draped a wrist over the top of the steering wheel and let out a low breath. "I'm a member of a team of six guys who're trained to talk people down from volatile situations."

"Mom said you were in the newspaper a couple of times."

"Mmm," he said.

"So you must be okay with the job."

"What are you getting at?"

She sighed and looked out the side window. "Nothing, really."

"Come on, Lena, I know you."

"Well, I, I guess it's hard for me to see you in control of your own emotions, much less someone else's."

"Oh," he said, "I get it."

"I'm not trying to tick you off, Mike. I'm just stating a fact."

"I don't think you know me anymore," he said coolly.

And then she couldn't help saying, "Tigers don't change their stripes."

He only shot her a hard look and then turned his attention back to the road.

Outside Flagstaff, as it was starting to grow dark over

the snow-capped mountains, Mike stopped at two gas stations and three motels, showing Kimmy's picture to anyone who'd been at work last Thursday night or Friday morning. He got nowhere. Then, only a mile down the road, he pulled off again at a string of motels, fast-food joints and gas stations. Lena sat in the car biting her lower lip, trying not to let panic swamp her.

It was after the sixth place he'd gone into that she snapped. "This is the biggest waste of time I've ever seen," she said hotly. "We should push straight on to Albuquerque and have your uncle's friend start checking on old panel wagons."

Mike turned to her slowly and deliberately. "I'm going to say this just once," he stated flatly. "It's not going to do us or Kimmy any good if we do find the owners of that car and they're not even in the state. This way, *my way,* we might just luck out and learn that they came this direction. Then we'll know." He put a silencing finger up. "And don't tell me again that the people in the station wagon might not even have Kimmy at all. I know that as well as anyone."

Lena glared back at him but kept her mouth shut until Mike pulled off again two miles later. "I don't believe this," she muttered, realizing that there must be a hundred motels and restaurants and gas stations in Flagstaff. She wanted to cry. "Can't we just go to Albuquerque? We could be there in a few hours and..."

Mike leaned into the car and swore. "I promise, Lena, one more word and I'll put you on a bus so fast your head'll spin. I'm dead serious."

She glared at him. "I'll report that you stole my car."

"Good God, woman, don't you ever let up?"

"Not when it comes to Kimmy," she fired back. "*You* I gave up on."

"You know, Lena, maybe if you had let me be a part of Kimmy's life, this wouldn't have happened," he retorted.

He might as well have stabbed her in the heart. Shocked, sick with anguish, she said, "You have the nerve to blame *me?* You were the one who put the gun against your head, Mike. And not ten feet from where my baby, *our* baby, was asleep. You're the drunk. Is that how you wanted her to be raised? Is it?"

He said nothing, and she knew she'd scored.

After another tense moment, he finally straightened. "I'm going into this motel to show Kimmy's picture. And then I'll go to the next place and the next. You can sit here and do nothing or you can take that other copy of her photo and start helping out. There's that gas station across the road and the minimart next door." He slammed the car door and strode into the motel.

She sat in the dark interior of the car for a few minutes fighting tears and exhaustion. They'd never get a lead on Kimmy this way; they simply had to get to New Mexico and take it from there. But there was obviously no stopping Mike. He had to cross all the t's and dot all the i's before going on.

She opened the passenger door, got out and stretched, feeling so tired and dragged out her head was starting to spin. Still, she rummaged around in the back seat for the other copy of Kimmy's photo, then headed across the road toward the gas station. The cashier inside said he'd been on duty, a double shift, last Thursday, but he didn't recognize the picture, nor did he recall an old wood-paneled station wagon.

"I'm sorry, lady," he said. "Good luck, though."

Lena thanked him and left, crossing the asphalt drive to the twenty-four-hour minimart.

The place was busy, and she had to wait in line to show Kimmy's picture. She yawned, felt that weary, desperate sinking sensation in her belly. Maybe she'd get a tall coffee to go. This was going to be a long, long night.

Finally at the register she explained the situation and slid Kimmy's picture across the counter to the older lady behind the cash register.

"This is her most recent photo," Lena said dully.

The woman pursed her lips and cocked her head, studying the picture. "Hmm," she said.

Lena looked up.

"You know," the lady went on, "I think, well, I'm pretty sure she was here."

At first Lena thought she hadn't heard correctly. "What?" she asked, her heart beginning to pound.

"Well, I think I remember the child," the woman said. "It must have been last Thursday night or really early on Friday morning. This woman, see, was carrying the child, you know, into the rest room. I remember because the little girl was real dopey, sleepy. 'Course it was late. But then when they came out of the bathroom, the girl was walking and the woman was tugging her along. I thought at the time it was kinda mean, yanking the kid like that. I guess that's why I remember and all."

Lena had stopped breathing, and all the blood had left her head. *Oh, my God!* she thought. *Oh, my God!* "Are you sure it was her?" she managed to ask, and she realized her voice was trembling.

"I'm pretty sure," the woman said, staring hard at her.

Lena flew out of the store and dodged cars as she raced to get Mike. *He'd been right—he'd been right!* She found him walking toward the GTO, and the words came tumbling out all at once.

"Okay, okay," he said, putting both hands on her

shoulders, "take it easy. I'll go talk to the lady and see if she recalls anything else."

"Mike," Lena breathed, "they really did take her. Kimmy's in New Mexico!"

"It looks that way," he said, and he ushered her toward the car.

He was back in ten minutes, and he slid into the driver's seat. He was smiling. "Not only does the woman think it was Kimmy, but she said that maybe the car was a wood-sided station wagon. They'd evidently parked right in front of the door and left the headlights on. She said she noticed that, always does because it's annoying. But she doesn't remember the woman very well. Too bad."

"Oh, let's go, Mike, please," Lena pleaded. "I'm ready to burst. This is the first hope I've had in so long."

"I know," he said. "Believe me, I do know."

But then, only about five miles on the other side of Flagstaff, he pulled off the highway and into a motel parking lot.

"What on earth are you doing?" she demanded. "There's no reason to show Kimmy's—"

"We're stopping," he cut in.

"*Why?*"

"Because we're both exhausted. We need a few hours' sleep and then we'll take off. And you've got to be as hungry as I am."

"We'll...we'll get food to go," she protested. "I'm not tired at all now, and I can drive while you—"

"No," he said. "We're stopping. Quit arguing. We'll put a call in for 5 a.m. if you want. But neither of us is in any condition to be driving."

"*Mike.*"

"No, Lena. And besides," he said, "we'd get into Al-

buquerque at one or two in the morning. There's nothing
we can do at that hour anyway.''

It was useless to argue. He parked and said he'd get a
room and be right back.

There was a restaurant-bar nearby, all lit up, one of
those false-front Western places. And then it hit her.
Mike wasn't tired and he wasn't hungry. He needed a
little pick-me-up. *Damn him!*

Shortly he came back with a key. Lena got out of the
car and stared at him. "One room?"

"There's a pullout couch. I'll sleep there. If I sleep at
all.''

"I'm supposed to share a room with you?"

"Okay, fine, I'll get two rooms. They're not cheap,
though. Does your budget run to that sort of thing?"

"No," she said sullenly.

Mike tightened his jaw. "I'm not going to molest you,
Lena. For God's sake, grow up.''

She looked up sharply and glared at him, refusing to
get into an argument.

"Ready to get something to eat?" he asked.

"Sure," she said icily. "And how about something to
drink, too?" Then she squared her shoulders and headed
toward the restaurant, feeling the daggers in her back.

GLORIA TORRES HAD spent the day catching up on er-
rands and bills and speaking to her boss at the restaurant.
She knew that any other employee probably would have
been fired by now, but her boss was a woman who had
three grandchildren of her own. She could not have been
more helpful or sympathetic. Just to be on the safe side,
Gloria also had the telephone company forward all calls
to a cell phone she'd rented a day after Kimmy's abduction. Still, whether she was at the post office or grocery

store, she worried—what if Kimberly somehow made her way home in the few hours she was gone?

Of course she hadn't, and Gloria had returned to Lena's, dodging a persistent reporter, at five that afternoon. She'd had several calls on the cell phone that day. They'd all been for Lena. Concerned friends, teachers, Larry Quinn touching base. And there'd been a message from the FBI, asking Lena to return the call as soon as possible. Gloria had spoken to the man, Special Agent Sabin, but she'd said nothing about Lena's having gone to New Mexico. Thus far the FBI had only been a pain in the butt to everyone.

At seven she turned on the TV for company and cooked a light dinner. Nevertheless, she kept staring at the phone, hoping against all hope that Kimmy would somehow escape from her captors and call.

It was shortly before eight that there was a knock at the door. Her heart leaped. Kimmy? Could it possibly be Kimmy?

It was not her granddaughter. Instead, standing ramrod straight and wearing dark suits, were two men. They both held up ID cards. "FBI," the shorter man said. "We'd appreciate it if you could answer one or two questions, Mrs. Torres. It is Mrs. Torres?"

Gloria stared at the official-looking ID cards and said, "Ah, yes, I'm Gloria Torres. Lena's still not here, though, and I…"

"It's not Miss Portillo we want to talk to," the shorter man said.

"Oh."

"May we come in, please?"

The short, wiry agent who stood as if he had a steel pole up his back, introduced himself as Special Agent

Alan Sabin and the other man, taller, heavier and almost white blond, as Agent Miller.

Gloria made them coffee. She would have offered the devil himself coffee or tea because it was in her nature to be hospitable.

They sat in the living room and she asked if they had any news on Kimmy.

"Well, now," Alan Sabin said, "that, of course, is why we're here."

"Something's happened?" she said excitedly.

"No, not with locating the child, Mrs. Torres."

"It's 'Gloria,' please," she said.

"All right, Gloria," he said. "You see, we've run into a snag with our investigation, and you may be the only one who can clear things up for us."

"Oh," she said.

Miller took up the conversation. "The problem is—" he smiled at her "—that we've only just learned that Mike Quinn is Kimberly's legal father."

"That's true," she allowed.

"We were curious," he went on, "why your daughter lied to the police."

Gloria gave a tight laugh and shook her head. "I assure you," she said, "there's nothing sinister about it. My daughter simply didn't want to involve him. When she divorced him, well, there were bad feelings. She's had no contact since."

"And is that why she took on your maiden name, Portillo?"

"Yes."

Alan Sabin nodded. "I wonder," he said, "were those bad feelings over Quinn's drinking?"

"I don't think that matters," Gloria said quickly. "The

issue here is Kimmy's welfare. Whether or not Mike had a drinking problem has nothing to do with—''

Miller cut her off. ''You could be very wrong there, Gloria,'' he said, and he gave her another friendly smile.

''I don't see…'' she began.

''The thing is,'' Sabin said, ''we've been hearing some disturbing things in our investigation.''

Gloria looked from one man to the other, uncertain.

Sabin went on. ''You must understand,'' he said, ''that Kimmy's welfare is our primary concern here. We only hope it's not too late, Gloria. And we need to ask you some tough questions. Please don't be upset. We all have the same goal in mind and, as her grandmother, you'll want to help no matter how distressing it might be.''

''I'm afraid you've lost me.'' Again Gloria looked from one to the other.

''It's really quite simple,'' Miller said. ''We've gotten some off-the-record tips that there may have been child abuse.''

She sat stunned for a long moment, and then she leaped to her feet. ''That's…that's ridiculous!'' she gasped.

''Please,'' Sabin said, ''please sit down, Gloria. We understand how upsetting this is to you. But we need your help if you're ever going to see Kimmy again.''

She did not sit. Instead she folded her arms stiffly over her chest, presenting a steely front to the men despite her small, trim stature. She was a pretty woman; some called her handsome. But when she was angry, her Latin temper flashed in her dark eyes and most people knew better than to push her. ''And just what are these off-the-record tips you're talking about?'' she demanded.

Miller said, ''Please do sit down, Mrs.…Gloria. If

there's been a mistake, then we want to clear it up. Your hostility won't help anyone, least of all your grandchild.''

Gloria eyed them warily, the blood pounding through her veins. She sat, looking down her nose imperiously at them.

"What we've learned," Alan Sabin said, "is confidential, of course. Our sources asked that their names be withheld.''

"That figures," she snapped.

Sabin went right on. "One of our sources is a neighbor of your daughter's," he said. "Apparently this neighbor has heard some very unsettling things coming from this house.''

"Oh, bull," Gloria said, her temper barely in check. "This is absurd. Lena would no more harm Kimmy than I would. What sort of jerk would make up such a story?''

"We realize," Miller said, "that you'd have no way of knowing any of this. But you need to look at reality here. For Kimmy's sake. Your daughter, who most likely was abused herself by Mike Quinn, has been under an enormous amount of stress since her divorce. She's a single parent, working long hours, barely making ends meet. It's understandable that she may snap from time to time. My gosh," he went on, "who wouldn't in that position?''

"Lena has never, ever laid a hand on her child," Gloria grated out. "You've been lied to. That's the only possible explanation." Then, abruptly, her eyes widened. "Oh, my God," she breathed, "you think...you think Lena did something to Kimmy! You think my daughter harmed her and tried to cover it up. Is *that* where this is leading?''

It was Sabin who said in a quiet voice, "I'm afraid so. It happens every day in this country. Too often. Either a single parent breaks under too much pressure or the other parent, the one denied custody, exacts some sort of revenge. No one, of course, means to harm the child, but things get out of hand.''

"Look," Gloria said, her heart hammering, "neither my daughter nor Mike is capable of such a thing. No one lost control here. If some busybodies told you otherwise, then they're lying." *Or you are,* she thought.

But Sabin and Miller weren't listening. Sabin said, "You could help us, Gloria. You could save Kimmy if it's not too late. You just need to take control of your emotions and look at the hard truth. If it's Lena or Mike, or both of them together, you need to help them, too. You can do it. The people we've spoken to tell us you're a very capable and moral person. We've come to you because—"

Suddenly Gloria stood up. "I...I need to call work," she said, thinking fast. "You don't mind if I take a minute to...?"

"Go ahead," Sabin said. "We'll wait."

Her fingers trembling, Gloria picked up the receiver while flipping through Lena's address book with her back turned to the FBI men. She found his home number and dialed Larry Quinn, Mike's dad. *Be there,* she prayed.

He was. "Who is this?" he asked.

"It's Gloria," she said. "I can't come into work. There're these FBI men here and this will take a while."

"What're you...?" he began, but then he caught on. "Oh, shit," he said. "Just hold on, Gloria. I'll be there in ten minutes. Don't tell them a damn thing. Hold on," he repeated, and he hung up.

The ten minutes crawled by in agonizing slowness. She offered the FBI men coffee again. She knew she was chattering but she couldn't help it. She hoped they'd attribute it to nervousness.

"They're so nice at work," she babbled, "letting me off like this. And I can't even tell them how long it'll be."

"Mmm, that's helpful," Sabin said. "Now, Gloria, we'd really appreciate it if you could tell us if you ever saw bruises on your granddaughter, say, on an arm...or burn marks."

"Bruises?" Gloria repeated, delaying, pretending to think. "Well, she fell down last week, you know, the way kids do, and..." She smiled nervously. "Do you mind if I go to the bathroom?"

She took a ridiculously long time, sitting on the edge of the bathtub, her heart racing as she counted the minutes. *Hurry up, Larry,* she thought, flushing the toilet. She felt crazily like some kind of undercover agent. A spy.

Finally she returned to the living room, and Miller started right in on her. "Gloria, we appreciate how upset you are at this time, but if you could help us, we might be able to find your granddaughter sooner. Wouldn't you like that?"

The anger boiled up in her again. "There's nothing I can tell you that will help you find Kimmy. Why are you doing this? Isn't it bad enough that she's gone?"

"As I said before, Gloria, hostility is really not at all necessary," Sabin said.

And so it went, Gloria holding them off, alternating between angry replies and inanities. *Hurry, Larry,* she kept thinking, trying not to look at her watch. And then finally, mercifully, she heard his knock.

She leaped to her feet. "I'll get it," she said, smiling

shakily. When she opened the door, Larry took her hands and gave them a reassuring squeeze.

"It'll be okay now," he promised, and he strode in past her, tossed his hat on the couch and plumped down next to Agent Miller. "Hi, guys," he said, "Detective Larry Quinn here, LAPD. So, what did they try to pull?" he asked Gloria, looking at the two agents.

"They told me they had some tips that Kimmy was abused. They wanted me to help. I guess they wanted me to say that Lena was given to fits of anger from stress or whatever."

"Mmm," Larry said. "Well, boys, I think it's time you take a hike. You're barking up the wrong tree, but what the hey, you usually do." Then he turned to Gloria. "What they do is tell you a good lie, and it's supposed to make you break down and confess. It works, too. I've used it myself. The trouble is—" he looked at the FBI men "—the person being interrogated has to be guilty."

Gloria was awash in relief. She watched as the agents stood, tight-lipped, and strode past her to the door. Special Agent Alan Sabin paused with his hand on the doorknob and glared at her and Larry Quinn. "The issue's not dead," he said to Larry. "You've got to realize by now that without a ransom demand, the odds are damn high that either your ex-daughter-in-law or even your own son is at the bottom of the kid's disappearance. Think about it, Quinn." He started out the door.

To his back, Larry said, "No, you think about it, Sabin. I've got better things to do."

When they were gone, Larry rose and gave Gloria a long hug. "They're creeps," he said.

She sighed in his big arms. "You want some coffee?" she asked. "I've got a pot on."

"You bet," he said. "We've got five years to catch up on."

CHAPTER NINE

MIKE SAT AT THE TABLE, pretending to read the menu, but Lena could tell he was angry. She knew him so well there was no mistaking the tautness in his shoulders and the pitch of his head. She wished now she hadn't said anything; she'd been trying all day to stay on his good side. What if he packed her back home?

Finally he put down the menu. "I told you I'm not drinking anymore," he said with careful control.

"Sorry," she mumbled.

"You're pretty damn tough, aren't you," he said under his breath.

"Look, Mike, I..." But she thought better of saying the words aloud—that she trusted him about as far as she could throw him. *Let it lie,* she thought. *Don't push his buttons.* It was enough that he wasn't drinking in front of her, that Kimmy apparently mattered to him.

"Go on," he said tightly. "What were you going to say?"

"Nothing, really." She looked up and shrugged. "I can't even remember now."

"Uh-huh."

They ordered barbecued-beef sandwiches. Lena had a Coke, and Mike ordered iced tea. She tried not to ponder the iron control he was displaying. It was enough that he was trying.

Back in the motel room, Mike pulled out the sleeper sofa and then said he was going to take a shower.

"I'm going to call Mom," Lena said.

"Okay. I'll have to make some calls, too. Got to let everyone know about the new lead," he said.

Then he disappeared into the bathroom, and she heard the shower go on, and she saw in her mind's eye, without a bridging thought, Mike's naked body under the hot spray. It only lasted a moment before she shut it off like a bad program on TV, then she picked up the phone and dialed her home number.

"Hello?" Gloria said.

"Mom, it's me. I'm in Flagstaff. We've stopped for the night. Listen, Mom, we have—we *might* have a new lead."

"What?" Gloria asked. "Honey, Larry Quinn's here. He's going to want to know, but tell me, quick. I can't stand it."

Larry Quinn's there? "Okay, we stopped at a million places and showed Kimmy's picture, and at one place, a minimart here in Flagstaff, the cashier thought she remembered Kimmy."

"Oh, my God," Gloria breathed.

"Yes, isn't that wonderful? She saw her—she actually *saw* her. Mom, that means she's alive!"

"I know, honey. Oh, I always knew, but..."

"It isn't a hundred percent positive, of course, but it looks good." She paused. "Mom, why is Larry there?"

Gloria told her about the FBI men and their "good lie." "So I called Larry and he came over and chased them away. Thank heavens for him is all I can say."

"Those guys actually told you they had tips about me abusing Kimmy?" Lena asked, outraged. "From my neighbors? I can't believe it. I..."

"I know, I know," Gloria said. "It's an interrogation technique. Larry told me all about it. Don't pay any attention to it."

"Goddamn them!" Lena said between her teeth.

"Listen, Larry wants to talk to you. Here he is."

"Cool down, Lena," Larry said when he came on the line. "Like I told Gloria, it only works on guilty parties."

"I'll sue them," she grated out. "I'll—"

"You won't do anything. Now, tell me about this lead."

Lena told him, aware that the water was no longer running in the bathroom. She'd let Mike talk to his dad, then, because she'd probably leave out some important details of the story.

The bathroom door opened. "Here's Mike," Lena said into the receiver, then she turned and held it out to him. "Mike, it's your dad. He wants to..." She swallowed. Mike wore only a towel around his waist, and water droplets beaded his skin. His hair was wet and slicked back. "He wants to talk to you."

Mike strode over, his bare feet leaving damp footprints on the carpet, and he took the phone from her. Lena backed away swiftly, then went to her bag, turning away from the sight of him. *Oh, God,* she thought. *Oh, God.* He looked the same—his skin, the shape and curve and heft of him. The muscles sliding under the smooth, pale skin, the height and size, the unconscious proud carriage that had captured her heart all those years ago.

He was talking to his father, and she listened, afraid to turn around.

"Yeah, Pop, it looks good. I've got the woman's name and address. She'd make a convincing witness if we ever need her. Very clear, sure of herself."

Then he was quiet, listening. Finally she heard him swear.

"Those pumped-up jerks!" he said. "Those..." Then he listened some more. "Okay, okay, but I swear, if they ever try that again, if they... Okay, Pop, yeah, I know." He said to Lena's back, "You want to talk to Gloria again?"

"No," Lena replied, still facing away. "Just tell her I'm fine and I'll call her tomorrow."

He hung up and grabbed some clothes from his bag. "I'll get dressed," he said as if he could read her mind, then he went back into the bathroom.

Lena let out a breath she'd been holding too long. She was okay with him as long as things didn't get too...personal, too intimate. It was only Kimmy who mattered, she reminded herself, not Mike, not their past relationship. Only Kimmy. And Mike had been right about how to find her. He'd been right, and she had to admit it. His hunch had panned out. Was it pure luck or was Mike Quinn really such a good cop?

He came out of the bathroom then, dressed, and Lena took the opportunity to shower. She let the hot water cleanse her, and she felt, for the first time in days, an immense relief, a burden lifted from her shoulders. Kimmy was alive. A voice whispered inside her head that days had passed since that sighting of Kimmy, and something could have...happened to her after that, but she tuned it out. She'd go on believing Kimmy was okay—she had to.

She put on the cotton-knit pajamas she'd brought along. Unsexy, thick enough to hide any curves, very modest blue polka-dot pajamas. The last thing on earth she wanted to do was to give Mike Quinn any ideas. When she emerged from the steamy bathroom, he was on the phone again, and she couldn't help overhearing his end of the conversation.

"Flagstaff, that's right. No, it's pretty chilly here. It's up in the mountains." Pause. "Well, we may have found something. A cashier in a store saw a little girl who looked like her. Yeah, the timing is right."

Lena knew instantly from the tone of his voice whom he was talking to. *It figures,* she thought.

"Listen, Jenn," he said, lowering his voice, "I'm sorry about that scene this morning." Pause. "I know, but I had to."

Lena's temper suddenly flared. How dare that woman stick her nose into this again?

"Jenn, please," he was saying. "It'll only be a few days. We'll be in Albuquerque tomorrow. We just stopped to get some rest tonight. I—" He stopped talking, obviously cut off by something Jennifer was saying. "Yes, I got one room," he said, and then he apparently had to listen again.

Ha! Lena thought. *Take that, you silly twit.* And then she wondered at her reaction. Why the heck should she care what kind of trouble Mike was having with his girlfriend?

"Okay, Jenn, take it easy. Yeah, me, too. 'Bye."

Silence settled over the room when he hung up. He didn't move from the chair next to the telephone, and finally Lena sneaked a glance at him. He was sitting, rubbing his temples with one big hand.

"Giving you a hard time, huh?" Lena couldn't resist saying with mock sympathy.

He lifted his head and looked straight at her. "What in hell are you talking about?"

Lena snatched her eyes away from his, unable to hide a small grin.

"Goddamn women," she heard him mutter, and then she slid into the bed and pulled the covers up.

JENNIFER HILTY WAS fuming. She got her kids into bed, turned out the lights in their rooms and then stalked around her house, raging inside. Mike had actually admitted that he and his ex-wife were sharing a motel room! Either he was incredibly stupid, which Jennifer knew wasn't true, or he was incredibly naive, which she was beginning to suspect. Or maybe he was incredibly brazen.

It wouldn't have been so bad if Jennifer hadn't accidentally seen the woman that morning, if she could still believe that Mike's ex-wife was the faded drudge, the low-class tart Colleen Quinn had described.

Lena was her name. Funny, she couldn't even recall Mike's mentioning it. Lena. And she wasn't a faded drudge—she was exceedingly attractive. Dark, exotic looking, tall and curved in all the right places.

Damn him!

She paced the length of her white-on-white living room with its pale sandstone fireplace and copper lighting fixtures, and she couldn't help picturing Mike in a motel room with *Lena*. They were both undressing, and she could see Mike's nude body in her mind's eye: a great body, big, broad, honed to perfection, curling blond hairs on his arms and legs, a patch of soft blond hair on his chest. In Jennifer's line of work she'd come to appreciate a good body, and she couldn't keep her hands off Mike's.

Could it possibly be as innocent as he wanted her to believe?

Jennifer gave one last exasperated sigh, then she went to the phone and called Colleen.

"Mike just phoned me from Flagstaff," she told

Mike's sister without preamble, "and Lena, his ex-wife…"

"What about Lena?" Colleen asked.

"Well, she's with him, and they're both in Flagstaff sharing a motel room."

"Oh, for Pete's sake," Colleen said. "Is he crazy?"

"I don't know. Honest to God, Colleen, I just don't know. What's he doing? Does he still like her?"

"I don't know. Wow, this is nuts."

"I'm going out of my mind. He acted like it was nothing, him and this…this woman in the same room. I can't figure him out."

"Listen, Jennifer, just calm down. Look, how about I come over and we can talk."

"It's late. I hate to bother you like this. I'd meet you somewhere, but there're the kids, you know."

"No problem. I've got this great bottle of Chardonnay, and we can open it and sit around and gab like roommates."

"Would you, Colleen? That'd be so great. And you can tell me everything about Mike and this…his ex-wife, okay?"

Colleen was there in twenty minutes, tall and blond like her brother, her face rather severe, a feminine version of Mike's. She was a career woman, vice president of a large insurance firm, and she had a no-nonsense way about her that called for obedience at her job.

She was a good friend, though, and Jennifer appreciated that Colleen had come over at this hour, smiling, unperturbed, with a sweating bottle of wine in her hand.

"So," Colleen said, going straight to the kitchen and rummaging around for a corkscrew, "what did my sweet baby brother do now?"

"Lena showed up at his place this morning and wanted

to go along on this trip of his to New Mexico. I drove by, you know, just to say goodbye, and she was there. They were arguing. I *thought* he refused to take her. When I left, at least, that's the way it sounded, but she must have convinced him somehow, because when he called tonight he told me she was with him.''

"What an idiot," Colleen mused, pulling the cork from the bottle and pouring two glasses. "Here, this is good stuff."

They sat on Jennifer's white sectional, Colleen's long legs stretched out in impeccable slacks, Jennifer sitting yoga-style in a sweatshirt and leggings.

Jennifer drank, the cool liquid sliding down her throat, then she held the glass in her lap, turning it in her hands. "Tell me about Lena, will you? I need to know her, to figure out what's going on here."

Colleen held her wineglass up to the light and squinted through it. "Oh, she's a hellion, all right. A real hot temper, kind of a tomboy. She likes cars. *Cars!* She has this old convertible, all souped up. She's had it since before she met Mike. In fact, that's how she met him. He stopped her for speeding and gave her a ticket."

"Cute," Jennifer said.

"I guess Mike thought so. They were married within a year. Lena was pretty young—too young, it seems."

"How young?"

"Well, she must have been about twenty-three or so."

"She's younger than I am," Jennifer noted.

"She had to grow up pretty quick. The baby, then Mike's drinking, then the divorce. She's done okay, though." Colleen took a drink and swirled the wine in the glass. "They were sure crazy about each other at first. I think Mike liked her energy. And she's smart, too. Manipulative."

"She sure manipulated him this morning."

"Uh-huh, she could do that. To give her credit, she did try after Jeff was killed. She couldn't deal with Mike's drinking, though, and she came to Dad." Colleen shrugged. "Mike was pretty impossible then. He's told you this, hasn't he?"

"Yes, sure he has. It must have been terrible."

"It was. But if Lena could have stuck it out... Well, you see how he quit drinking and all. I never quite understood why she just ended it like that."

"Does she know Mike doesn't drink anymore?" Jennifer leaned forward, elbows on her knees.

Colleen shrugged. "Probably not."

"If she found out, would she want him back?"

"I don't know. Maybe. But it's been five years...."

Jennifer unfolded her legs and stood up in one easy motion. "Damn it, Colleen, I'm here and he's there, with *her,* and he's probably telling her in that real sincere way he has how he's been sober for five years, and how he's changed. She's probably listening, out of her mind worried about her kid, and there he is, big, calm, understanding Mike Quinn, right there to comfort her. Oh, damn it!"

"Sounds like a possibility," Colleen said, nodding.

"What in hell am I going to do?"

"Go to Albuquerque. Tomorrow. Leave the kids with your ex and just go."

Jennifer stared at her for a long moment. "You mean just show up? But I don't know where he is."

"Easy. Call the Albuquerque police and ask for John Hidalgo. He's Uncle Ted's friend, Mike's contact. He'll know where Mike is."

"Just show up out of the blue?" Jennifer repeated.

"It might not be a bad idea," Colleen said thoughtfully.

"Won't Mike be ticked off? I could make matters worse."

"You don't know Lena the way I do," Colleen said. "You might just want to make that trip, Jennifer."

MIKE WAS HAVING a helluva time getting to sleep. The pullout bed was lumpy, but that wasn't it. Nor was it the television, which Lena had left on low before she fell asleep. He was hesitant to turn it off, because it might wake her up, and he knew how exhausted she was. She'd been a trooper, though, doing a lot of the driving. Finding the woman in the minimart—that'd been incredibly lucky.

He tried to sleep, closing his eyes, wrestling with the blanket and pillow, endeavoring to be quiet so he wouldn't awaken Lena.

Everything about her was achingly familiar, and if he'd let himself realize that this enforced proximity was going to be so damn difficult, he'd have gotten two rooms—no matter how much they cost.

The way she moved, every gesture, was a stake driven into his heart. He thought of how she'd emerged from the bathroom with a towel wrapped around her wet hair. How many times had he seen her like that when they'd been married? And how many times had he gone to her, pulled the towel off, enfolded her damp body in his arms and they'd fallen onto their bed together, Lena all soft and warm from her shower?

The TV set droned on, flickering blue light on everything, on Lena where she lay on the bed, curled up on her side, the same way she'd always slept. She'd fit into the curve of his body as if they'd been molded together.

He recalled without wanting to the many nights they'd slept together like that and he'd smelled the scent of her hair as he fell asleep.

He opened his eyes and sat up. He couldn't sleep. He searched for her shadowed form, and while he watched she moved restlessly, the blanket falling away from her foot and her calf. A slim beautiful foot and a smoothly curved calf. He could feel her skin under his hand, feel the satiny warmth of her, still, after all this time, and he burned with shame and desire.

He'd hated her for a long time for leaving him when he was falling apart, but then he'd come to realize that he hadn't allowed her, or anyone, to help him. It wasn't until later that he'd been ready to accept help, and then it had been far too late for reconciling with Lena. Joe Carbone had been there for him, thank God, and Joe had made him understand that Lena had done what she had to do in order to survive.

It had been his fault, he'd come to realize, but that was all water under the bridge now.

They'd been okay together all day, once the clash that morning had been over, but that remark she'd made about his getting a drink had cut right to the core. She didn't believe he was sober now, but then, she had reason to suspect his truthfulness. Alcoholics lied routinely, or evaded the truth or conveniently forgot what they'd promised; he knew that now, and he tried to see the situation from Lena's point of view.

Was she dreaming? Or was she having nightmares? He heard her make small noises in her sleep, soft, distressed sighs, and she seemed restless. She was single-minded in searching for Kimmy, that powerful maternal instinct, and she was probably too preoccupied with that to give him much thought. It was just as well, he mused. He had his life and Lena had hers. Maybe there was some guy, as well, for all that she professed not to date. An attractive woman like her.

It seemed she was doing okay, too, with her job and her house and her friends. Better than okay.

He watched her sleep, and regret washed over him. It was warm in the room, and he threw off the cover and lay with an arm behind his head, staring up at the ceiling, trying not to hear the rustling and murmuring that came from Lena's bed.

Next time he'd definitely get two rooms.

THE FOLLOWING MORNING they left early, getting back on Interstate 40, heading toward Gallup, New Mexico, then the final leg into Albuquerque. It would take most of the day, what with stopping to show Kimmy's picture along the route.

Mike was tired, a result of his restless night, and he let Lena drive while he dozed, head back on the seat. They stopped wherever there was a gas station or café or Navajo curio shop, and both of them fanned out to display Kimmy's photograph.

It was a desolate stretch of highway, past the giant meteor crater outside of Flagstaff, past ocher-and-dun-colored hills covered with dry brush and stunted trees. They descended, leaving behind the mountains around Flagstaff, only to rise again as they approached Gallup, just south of the huge Navajo reservation. They ate lunch at a burger place right off the highway, where they'd stopped to show Kimmy's picture. No one had seen her, though. No one had seen her all day.

"Maybe they didn't stop here," Lena said, sighing. "Or maybe no one we talked to was working last Thursday or Friday, or maybe…"

"Don't torture yourself," Mike said. "We had one lucky break. Can't expect another so easily."

He took over the wheel when they left Gallup, with its honky-tonk bars and Indian trading posts, and to keep himself awake he asked Lena what Kimmy was like.

"What's she like?" Lena repeated, staring out the side window. "That's a tall order."

"I missed her growing up," Mike said. "I only remember a little baby. Big brown eyes, fat wrists. She'd just learned to say *dada*."

"She's a very serious little girl. Oh, she plays like crazy," Lena said, "and she giggles with her friends. She listens, though, and she seems to have a real mature sense—oh, gosh, it's hard to explain, but she seems to understand how people feel. She's sensitive. And she loves her grandma and Al and the guys at work. I think she's a pretty well-adjusted kid."

"Sounds like you did a good job with her."

"All I did was love her, Mike. She felt that from the day we brought her home."

"I loved her, too."

She didn't answer, and he felt regret eat away at him.

"If...when we find her, I don't know what to tell her about who you are," Lena finally said in a small voice.

"What *have* you told her about me?" he asked, his heart sinking.

"I just said you had to go away because you were sick. I said you always loved her."

"Mmm." It could have been worse, he thought. Lena could have said terrible things about him.

"I guess I've been overprotective in some ways," Lena said defensively, "but I couldn't let anyone, anything, hurt that child, not after what she'd been through."

Was this Lena's attempt at rationalizing her behavior? Or could it be a stab at an apology?

"She had a loose tooth," Lena said. "I was going to pull it out for her, and then we were going to put it under her pillow for the Tooth Fairy. I wonder..." Her voice broke, and she put her face in her hands.

"God, Lena, don't," Mike said, and he reached out a hand and touched her arm.

"I can't help it," she said, her voice muffled.

"We'll find her," he promised. "And you can introduce her to me. You can tell her I'm her father and that I'm not sick anymore."

Lena took her hands away from her face and said fiercely, "If you ever hurt her, Mike, if you ever lie to her or let her down...I'll murder you with my bare hands!"

"For God's sake, Lena, give me some credit," he said heatedly.

"Why?" she asked, and then she settled back against the seat and turned her head away from him, watching the rough, arid landscape slide by. Mile after monotonous mile.

CHAPTER TEN

JANE STOOD in the cramped bathroom and touched the swollen corner of her eye. It was turning purple already. She choked back tears. She'd been struck before, and not just by Danny. The bruises always went away.

It had started over the empty cereal box in the cupboard. He'd gotten up late and in a bad mood, hungover and hungry. He'd rummaged around in the fridge, looking for eggs. There were none. Then, swearing, he'd gone for the cereal, and there had only been a few spoonfuls left.

"Do you ever go to the goddamned store?" he'd yelled, breaking a coffee mug in the sink. Then he'd turned on her and, without any warning, he'd punched her.

Kimmy had seen it, too, and she'd cowered in the corner, crying. He'd almost gone for her then, but instead he'd grabbed Jane's purse, taken her money and said the guys were picking him up in a few minutes and he'd just stop and eat somewhere. "When I get back, there'd better be food in the house, you hear me?"

Jane had whimpered that he'd taken the last of her money. He'd thrown some bills onto the kitchen table and stormed out, and the last she'd seen of him, he was sitting on the curb, waiting for his buddies, smoking a cigarette.

She looked at the bruise again. *I hate him,* she thought.

And she knew what he was up to today with that bunch of creeps he called friends. They were making last-minute arrangements to use a no-questions-asked rental house up in Espanola—the house where they were going to do the film with Kimmy.

Jane washed her face and shut the thought out of her head. They were flat broke, and there was no other way. She didn't even know if she had enough money to buy enough groceries.

While Kimmy lay on the bed in the back room, locked in again with the TV turned on, Jane cleaned the broken glass out of the sink, then fixed a cup of instant coffee, which she proceeded to lace with whiskey because yesterday she'd run out of the drugs she kept stashed in the bathroom. Just thinking about having to do without them made her sweat. She drank the coffee quickly, then fixed another cup, pouring in more whiskey, not giving a damn that Danny would notice the bottle was now two-thirds empty.

By noon she was drunk. She unlocked Kimmy's door and stood over the bed, watching as the child lay dozing, last night's sleeping pill still in her system.

"Hey, wake up, kid," she said, slurring. "I gotta go to the store. Wake up."

Kimmy stirred and rubbed her eyes. "Is he...gone?" she asked.

"Yeah, he's gone. For now. Hey," Jane said, "you gotta be a good little girl while I run to the store. No tricks. Okay?"

Kimmy sat up. "You're leaving?"

"Store's only a few blocks away. I'll be right back. Your door'll be locked so..."

"I don't want to stay here," Kimmy cried suddenly,

and she wrapped her arms around Jane's waist. "Please don't leave me alone!"

Jane sat on the bed completely at a loss, the kid clinging to her. She felt a rush of warmth in her stomach. Her kid, her *own* kid, was hugging her.

Maybe it was the alcohol flowing in her blood, or maybe it was maternal instinct, but abruptly she made up her mind. "Okay," she said, "I'll take you along. But you've gotta be a real good little girl. No talking to anyone. Okay?"

Kimberly looked up. "Okay," she said.

"You gotta promise."

"I promise."

Danny had ridden with his buddies, so Jane took the station wagon. She was really too drunk to be driving, but she was past caring.

"Okay," she said when she parked the big wagon near the front of the store. "Here we are. You keep your mouth shut. I mean it. And no telling Danny about this, either."

"All right," Kimmy said, opening the passenger door.

It felt strange and special to walk into the familiar grocery store with a kid holding her hand. How many times had Jane seen mothers leading their kids along, letting them push the big carts? This was her kid, too, her flesh and blood.

Kimmy was awfully well behaved going down the aisles, but she did keep asking for stuff Jane couldn't afford. Once Jane had to take her by the shoulders and scold her. "Put that back. Who said you could have that?"

Then Kimmy shied away and said, "Your breath smells."

"Just be quiet," Jane snapped, and she moved along.

It happened in the cereal aisle. One minute Kimmy was right behind her, the next she was gone.

Jane's heart lurched when she realized it. Quickly she hurried up the aisle and down the next, then backward, pushing the cart, frantic. Where in hell *was* she? *Oh, God,* Jane thought, maybe the kid had conned her!

She left the cart and rushed outside, stumbling once, righting herself, desperately searching the parking lot. Damn it. Danny was going to murder her!

She dashed down one row of parked cars, past the station wagon, then up another, her breath rasping with the exertion. Where in hell was that brat?

Then she spotted her, and the rush of relief almost made her pass out. She raced toward the street, where Kimmy was standing, waiting for the light to change, ready to cross and run away.

"Kimmy!" Jane yelled. "You get the hell back here! Kimmy!"

She caught her and spun her around, then started to drag her back toward the car. The damn kid was sobbing and crying that she wanted her mother.

"Shut up!" Jane kept yelling, pulling at her. "Shut the hell up!"

Jane had almost reached her car, when a lady shopper walked over. "Is everything all right?" the woman asked, eyeing Jane and Kimmy.

Oh, hell, Jane thought, and she pushed Kimmy toward the car.

"I want Mommy," Kimmy was crying.

Considering her state of inebriation, Jane reacted quickly. "Get in the car," she ordered, then she turned to the woman. "That kid," she began, "she's been a pain all week. She's my niece, see, and I'm baby-sitting." Then she turned away.

The woman stared at her for another moment and then walked toward the store, looking back over her shoulder a couple of times. Jane got into the car, gulping in a breath of relief. Then she grabbed Kimmy's arm and dug her nails in. "You sneaky little brat!" she said, shaking her. "You tell Danny about this and I swear you'll get the spanking of your life. You hear me?"

She didn't remember the groceries till she was halfway home, nor did Jane realize that the woman who'd confronted her had gone into the store and immediately asked where she could find the manager.

IT WAS NINETY MILES to Albuquerque, and Lena was driving again. They hadn't spoken much since Lena's last outburst, and she was desperately casting about for something to say, something that wouldn't get Mike's back up. She felt like a crazy yo-yo, alternating between polite conversation and five years' worth of harbored resentment. Things just burst out of her, and she couldn't help it. But she kept trying. They had to stay together, after all, until they found Kimmy.

The subject she chose was not a good idea, and she knew it the second the words were out of her mouth. But it was too late by then. "So," she said, modulating her voice to careful neutrality, "what's with you and Jennifer. Are you going to get married?"

"Huh," he said, and the reply held a wealth of irony and doubt but no surprise.

"What does 'huh' mean?"

"It doesn't mean anything."

A devil inside Lena wouldn't quit. "Well, are you? Are you madly in love?"

He gave her a sidelong glance. "Awful curious, aren't you?"

"Just trying to make conversation."

"You want to pick another subject?"

She was glad she was driving; she could keep her eyes on the road, her face straight ahead. She shrugged. "Sure, whatever." But inside, the devil plied his pitchfork. Yes, she had to admit to herself, she was curious, damn curious. And, even worse, she was just a tiny bit jealous. God, she hated that lack of control on her part.

"You might want to slow down," he suggested.

"No," she said. "I figure if I get pulled over, you can flash your ID and get me out of a ticket."

"This is New Mexico," he growled.

"You'll get me off," she said complacently. His grousing about her speed had never gotten him anywhere, and it wouldn't now.

The interstate rose again as they neared the Continental Divide. The distant peaks to the north were already snow-capped, but here the land was still dry, and the few stunted trees had to fight for a patch of dirt in which to grow.

Shortly after four they began to descend as they approached Albuquerque. They drove through the Acoma Indian Reservation and then the Laguna Reservation. Ahead was the Rio Grande, a green line bisecting the high, arid plain, and from its banks Albuquerque sprawled eastward to the dry Sandia Mountains.

Lena and Mike turned off the interstate at a downtown exit, and they were instantly lost among the hodgepodge of old colonial streets: San Pedro Drive, Lomas Boulevard, Indian School Road. Mike had to use the cell phone to call police headquarters and get directions. It was located near the central plaza and the convention center in the heart of the city. It was also a stone's throw from gang-infested neighborhoods.

Lena looked for signs to the Galleria Convention Center. "Do you think this detective friend of your uncle's...what's his name?" she asked.

"Hidalgo," Mike said, "John Hidalgo."

"Do you think he'll be there?"

"I really don't know."

"If he isn't... Well, do you think the police will help? We're out-of-state, after all, and..."

"Stop worrying," Mike said. "It's a reciprocal thing. Cops help one another. Doesn't matter where they're from."

Lena let out a low whistle. "I just hope the FBI doesn't try to butt in."

Mike laughed humorlessly. "So do I, so do I."

Detective John Hidalgo was at headquarters when they parked in the visitors' lot, strode into the tall building and checked in with the desk sergeant. He came down to meet them, and Lena had the instant impression of an attractive, smart, self-assured man about her own age.

On the drive Mike had told her what he knew of John Hidalgo. He'd met Ted Quinn at a police convention in Colorado in the winter, and a group of cops had tried skiing, including John and Uncle Ted. They'd struck up a friendship. He was of Spanish descent, from one of the original seventeenth-century land-grant families. Despite herself, Lena had been impressed. Her family had been from Spain, but they sure hadn't owned any land grants.

Lena studied him, the pale complexion and perfect razor-cut dark hair, the long, narrow Don Quixote face. His dark eyes had depth and intelligence. He was wearing a sport coat and light wool trousers, while the other guys were mostly in jeans.

"I've been waiting for you," John said, shaking both their hands, escorting them through the security doors, up in the elevator and into the enclave of police headquarters. As they walked, he explained that he'd done some preliminary work on the case. "I had motor vehicles run a printout on every old wood-sided station-wagon model registered in the state," he told them as they arrived at his desk in a large, open room where the vice detectives were stationed. "There're eighteen or so. The question is, did these characters in the car even return to New Mexico?"

Mike sat next to Lena across from Hidalgo and explained about the clerk in the minimart.

"All right," John said, "good legwork there, Quinn. At least we can assume they're back in the state. That's a real break."

"And Kimmy's...alive," Lena put in, closing her eyes for a moment. Even the notion of the alternative was too difficult to contemplate. She felt Mike's brief, gentle touch on her shoulder, as if to say it was okay, they were all having the same thought.

John pulled the motor vehicle printout from under a file and held it up. "This is it," he said. "I know eighteen doesn't sound like a lot, but it'll take a while to check them all out. New Mexico's a big state. Lotta territory to cover. We'll get them, though. If they're here, we'll get them."

"Can we start now?" Lena asked expectantly, but Hidalgo said this couldn't have been a worse time at headquarters.

"It's what we call a roundup day. Happens every twelve months or so. Trouble is, I've got to help with the arrests. It'll take the whole damn evening to process them. But tomorrow morning, bright and early, we'll meet here and divide up the list on those station wagons, start making calls. I hope that's okay."

Lena felt disappointment settle in her stomach. There was nothing she could do, though. Kimmy had been unharmed when the lady at the minimart had seen her. Surely she was still okay. How could anyone hurt such a sweet, loving child?

"Tomorrow morning," Lena said, "I want to help make those calls."

"Lena—" Mike began.

But John smiled and cut in. "I don't see why not," he said. "I can find you an empty desk and a phone and you can take some of the names on the list."

"I'll need to know what questions to ask," she said. "I assume we won't be calling to ask if anyone kidnapped a little girl out in California."

"No, we won't. I'll make up some cock-and-bull story and give you a prompt sheet," John said.

"Okay," she said, and she was able to smile. She'd be doing something, actually helping to get her child back. "Thank you," she breathed.

"My pleasure," John said, and then abruptly he snapped his fingers. "Damn, I almost forgot." He pushed aside papers and files and then snatched up a note. "Here it is. Came in for you this morning, Mike. It's from a Jennifer Hilty. I guess she's here in town, checked into the Desert Inn. She wanted you to call when you got in. Number's right at the bottom." He handed Mike the note.

Mike stared at it. "Oh, boy," he said, then he looked up. "Mind if I use the phone?"

"Sure," John said. "Just dial nine for an outside line."

Lena sat in shocked silence, staring at Mike as he dialed. She couldn't begin to imagine what he was thinking. Was he happy? Angry? Surely he must find this pretty darn unusual—possessive, she thought.

She tried not to listen, but it was hard.

"Jenn?" he said, and he turned away, the phone against his ear. For a moment he listened, then he said, "This is crazy. I mean, I'm going to be maxed out here." Again, he listened. "Well...yes, I suppose we could do that. But I really don't have much time." There was another period of listening, then he said, "All right. But you'll have to wait in your room. I'll call when I can." A pause. "No, haven't had time to get a room...two rooms, that is," he added.

John met Lena's eyes and shrugged, a quirk of a smile on his lips. Lena kept her countenance expressionless, but inside she was both amused and irritated. This woman had no right to take up Mike's time during a crisis like this. No right at all. Still, it was kind of funny how jealous his lady friend must be. If only she knew.

John had to get busy helping with the roundup, so after Mike's call he walked them out to the parking lot, promising to meet them back at headquarters at 8 a.m.

Then he saw Lena's car. "Is this yours?" He walked around it. "Wow, this sucker is great. What's the horsepower?"

Lena told John all about her prize vehicle, where she'd bought it, how she'd fixed it up.

"I'll bet you get your share of tickets in this," he said, hands in his pockets.

"Oh, not too many," Lena said.

"Right," Mike put in.

Hidalgo laughed. "I'd better get going," he said. "If you're looking for a good deal on motels, try the Red Rocks out on Route 66. It's clean, too. They've got a few two-bedroom suites, if that's what you're looking for," he added diplomatically.

Mike groaned.

"See you *mañana*," John said, and he left.

Lena got behind the wheel of her GTO and started it up. "Look," she said, "I can drop you at this Desert Inn place and then I'll go get us a couple of rooms. Or maybe you want to, you know, just stay with your friend and I'll pick you up at a quarter to eight tomorrow."

But Mike was shaking his head. "No," he said, looking straight ahead. "Let's go check out this Red Rocks Motel. I'd feel better if I knew you were safely in a room. If they have a suite, that'll work."

She cocked a dark brow. "Then you won't be staying with Jennifer?" she asked in a neutral voice.

Mike shook his head. "No, I won't. As soon as you're settled in, I'll borrow the car, though, if you don't mind."

"No problem," she said, and she backed out of the parking space. He wasn't going to spend the night with Jennifer, then. *Interesting,* Lena thought, and she squelched a momentary stab of satisfaction before driving off, her mind settling back on Kimmy.

CHAPTER ELEVEN

MIKE STARTED LENA'S GTO, his thoughts on what he was going to say to Jennifer. He had directions to the Desert Inn but had to concentrate so hard on finding his way through the unfamiliar streets of Albuquerque that by the time he pulled up at the posh glass-and-stone façade of the motel, he still had no idea what he was going to say or why Jenn was there.

He asked at the desk, found her room and knocked. She didn't answer immediately, and he stood there waiting, resenting his need to do this, and at the same time feeling guilty for his resentment. Damn. How in hell was he supposed to handle this?

She finally opened the door, and her perfume wafted out around him.

"Mike, oh, Mike, I missed you so much, darling," she said in that lovely, throaty voice that could send ripples of desire through his gut, and she pulled him inside and clung to him.

"Hey, Jenn, what's this all about? I haven't even been gone for two days," he said.

She leaned back in his arms and looked up at him. "It was your being so far away. I almost went crazy missing you."

He wasn't sure whether to be flattered or irritated. "Where are your kids?" was all he could think of to ask.

"Bob took them. He was a sweetheart about it. I just hopped on a plane and here I am. Aren't I bad?"

"Well, Jenn, like I said, I really won't have any time to see you. Tonight's the only free time, because Hidalgo's tied up, but starting tomorrow morning, hell, I'll be lucky to get a bite to eat."

She pouted a little. "Mike, I came because I want to be here for you. Don't you understand? This is a terrible thing for you to be going through, and you need someone here for support."

"That's great of you, Jenn. It's just that I'm going to be so busy."

"Then I'll wait for you. I'll be here whenever you have the time. That's what a relationship is—or at least that's what I always *thought* it was."

Mike held her, one hand on each of her arms, and he studied her face, trying to read her, trying not to hurt her feelings. "Look, this isn't about relationships. It's about Kimmy and about police work."

An expression he couldn't name flickered across her face, then disappeared. "So why is Lena here with you? She isn't a policeman."

"She's Kimmy's mother. She was half out of her mind. I couldn't leave her behind."

"That's not what it sounded like yesterday morning."

"No, I...ah...it's complicated, Jenn. You'll just have to trust me on that."

"Did you really share a motel room with her last night?" Jennifer asked, coyly fiddling with the end of the zipper on his leather jacket. "Are you sharing one with her tonight? Is that why you don't have time for me?"

"Jennifer," he said, "for God's sake, you're getting all upset over nothing. I don't have time for this. We have separate rooms, okay?"

She looked up at him, searching his face. "You're mad. I blew it, didn't I?"

"Nobody blew anything. I'm just trying to explain to you..."

She threw her arms around him then and laid her head on his chest. "I love you," she breathed. "I can't help it."

He stroked her hair. "Take it easy, Jenn. I'm not angry. I'm just, you know, preoccupied." He put a finger under her chin and tilted her face up, and he saw with dismay that there were tears shining in her eyes. "Come on, let's get something to eat. We'll talk."

They ate in the Desert Inn steak house, off the lobby of the motel. The food was excellent, the decor very Southwest, and romantic notes from the piano bar accompanied the mouthwatering smells of grilled meat.

Jennifer ordered chicken—she never ate red meat— and Mike ordered the filet, medium rare.

"What a change from burgers and pizza," he said, cutting the butter-soft steak.

Jennifer was still busy with the plate she'd heaped high from the salad bar. She ate silently for a time, then put down her fork and asked him directly, "Do you still love Lena?"

He almost choked on his mouthful of filet. "Damn it, what kind of question is that?" he retorted.

"Kindly answer my question," she said coolly.

"No, I do not love Lena." He glared at her. "This is how you give me *support,* Jenn?"

"I think I have to know, don't you?"

"Well, now you know."

"Why'd you break up?" She leaned over the table, her face lit by the candle in the glass cylinder. "Why did you leave her?"

"I told you all that. My drinking. Look, can we eat in peace? I *was* enjoying this meal."

"What kind of marriage did you have? I mean, was it wildly romantic, practical, purely physical?"

"You're not going to let up, are you?"

"No. I need to know, Mike. I mean, you just took a leave, left L.A. with your ex-wife, and I don't understand it."

"I wish I could tell you in twenty words or less what kind of marriage we had. Hell, it only lasted a few years. We were in love, we thought it could work, it didn't." He shrugged and turned back to his food.

"Was your drinking the only problem? Or was it money or your job or something else?" She toyed with the salad, then picked a crouton off the top and ate it slowly.

"It was my drinking, as far as I know. You've heard all this, Jenn. Why the third degree?"

"Because she's back in your life."

"Only out of necessity. Believe me, she doesn't like it any better than I do."

"You're sure of that?"

"Yeah, I'm sure. She hates my guts."

"Hmm," Jenn said, and then she dropped the subject, and the meal went much, much better.

He was really glad she hadn't pushed any more, because he didn't much like recollecting the sordid details of that final scene of his marriage. Only he and Lena and Joe Carbone knew, and he'd like to keep it that way.

She started again, though, over coffee. "Was it the baby that put pressure on your marriage?" she asked. "I mean, with her being adopted and sick and everything?"

"No," he said. "Believe me, Kimmy had nothing to

do with it. We both loved her. We wanted more kids, too, but... Well, that never came about.''

''I think you were very brave to take that baby.''

''We never thought of it that way,'' he said. ''But the media made a big deal of it. We were really surprised, but I guess it was a human-interest kind of story. It was sort of embarrassing.''

''You're too modest.''

''You wouldn't believe the fuss. Phone calls from papers and TV shows all over the state. We had to change our phone number, for God's sake. Lena was going nuts trying to get in and out of the house without being followed.'' He laughed and shook his head, remembering.

''Didn't it make you feel good?''

''Hell, it was a pain in the butt.'' He thought back. ''The only time I remember enjoying the publicity was the day we went to the hospital to bring Kimmy home. We'd tried to keep it secret, but someone at the hospital must have leaked the information, because there were some photographers and video guys around when we left. And we did let them take some pictures. I still have the newspaper article. It has a nice picture.''

''I didn't know you were famous,'' Jenn said playfully, reaching over the table to put her hand on his.

''It was just for a little while. But it *was* a nice picture. Lena and me, and she was holding the baby, and Gloria was there, grinning like crazy....''

''Gloria?''

''Lena's mother. We looked so damn happy in that picture. It was on TV, too.''

''Mmm, that's nice.''

''Yeah, it was.'' He could close his eyes and recall the scene as if it were yesterday—Lena holding Kimmy proudly, him standing behind her, Gloria beside her, and the caption: Policeman and Wife Save Baby. And their names and...

Gloria's name! Gloria Torres, right there in the article, and it even said she was from Woodland Hills, where she still lived! Someone could easily have found Kimmy through Gloria, who picked her up at school every day. Someone who followed Gloria to the playground and saw her pick her granddaughter up and then went early one day and grabbed Kimmy and...

Mike was vaguely aware of Jennifer saying something and the muted tinkle of china and silverware and conversation, but his whole being was focused on this new hunch, this *cop's* hunch. After six years, someone had found Gloria and then Kimmy through that newspaper article. And who would still have that? Who and why? The who was pretty easy—Kimmy's birth mother, Jane Cramm. She might have abandoned her baby, but she might not have been entirely without feelings. She would have seen the newspaper and kept the article, and since Lena was virtually untraceable, she'd searched out Gloria.

"Mike?" Jenn was saying. "Mike, what's wrong?"

"Nothing," he muttered.

"You didn't hear a word I said. I asked if you—"

He cut her off. "Listen, Jenn, I've got to make a call. I'll be back in a second."

"Mike, what...?"

But he'd pushed back his chair and was striding out to the lobby. He went straight to the public phone and dialed his folks' number. His mother answered, and he had to talk to her for a minute before she put his dad on, and he tried not to sound impatient. Finally Larry was on the line.

"Pop," Mike said, "it came to me. Who it is, who it

probably is. It was that newspaper picture of us getting Kimmy at the hospital.'' He explained the whole thing. ''So it could be her, Jane Cramm.''

''By God, you're onto something there,'' Larry said. ''It's worth a try. There's got to be a record of her somewhere. I'll push the FBI. She has to have left a trail.''

''Do that. They may find something. We're going to work the vehicle angle at this end. Hidalgo's got the list of wood-sided wagons for us. We'll go to work on it tomorrow. And hey, Hidalgo says to say hello to Uncle Ted.''

''I'll tell him. How's...uh, Lena?''

''Okay,'' he said offhandedly. ''Why—how's she supposed to be?''

''Well, since Jennifer's there, I wondered...''

''How in hell do you know Jenn's here?'' Mike asked angrily.

''Colleen told me. Why—is there a problem?''

''Damn it! I *knew* there was something... Colleen set the whole thing up—I know it.'' He took a deep breath to stave off his anger. ''Tell that sister of mine to mind her own business,'' he said.

''Maybe you'd better tell her,'' Larry said. ''I'm sorry I ever mentioned it.''

''Okay, okay,'' Mike said, trying to stay calm, ''forget the whole subject. I'll call you tomorrow about the case. And now I've gotta go and try to convince Jennifer to go home. Nice job, huh?''

''You'd rather walk on hot coals?'' Larry suggested.

''Something like that, Pop.''

Mike wasn't sure whether to be more aggravated by Colleen or Jennifer, but he sure wasn't in a very good mood when he sat down across from Jenn.

''Business,'' he muttered. ''Sorry.''

"Something about the case?" she asked carefully.

"Yeah." He'd decided not to say a word about Colleen. It would only cause an unpleasant conversation, and he didn't feel like dealing with it.

Jennifer insisted on paying for dinner; they argued about it and finally decided to split the bill. It was just another irritation in an evening that was degenerating moment by moment.

He walked Jenn back to her room, and she turned to him, her eyes luminous, and said, "Do you want to come in for a while?"

It was a laughable come-on, seeing as he and Jenn weren't exactly strangers to each other, but frankly he wasn't in the mood.

"Look, Jenn, I'd love to, but it's late, and I've got to get up early tomorrow. Helluva day ahead of me. I'm beat."

She looked at him, her mouth a tight line.

"How about I drive you to the airport in the morning?" he suggested, hoping to soften the blow.

"So I'm getting dumped?" she asked, stepping back from him.

"No," he replied wearily, "you're just going home." Then he kissed her on the cheek. "I'll see you in the morning."

She turned her back and unlocked her door.

"Good night," he said softly.

The door closed in his face. He stood for a moment, looking at it, then shrugged and walked off down the hall, and before he'd even reached Lena's car, his mind was whirling with ideas, plans, possibilities. Jane Cramm, eighteen vehicles to trace, records—the phone company, driver's license? Credit card? Probably not, if she was a druggie. Social security? Drug arrests?

Maybe the station wagon was a dead end, or maybe it was connected. He didn't know yet; he only knew the pieces of the puzzle were starting to fit together—only the outside rim of it for now, but he'd find more, and eventually the whole picture would emerge. And there, at the center, he'd find Kimmy.

Back at his motel, he let himself into the suite quietly, yawning, figuring Lena was in her own room, fast asleep.

She was asleep, all right, but she was on the couch in the living room, the TV still on. He crossed the floor and stood looking down at her. She'd fallen asleep on her side, her head resting on one hand. She had her pajamas on, the polka-dot ones, and she looked so young, so peaceful, lying there. Her dark hair spread over the cushions, and the light touched her features, as if a finger brushed them with gilt here and shadow there. He gazed at her too long, a feeling of regret for the past, for what he'd lost, tightening in his chest.

Then he leaned over and shook her very gently. "Lena," he said, and her eyes flew open and she gave a startled gasp.

"Lena," he said again, "you fell asleep here."

She rubbed her face. "Oh, God, sorry, I..."

"Go to bed."

"Uh-huh." She sat up. "I was dreaming that we found Kimmy and we were back home, and I was so happy. Oh, Mike, I was so relieved and happy."

"Mmm," he said.

"Will we find her?" she asked imploringly.

"Yes, Lena, I already told you that."

"It's the only thing keeping me sane," she breathed.

"Go to bed," he said gently.

She got up and gave him a shaky smile. "Good night."

"Mmm," he said again, and he watched as she padded

across the floor, barefoot, and disappeared into her bedroom, closing the door behind her.

Two doors shut in his face tonight, he thought. *Good work, pal.*

THE NEXT MORNING over breakfast he told Lena about how Jane Cramm might have traced Kimmy. She held a mug of coffee, her elbows resting on the table, and watched him with her dark, slightly slanted eyes.

"The newspaper article had Gloria's full name in it. They couldn't find you or me, so they located Gloria, followed her, maybe staked out her house for days," he said.

"Why?" she asked.

He shrugged. "Some kind of belated maternal instinct? A ploy to get welfare maybe, aid to dependent children, something like that?"

"Kidnapping is a federal crime, a capital crime. Wouldn't she know that?"

"Ah, who knows what's going through her mind—if it's her." He went on. "It'd be too much to expect the wagon to be registered to her. Probably the guy's."

"You mean the guy with her, the 'mean man' Marcia saw."

"Yeah, whoever he is."

"I hope these leads aren't dead ends," Lena said, frowning. "We've wasted so much time on them."

"It's all we have to go on. Lena, don't worry. I've got a hunch the connection is this Cramm woman."

She gave him a quick smile that disappeared so swiftly he wasn't sure he'd seen it.

"I like your hunches," she said softly.

He dropped Lena at police headquarters just before eight. "Tell Hidalgo I'll be back soon."

"Okay. Maybe we'll have already found the car," she said, trying to be cheerful. "At least I can *do* something."

He watched her walk into the building, her shoulders set, her jeans tight over her rear end, a perfect fit. Then he pulled out into traffic and drive to the Desert Inn to pick Jennifer up and take her to the airport.

When she didn't answer his knock at her door, he looked in the coffee shop to see if she was eating breakfast. She wasn't there.

The clerk at the front desk answered his inquiry by punching keys on his computer. "Mrs. Hilty, Jennifer Hilty?" The clerk looked up from the keyboard. "She checked out an hour ago, sir. Asked me to call her a cab."

DANNY HAYDEN WAS on the phone, trying to clinch the movie deal, and Jane was doing a pile of dishes left over from the night before. She was making too much noise, fumbling, dropping things right and left, and Danny knew she'd been sneaking booze again. It made him mad as hell.

The little girl was sitting at the table, eating cereal out of a bowl, real quiet and scared, her big brown eyes just showing above the bowl. She was starting to look pale with shadows under her eyes. They'd better make that damn movie fast.

"Okay," he said into the phone, "so you got all the equipment lined up?"

"Don't worry about our end of things," the man said. "You just deliver the kid, all clean and nice and smiling."

"No problem," Danny said. "And the money?"

"Like I said, half when we start, half when it's done."

"Cash?"

"Cash."

When he hung up, he whirled around and yelled, "For God's sake, keep that racket down, will you?"

Jane dropped the lid of a pot, and it clanged in the sink. "Sorry," she whispered.

He shook his head in disgust, deciding not to bother swatting her because it made the kid cry, and he couldn't stand the goddamn screeching all the time.

Yeah, Jane was drunk again. And he knew why. Well, besides the fact that there was no money for drugs—it was the damn little brat. Jane wanted to keep the kid.

Once he'd realized that she really meant it, he played along just to shut her up. A kid. Sure, she was a cute kid, and for a minute here and there he'd thought it might be fun to have a kid, like a puppy or a kitten, but he knew it was far too much trouble to take care of her, not to mention too expensive. And what would happen when she grew up and starting asking questions and talking back?

No, fatherhood was not in the stars for Danny Hayden. Jane, of course, was a different story. The kid was Jane's real child.

He'd been pretty damn clever once Jane had told him she'd had a baby that she'd given up for adoption. He'd worked on that maternal instinct, and it had been easy as pie. The grandmother was right where the newspaper article had said she was—unbelievable luck—and all he'd had to do was call Information to find that out. Almost too easy.

Jane was staggering around the kitchen with that stupid grin on her face, the one she got when she drank. And her one eye wandered, walleyed, so you couldn't tell exactly where she was looking.

"Go take a nap or something," he said. "You're driving me nuts."

"In a minute," she said.

"*Now.*"

She shot him a frightened look. "But I told Kimmy we could go out for a walk."

"In your condition?" He laughed.

"I'm okay, Danny."

"The hell you are. Go on, like I said. I'll take care of the kid." He was aware of the girl looking at him, scared, dropping her spoon.

"Danny…"

He walked up to Jane, stood chest to chest with her; he wasn't much taller than she was. "I said," he breathed, low and deliberate, "go take a nap."

She switched her eyes to Kimmy, once, hesitated, then her shoulders slumped and she turned and shuffled off.

"Okay, kid," he said. "You finished?"

"Yes," the little girl whispered.

"Let's go."

She walked down the hall in front of him, went into her room. Then she looked up. "Can I go for a walk with Jane later?"

"Maybe," he lied. Like hell he'd let the neighbors see this kid—or any cops who might be driving down the street. For all he knew there was a nationwide APB out on her, with her picture and everything.

"When can I see my mommy?" she asked in that little, piping voice of hers.

"If you're good for the next couple of days, maybe you can see her then."

"Promise? Cross your heart and—"

"Yeah, yeah, sure, kid," he said impatiently. "Cross my heart and hope to die."

CHAPTER TWELVE

IT WAS ALREADY A ZOO at police headquarters when John Hidalgo met Lena at the security desk downstairs.

"Lawyers," he said, shrugging. "After yesterday's busts, there must be fifty lawyers in here arranging bail."

"I'll be in the way," she said, apologetic.

"Nonsense," he replied. He took her arm and led her to the elevator and the maze of offices while she explained, as best she could, where Mike was.

"You were once married?" John asked en route to his desk.

Lena nodded.

"And Kimmy's adopted, by both of you?"

"Yes," she said. "It was Mike and his partner who took Kimmy to the hospital when she was only a day old. The guys were really concerned. Mike and Jeff tried to visit her every day. She was a crack baby, and the doctors weren't sure if she'd make it."

"So you and Mike adopted her. That was a...very special thing you did."

Lena shrugged. "We were lucky to get her." She told John about Mike's hunch, how Kimmy's birth mother might have kept track of her through Gloria, who still lived in Woodland Hills and was a big part of the child's life. "That's what Mike thinks, anyway," Lena said.

"But you don't?"

"Well, I don't have that cop's nose, you know. But

he has his dad out in L.A. stepping up the search for the
woman. Jane Cramm's her name. At least it was then...."

"Is the FBI...?"

"Oh, yes," Lena said. "They're supposedly conduct-
ing their own investigation. But what they're really con-
ducting is a farce. A sick farce." She told him about
Special Agent Sabin's visit to Gloria. "That moron," she
said under her breath.

Hidalgo laughed.

He shuffled files at his desk, then found what he was
hunting for—the prompt sheet he'd made up for Lena.
"Ah," he said, "here it is. Why don't you sit here a few
minutes and look this over while I try to find you an
empty desk and a phone."

She sat in the wooden chair across from his desk and
began reading the prompt sheet, familiarizing herself with
the questions he'd concocted for the phone interviews
with the station wagon owners. While she read, she was
aware of a lot of male eyes on her. They were no doubt
wondering who she was. John's girlfriend? Someone he
was interviewing? A poorly dressed lawyer?

Lena couldn't help smiling. Lots of times, long before
Mike had joined Hostage Negotiations, she'd visited him
or met him at his station. She'd known most of the guys
then, and they'd all been teases. "Soon as you dump that
creep Quinn, I'm next in line. Okay?" they'd said.

Back then she'd liked cops. Just as she enjoyed the
company of her fellow workers at Al's. Sometimes they
seemed to her to be no more than little boys playing
games: cops and robbers or race car drivers. She found,
too, that the boldest and most flirtatious of them turned
to mush if she called them out on their teasing. She'd bet
this lot of Albuquerque cops was no different.

"What do you think?" John asked.

She started, realizing she'd been daydreaming of bygone days, missing the life, and she was surprised. "Oh," she said, "the phone questions. They're good, John, really."

He found her a desk and phone near the window overlooking the plaza below. "This is Swartz's spot," he said. "He's on vacation." John then produced the list of eighteen names and addresses. Some had phone numbers; others didn't. "Why don't you take, say, five of these and start from there. Try Information if you haven't got a number. Okay?"

Lena took the list he handed her and nodded. "I hope I do this right."

John put a hand on her shoulder and said, "You'll do fine. Just keep good notes and we'll see where it all leads."

She smiled and took a breath. "Okay," she said. "Just leave me alone or I'll get even more nervous than I am."

"Done," he said, and he left her there with her list of names.

The first person on Lena's list, a man from Alamogordo, wasn't home. She didn't even bother to leave a voice message. What would be the point? Next to his name she put a star and a notation: try after work. It was going to be a long day.

She picked up the phone again, ready to try the next number, but found herself glancing toward John's desk. Mike wasn't here yet. And she wondered if he was still at the airport with Jennifer. Was he waiting for her flight? Having coffee with her, leaning close over a little table? She thought about last night. He'd been home relatively early. Still, he'd had plenty of time with Jennifer to...to go to bed, she thought, trying to tamp down the image. *Had* he made love to her?

Get a life, she told herself, and she shook off the images and dialed the next number.

She reached Hannah Grueter in Farmington on the second ring.

"Hello?" said an elderly woman.

Lena's heart quickened. *Do this right. Concentrate,* she told herself firmly.

"Good morning, Mrs. Grueter," Lena began. "My name is Anne Berringer, and I'm from Roper's National Survey. I wonder if I could have a minute of your time."

"Is this one of those sales calls?" the woman snapped.

"No, it isn't," Lena went on. "We aren't selling a thing. In fact, Roper's is being paid by the automobile manufacturers to conduct a very important survey that will be a benefit to car owners such as yourself."

"Go on," the woman said, albeit suspiciously.

Lena took a breath. "I understand that you still drive a 1961 Ford station wagon, ma'am."

"Yes, I do."

"Good, good. And could you tell me how many miles are on your odometer?"

"Oh, for heaven's sake, I have no idea," Hannah Grueter said.

"Over one hundred thousand? Two hundred?"

"Over a hundred. Maybe it's around a hundred fifty."

"That's fine," Lena said, ad-libbing, beginning to feel more confident. "And are you the sole driver, Mrs. Grueter?"

"It's *Miss.* And, yes, I'm the only one who drives my car."

"I see. Then there's no nephew or niece who would borrow your automobile occasionally?"

"No. My nephew's a bum. I wouldn't let him touch it with a ten-foot pole."

Lena allowed herself a friendly laugh. "How about your mechanic?"

"Slacks? Well, sure, to test it or something."

"Slacks?"

"Slacks Kerry."

"Mmm. Okay. Do you often have to leave your car for a few days with him?"

"Sometimes. Transmission went out a few years back. You know."

"Okay," Lena said, underlining the name Slacks Kerry on her notepad. "Has there been a recent breakdown, Miss Grueter?"

"Had my winter tires put on, is all."

"And that was…?"

"My show's coming on," Hannah Grueter said, annoyed.

"Only two more questions," she said pleasantly.

"Oh, all right."

"Have you taken your car on a trip recently?"

"Yes."

"To…?"

"Colorado Springs."

"Uh-huh. And it ran well?"

"Just fine, young lady, and now I'm going to watch my show."

"Thank you for your time," Lena said, and she hung up. *Phew!* she thought. She'd had to wing it a lot. But then, she spent half her days on the phone at Al's. She knew how to talk cars.

She called the next number on her list, having to get it from Information. It belonged to a Daniel Hayden of Santa Fe. There was no answer and no recorder. She put a star next to the name: call later, no answer.

It was then that Lena noticed Mike at John's desk,

talking to him. He was standing, leaning over with his hands on the desk, one knee flexed, and she couldn't help noting that Mike was as tall as anyone in the room, and certainly as handsome in his jeans and pink shirt with the cuffs rolled up. She'd always liked looking at Mike, the way his dark-blond hair fell softly over the top of his ears and curled a little at the back, the way he carried himself, the pitch of his head when he was concentrating, as he was now. She couldn't help wondering if Jennifer saw those same things in him or if his nearness made her stomach tighten the way Lena's used to.

Mike turned his head, as if sensing her eyes on him, and their gazes met for a moment before Lena collected herself and looked back at her notes. And then she was aware of him approaching her, but she kept her head down, studying the list in front of her.

"How's it going?" he asked.

"Oh," she said, as if surprised. "Well, I got one person so far."

"Good," he said. "Good."

"She doesn't look like a suspect."

"Mmm."

"So—" she clasped her hands on the desk and looked up "— did you get Jennifer off all right?"

"Oh, yeah, sure," he mumbled.

"Good," she said, idiotically repeating Mike's words. "Well—" she smiled brightly "—I'd better get back to work here."

"I guess so."

She switched her gaze to her notes, aware of Mike moving away. Still, she couldn't help searching her feelings, and it was rather like probing a sore tooth with her tongue. Was she glad he'd shipped his lady friend off? *Yes,* she thought, trying to convince herself it was only because Mike needed to concentrate on the job at hand. Yet she couldn't help remembering that he'd come home early last night. *Had* he slept with the woman?

Damn it, she thought, letting out a breath. How could she possibly have room in her mind for such triteness? Kimmy was what mattered. She was *all* that mattered. And yet, somehow, there was room in Lena to wonder about Mike and his life. And she hated that.

With determination, she forced her thinking back to Slacks Kerry, the mechanic. If he had access to Hannah Grueter's car, he *could* have driven it to L.A. and back in two days. He might warrant checking out.

She dialed another number, someone named Ralph Martin right here in Albuquerque. He answered, and she went through her routine.

"If you're trying to sell me a new car, forget it, lady. I like what I have. I'm out of work, too, so trying to get money out of me won't fly."

"This really is a survey, sir," she said. *Nasty man. Angry,* she scribbled on her notepad. "We merely want to determine how many of these wagons are still on the road. It helps the auto manufacturers with engine design, torque, suspension, all those things."

"Yeah, so?" he said.

"Could you tell me how many miles are on your engine?"

"Two-forty-five."

"That's a lot of miles. Is the engine the original or a rebuilt one?"

She went along those lines until she was sure he wasn't suspicious of the call. Then she switched gears. "Are you the only driver, Mr. Martin?"

"Yeah, sure. Well, sometimes my wife uses it."

And then Lena ventured, "Is that your wife, let's see, Jane?"

"Where in hell do you people get your information? Her name's Polly."

"I'm sorry. I'll make that correction, sir. Now, do you feel comfortable driving your '68 wagon on a trip?"

"Would you?" he said curtly. "Hell no. We take my wife's car. It's a Buick, by the way."

"I see. So in, say, the last six months your car hasn't been out of New Mexico?"

"Hasn't even been out of this damn city," he grumbled.

"Thank you, sir. That will do it," Lena said.

"Yeah," he said, and he hung up.

Just before lunch Lena tried the first number she'd called and still got the recorder. She tried Daniel Hayden again, too. No answer. Then she tried the last number on her list, but the car owner had passed away last June and the car was at the junkyard. Lena put a line through the name.

She finally stood and stretched, aware, after the fact, of every eye in the room turned to her. She was wearing jeans and a white round-necked T-shirt with long sleeves, and she realized it wasn't much of a cover-up, not around this group.

Mike was looking at her, too. He was at a desk near John's, on the phone with his own list, talking. Nonetheless she felt his gaze, and a hot ripple of tension ran along her limbs. She felt suddenly as if she were betraying herself.

She walked to John's desk, her list and notes in hand. He wasn't on the phone, so she sat and asked how his calls were going.

Hidalgo frowned. "Not so good. Yours?"

"Well," Lena said, aware of Mike hanging up the phone and coming toward them, "two I can't reach yet. One's deceased, the car's junked. There was a man—" she glanced at her notes "—a Ralph Martin, whom I'd say is not a possibility. But there was this woman, a Hannah Grueter, who's got a mechanic who could possibly be our man. I know it's not likely, but I've got his name. He's in Farmington."

"If we have to, we'll check him out," John said. Then he looked up at Mike. "How's your list going?"

"About like yours," Mike said. "The trouble with me is I'm afraid I don't come off very well as a telephone surveyor. I had two people cuss me out and hang up."

Lena looked down at her hands and cleared her throat. "I...well, I seem to be doing okay on that end. I mean, I do spend half the day on the phone at my job. Maybe I should, you know, take a few more names from you guys." She studied her nails.

"Well, now," John said, "what do you think, Mike?"

She heard Mike give a short laugh. "What the hell," he said. "When it comes to cars, Lena really can hold her own."

"Okay, then," John said. "Let's get a bite to eat and then, Lena, well, you can have at it."

"Really?" she said, perhaps too eagerly.

"Really," John said.

They ate at a popular local diner, a real blue-plate-special joint. The restaurant wasn't old, but it was decorated in the style of the 1950s. The menu, too, was reminiscent of the fifties: burgers, hot dogs, grilled cheeses, BLTs, fries, malts and shakes and cherry or vanilla Cokes. The prices were 1998.

Lena had a grilled cheese; the guys chomped down on chili burgers. They all had iced tea.

John was easy to be with. He had a quick smile and sharp, humor-filled black eyes. His jokes were bad, though, a little too raunchy for Lena, who had already heard most of them at Al's. She told the only joke she remembered, a feminist joke. Lena laughed, but John said, "I don't get it." Then all three laughed.

"I didn't know you'd become a feminist," Mike said, staring at her, his head cocked.

Lena took a drink of iced tea and raised her eyes. "There's a lot you don't know about me, Mike Quinn," she said levelly.

After lunch they walked back to headquarters under a perfect October sky. Lena commented on how blue it was.

"It's from the dryness," John said. "A lot of desert out there."

And then the reason she was here, walking with these two policemen, came crashing back into her head, and she couldn't believe she'd actually forgotten it for a few minutes. *Kimmy.* Perplexed at herself, she started across the street against the light.

Mike grabbed her arm and pulled her back onto the curb. "God, you trying to get killed?"

She let out a breath and had to shake off her thoughts. "Sorry," she said. "I was thinking about Kimmy."

She could feel the warmth of Mike's hand on her arm, the strength, and she wanted to lean on him, to put her hand on his chest and beg him to tell her it was all going to be okay. She felt the warmth of his fingers still gripping her arm, a searing heat that turned her flesh to liquid. *No, no, no,* her brain kept repeating, a mantra that her heart ignored. And when he finally released her and they crossed the street, she was certain her knees were going to buckle. After all these years, all these days and months and years, how could this be happening?

Back at the station she was immensely grateful to have the lists to occupy herself, to drag her mind back to reality. Between her, Mike and John, they'd spoken to eleven of the eighteen station wagon owners, and according to everyone's notes, there were only two questionable car owners, and neither of them seemed too promising.

Before going on to a few of the names from the other two lists, Lena redialed the car owners she hadn't been able to reach earlier. Again she got the recorder on one of them. But the other picked up.

It was Daniel Hayden's number in Santa Fe.

A woman spoke. "Hello?"

Lena went into her routine patiently, being very careful not to arouse suspicion. The woman was a bit of a pain, too, a little paranoid, one of those people who were sure everyone was out to sell them something. She wouldn't even give her name, only said she was a friend of Daniel Hayden's.

"You're familiar with his station wagon?" Lena asked.

"Uh-huh."

"I wonder if you could tell me approximately how many miles are on it."

She didn't know.

And so the Q-and-A session went. The woman was timid, her voice uncertain, and Lena jotted down in her notes: confused.

"Just a couple more questions," Lena finally said. "Does Mr. Hayden trust his car on long trips?"

"I don't know."

"Does he take trips, say, out-of-state?"

"Well, maybe, sometimes."

"Hey," Lena said, "it must be a great old car."

"Uh-huh."

"Do you sometimes go along with Mr. Hayden?" Lena ventured.

"Sometimes."

And then she pushed; even though John had warned her about not arousing suspicion, she pushed a little harder.

"Would Mr. Hayden trust his car on a trip as far as Chicago or perhaps California?" Lena asked matter-of-factly.

There was a pause, then the woman said, "I gotta go," and she hung up.

Lena sat back in her seat and whispered, "Wow." It certainly crossed her mind that this woman—the very woman she'd just spoken to—could be Jane Cramm.

She took a moment to collect herself, then she rose and went over to John's desk, where he and Mike were compiling notes.

"I may have something," she said neutrally.

Both men stopped and looked up.

"It was this woman, up in Santa Fe." She went on to tell them about the conversation, referring to her notes. "I mean, she could have been tired or hungover or even stoned. I don't know."

"Interesting," Mike said. "Very interesting." He glanced at John. "How far a drive is it up to—" he was saying, when abruptly he stopped, his attention drawn to something over John's shoulder. He swore.

Lena followed the path of his gaze and her heart froze. Coming straight toward them were two men in dark suits, both men wearing sunglasses. "Oh, no," she breathed. "It's them."

John swiveled in his chair. "Swell," he said.

Before any of them could say another word, FBI Special Agent Alan Sabin and his sidekick, the big blond Miller, were at Hidalgo's desk. Lena felt her limbs go stiff and her pulse grow heavy.

Taking off his sunglasses with measured practice, Sabin introduced himself and Miller to John. Lena just glared at him, and Mike rose to his feet, towering over Alan Sabin.

"I can't say this is a pleasure," Mike said coolly.

Sabin smiled. "Thought we'd drop by and compare notes. It's still our case, Quinn, and for your information, interfering with an FBI investigation is a federal crime."

"Who's interfering?" Mike said. Then he added, "That was a nasty little trick you pulled on Gloria Torres. Big man, aren't you?"

Lena had had about enough male posturing. "Do you have any new information on my daughter's kidnapping?" she asked Sabin. "Or would you rather trade insults with these guys?"

Sabin eyed her up and down and took his time answering. "It so happens we do have a lead," he finally said insolently.

Lena's breath stopped. "Tell me," she said, "what is it?"

"Well, now," Sabin began, "you haven't exactly been cooperative, Miss Portillo, or is it Mrs. Quinn? Never really got that straight, did I?"

"What is it?" she demanded, her cheeks hot, fury battling with exhaustion, desperation clawing at her.

He grinned, taunting her.

"Tell me," she said harshly, and all her control fled in that moment. She started toward him, not knowing what she was going to do, not caring, only determined to force him to tell her what he knew.

There was a hand on her arm, and Mike spoke into her ear, "Take it easy, Lena."

She pulled in a deep, rasping breath, her hands in fists, trembling with emotion, then she whirled abruptly and walked swiftly into the ladies' room, banging the door. She stood for a time, eyes closed, calming herself, then she bent over a sink and splashed cold water on her face.

Mike opened the door, stuck his head in and looked around.

"Lena?" he asked uncertainly.

"I'm okay," she answered.

He came in and stood next to her, his expression concerned.

"You're not supposed to be in here," she said dully.

"The hell with that. Listen, the FBI found out that Jane Cramm had a waitress job four years ago. She paid taxes. Place called Malaga." He put his hand on her arm and brought her around to face him. "Malaga, New Mexico."

It was a moment before his words sank in. "Then..." She licked dry lips. "Then this Jane Cramm really is here? Here in New Mexico?"

Mike was smiling softly. "Looks like it. Looks like she gave up the baby six years ago and then, for whatever reason, she stole her back. And," he added, "I can't think of one single reason she'd want to harm her."

The tears came then. A flood of relief and worry and desperation. She fell against Mike's chest, her fingers convulsively gripping his shirt, and she let herself cry. She wasn't aware of Mike's fingers in her hair or the look of pain and regret etching his face.

When Lena and Mike emerged from the bathroom everyone avoided eye contact with them. One of the women officers edged past them and went into the ladies' room. "Ah, excuse me," she said, and Lena wished a hole would open up and swallow her.

Mike was forging a path back to Hidalgo's desk, to the FBI agents. *The goons,* Lena thought. She forced her feet to move and told herself firmly to get it together. Now was not the time to fall apart. And they had a lead on Jane Cramm. The woman had been in New Mexico. Years ago, true. But she'd been here, and Lena prayed she still was. With Kimmy. Yet, amazingly, when they reached John's desk, Sabin and Miller were back on the same refrain.

Lena overheard Miller saying, "That vehicle list you're checking out is a wild-goose chase."

And John. "How's that?"

"Statistics," Miller went on, and he gave Lena and Mike the once-over.

Sabin took up the conversation. "Jane Cramm or no Jane Cramm, statistics say it's usually the parents behind a kidnapping."

Lena stared incredulously at him while feeling the sudden energy flowing from Mike. He seemed to swell, to grow larger than life. It was almost as if she could see him gathering himself for a confrontation, but John Hidalgo forestalled him.

John said, "There's no evidence whatsoever that this is the case. If you'll recall, Kimberly was even spotted by a clerk at a minimart in Flagstaff. I don't see how you can—"

"Oh, right," Sabin chimed in. "And who did the clerk *allegedly* tell this to? Quinn? Miss Portillo here? I don't suppose you checked it out yourself."

"Now, look—" John countered.

Sabin cut him off. "These two have put up a good

show, I'll give them that. But my money's on that poor kid still being in L.A. They probably dumped her—''

Lena gasped at the very moment Mike lost it. One second he was standing next to her, hands in his jeans pockets, the next he had the FBI man sprawled across the top of John's desk, papers and files flying, his fist raised to strike.

"Take it easy, Quinn!" one of the cops yelled, and three more joined him to pull Mike off. They had to hold him and talk him down while Sabin righted himself and puffed out his chest, straightening his shirt and tie.

He glared at Mike. "I'm pressing assault charges, Quinn, right here and now," he rasped.

"Be my goddamned guest, you bastard," Mike shot back, and he struggled against the cops who still held him.

Sabin turned to his partner. "You witnessed that, Miller. You can corroborate this officer's assault on me."

"Yes, I certainly can," Miller intoned.

Sabin swung around to John. "You saw the whole thing. Write up an arrest report."

John shrugged. "I didn't see a thing."

Sabin glared at him, then pivoted, facing another one of the crowd. "You saw what he did!"

"Not me, buddy."

"Then *you* saw it!" Sabin snapped at another onlooker, a woman.

"Saw what?" she said.

Lena watched the whole thing, frightened by the violence, by the atmosphere of pure male testosterone, but glad that Mike had stood up to Sabin. She was sickened by the necessity but perversely thrilled by the vanquishing of the FBI man.

When the FBI men were gone, John looked at Mike,

who was tucking his shirt into his jeans. "That was cute, Quinn."

Mike, his face still flushed with anger, shrugged. "He's lucky I didn't kill him."

Drawing in a deep breath, her hands shaking, Lena picked up the papers and files scattered on the floor, placed them on John's desk, then headed back to her own private spot. There was still work to be done. Later, when Mike was calm, she'd tell him that if he hadn't tried to punch Sabin, she would have done it herself.

The afternoon waned. Lena reached three more people on the list, but no one fit the bill. By five she'd only reached one more. That car, too, had been junked this past year.

At five-fifteen, Mike came over and interrupted her. "'Scuse me," he said, standing in front of the desk. "I got hold of the owner of the restaurant in Malaga where Jane Cramm worked. No luck. He said they get a lot of transients, go through waitresses by the dozens. He can't remember Cramm at all."

"You know," Lena said, "we don't have one single station wagon registered there, either. Of course, we know it's not registered in her name, anyway."

"That's true," Mike said. Then he gave her a half smile. "You'd make an all-right cop, Lena."

"Really," she said, shaking her head. "I think I'll stick to cars, though. A lot less stress."

"You're doing okay," he stated. "I always knew you would."

Lena looked up. "You checked, though, Mike. You kept tabs on me."

"Only to see if you were okay. You and Kimmy. I make no excuses."

"Mmm," she said.

Mike changed the subject. "John's going to have Hayden and that Slacks guy run through the computer first thing in the morning, see what turns up."

"Something's got to give," she said, sighing.

"It will. Always does."

At seven they called it a day. They'd reached sixteen of the eighteen car owners. That was good. What wasn't so good was that other than the two John was going to do a computer check on, they had zip. Lena held on to the fact that the woman at the minimart had identified Kimmy, and the fact that Jane Cramm had once worked in New Mexico. She had to still be here. She simply had to be the one who'd taken Kimmy. And Mike said, over and over, that they'd find her.

"Let's get a drink," John suggested when they were through for the day.

Lena's heart skipped a beat. *Oh, no,* she thought. He'd take them to some cop hangout. She knew it. And what would Mike do? He'd been awfully good this past week, but in a cop bar?

Still, she herself could use a drink. Two, maybe. Her nerves were raw, and every muscle in her body thrummed with weariness.

"Well?" John asked. "How about that drink?"

"Okay," Lena said, and she picked up her sweater, threw it over her shoulders and glanced at Mike.

"Fine," he said.

John took them to a nearby bar, one of those narrow, shotgun places with pool tables lining one side, the long bar on the other and tables in the back, near the kitchen. It was dim and smoky and jammed with cops. Loud. All three pool tables were busy, and two electronic dartboards were in use. A big matchup was in progress.

"I'll find us some barstools," John said over the din.

But Mike put a hand on his arm. "Let's just get a table. That okay?"

"Sure," John said. "They've got great food in this joint."

"I smell garlic," Lena said, following John toward the rear.

"Spaghetti, garlic bread," he said over his shoulder. "And the lasagna's the best in the city."

It had occurred to Lena that if Mike and John began on beers and shooters—Mike's favorite—the car was only four blocks away, at police headquarters. She could always leave, drive to the motel and order food in. No big deal. She just hoped Mike wasn't hungover in the morning. That would be the icing on the cake.

A barmaid came over when they were seated. "The usual?" she asked John.

"Yeah, in the bottle. And back it up with a shot of tequila. Don't forget the lime, eh?"

"I look like a moron?" she said. She turned to Lena and raised her brows. "And for the lady?"

"Ah, how about a vodka and OJ."

"One screwdriver comin' up." She turned to Mike. "What do you have for nonalcoholic beer?" he asked. She rattled off three brands.

Mike chose one.

Lena cocked her head.

"Don't drink?" John asked.

"Let's see," Mike said, looking at John. "It's been sixty-one months and... Hell, I don't know how many days anymore."

Lena sat there mute, stunned. Sixty-one months? That would have made it... *Oh, my Lord,* she thought. Mike was saying he hadn't had a drink since that night? She stared at him. Sixty-one months.

CHAPTER THIRTEEN

IT TOOK A WHILE before Lena's mind stopped whirling with the new realization, and she wondered if Mike and John noticed how quiet she was. She sat there and sipped her drink and was glad for the dim light that hid her expression. She kept staring at Mike across the table, studying him, and she wondered with a sense of shame how on earth she could have missed the signs of his sobriety.

She hadn't believed him. But how could she have? The one thing in a relationship that alcoholics eroded most was trust. Only once did he glance in her direction, and their gazes met and held for a mere breath of time before he looked back to John and replied to something the detective had asked him.

They ordered dinner from frayed old menus—John didn't even need to look—and still Lena watched Mike, thinking back over the past week. How could she have failed to notice how healthy he looked? The alcohol bloating gone, the clear eyes. And he'd never smelled of liquor. Had she just not wanted to see it?

My God. Five years and Mike hadn't had a drink and she hadn't known.

He was talking to John, something about the FBI, and she saw his brows draw together. John replied, obviously something humorous, because Mike's expression cleared and he flashed a smile that lit up his face like a boy's.

The waitress came with their dinners and asked if they wanted refills on the drinks. Lena nodded. She needed to relax, to erase from her mind the awful ups and downs of the day, to try to wind down.

"You want to work the phone again tomorrow?" John was asking her.

"Oh, yes, of course."

"Okay. You did a good job," he replied, smiling, his long Spanish face creasing pleasantly.

"Do you think that Daniel Hayden could really be a good lead?" she asked anxiously.

"Maybe. It's worth the computer check, and we'll run that Slacks character along with Jane Cramm. It's too bad we couldn't trace her through that restaurant, but we'll keep trying. At least we know she was in New Mexico."

"Years ago. She could be anywhere," Lena said, playing devil's advocate.

"We'll find her," Mike stated.

She gave him a rare smile and thought there were so many things she should say to him now, needed to say. An apology to start with. And maybe, just maybe, she and Mike could be friends, and if, *when,* they got Kimmy back, he could indeed be a father to her.

They ate, Lena quiet, the men trading police talk. She was impatient, she realized, for dinner to be over, for her and Mike to return to their motel alone so that she could say the things that were building up inside her.

She didn't eat much, but she finished her second drink, and eventually she relaxed, her limbs liquid, a slight buzz in her head. Maybe she'd be able to get a good night's sleep.

It was eleven before John walked them back to the parking lot to Lena's car.

"You drive," Lena said, handing Mike the keys.

He didn't say anything, only waved good-night to John and started the car. Lena rested her head on the seat back, her eyes closed, and listened to the reassuring rumble of the engine.

"You're the only person I ever let drive this car," she finally said.

"That so?"

"Uh-huh."

"You mean, in all these years you never let anyone else touch it?"

"That's right."

"What about the men you dated?"

"Fishing, Mike?"

"No, dammit, just plain curious."

"You can count on the fingers of one hand the men I've dated, and they all had their own cars."

The car slowed and turned, and Lena rested, her eyes still closed. She was thinking about what to say, how to ask, but the words came out before she framed the right question. "Why didn't you tell me years ago, Mike?"

"Tell you what?" he asked maddeningly.

"That you really stopped drinking."

"Would it have done any good?"

She had to think for a minute, and, ruefully, she had to reply no.

"Question answered."

"Maybe you should have tried, told Gloria, had your mom or dad tell me... Well, try to tell me."

"I thought about it, but you disappeared, and frankly, I didn't have the energy or the nerve. I was fighting my own battle. And then it was too late."

"I ran," she mused. "I ran for my life."

"I know," he said. "I understood after a while, and I figured it was better not to dig up old bones."

"Maybe you were right," she said. "Or maybe..." Her voice died.

He pulled into the motel parking lot and stopped the car. "We're here," he said quietly.

She stayed there, unable to summon the energy to move. "I'm so tired, Mike," she said.

"Come on, let's get inside and get you to bed. You sure are a cheap drunk, Lena."

"I'm not drunk."

"No, only comatose."

He came around to the passenger side and opened her door, and she roused herself to open her eyes and stand and breathe in the fresh night air.

"You're not going to be sick, are you?" Mike asked. She shook her head.

Inside, she sank onto the couch.

"Lena, it's late. Go to bed."

She looked up at him. "Should I have stayed with you?"

He sighed in exasperation. "Is this really the time to discuss it?"

"Should I have?"

"I don't know. I honestly don't know."

"Maybe I should have, but I was so scared. I couldn't deal with it. After my father... And I loved Jeff, too, you know."

A shadow crossed Mike's face. "I know you did. It was a real bad time, Lena, for all of us."

He paused, and she could see the effort he made to smile.

"But we survived, we managed, didn't we? And we're both doing okay."

"I owe you an apology," she said, her gaze on his. "I'm sorry."

"Not necessary."

"Oh, but it is. For years I thought every bad thing there was to think about you. I hated...I thought I hated you."

"Forget it," he said gruffly. "It was my fault. I was the one who drank. I almost killed myself. I chased you away, almost lost my job. I deserved everything that happened."

She looked down at her hands. "I'm ashamed of myself. I didn't believe you. I'm so damn stubborn. I couldn't give you credit for changing, and I..."

"Stop it, Lena."

"It isn't *me*," she went on. "It's Kimmy. I deprived her of her father. I'm so sorry, Mike."

"Lena..."

"No," she said, waving a hand, "let me say it. I made you miss all the years she's been growing up. It was a terrible thing I did."

"You did what you thought was right."

"Why are you being so damn nice to me?"

"Why shouldn't I be?"

"Oh, Mike. Maybe you'll never get a chance to know Kimmy now. Maybe she'll never get to know her father. Maybe it's too late, and it's all my fault," she said wretchedly.

"Lena, don't torture yourself. It's the booze talking. We'll get Kimmy back."

"You could be wrong. What if it's too late and she's..."

"Stop it, Lena," Mike said sharply.

She tried, but every horrible possibility she'd ever imagined flashed before her eyes. Her baby, her little girl, tortured, dying, screaming, her little body lying... No, she couldn't allow herself to think those things. She closed her eyes for a minute, taking deep breaths, feeling the hideous shuddering terror retreat into a corner of her mind.

"Lena, you okay?" Mike asked.

"Yes, sure, I just... I'm going to take a shower," she said, forcing her voice to remain calm.

She thought the shower would be soothing, but it wasn't. It was as if all the tears inside her were raining down on her skin, and slowly she slid down the tiled wall to sit crouched, face in her hands, moaning in anguish, the water pounding on her back.

A knock on the bathroom door barely roused her. She heard Mike calling her name, asking if she was all right, but it didn't seem to matter; she couldn't stop crying.

The door opened, and he came in. She was aware of it, but it had no reality; only her pain was real.

"Lena?" he asked in an anxious voice, then, "Damn, I knew those drinks were too much... Lena?"

She couldn't move. The water was hot, but she was shivering; that didn't matter, either. Then the glass door slid back, and Mike reached in and turned the water off.

"Come on, Lena," he said softly. But she couldn't respond; it was too much effort.

A towel was thrown around her, and she was pulled upright. His strong arm supported her, and she surrendered to her need and clung to him, not caring that she was wet and naked and water was streaming into her face from her hair.

"Mike," she sobbed, "I can't go on if anything's h-happened to her. Oh, Mike."

He held her and stroked her hair. "Shh," he said. "It'll be all right. I promise you. You're just tired. It'll be better in the morning."

She trembled convulsively from cold and fear, and she

shook her head, droplets of water flinging off her hair. "No, no, it won't be better till I have her back."

"You will. You'll have her back."

"Oh, Mike," she cried, tilting her face up to his, "if only I'd known you'd changed! If I'd let you be a part of her life, maybe this wouldn't have happened."

"Don't be silly, Lena. It could have happened if I'd been there. It isn't your fault. It isn't anything you did wrong."

She buried her face in his chest, wetting his shirt, but he only pushed her hair back and tried to dry it with a corner of the towel. Gradually she stopped shaking, and as she felt his heart beating against her cheek, she calmed down, her tears stopped. She took a deep, quavering breath.

"Better?" he asked.

She nodded wordlessly.

He held her still, and his arms, his chest, felt so good she never wanted to leave their shelter.

"When you hold me," she whispered, "I can almost believe everything will be all right."

"It will."

She knew she had to let go of him—this had only been an interlude—but she couldn't bear the desolation it would bring.

"Lena," he began.

"I'll go to bed now," she said, but she didn't move.

She felt him shift his position; he was going to disengage himself from her, he was... But his head bent and his cheek brushed hers and somehow, miraculously, his lips were on hers.

A voice in her head cried danger, but she didn't care. His smell, his warmth, the strength of his hand on her back, the wetness of his shirt from her tears and her hair—they were too important, too vital to her existence. He murmured something, and she felt his hardness against her nudity, and he pulled her closer.

She opened her mouth to receive him, and it was as if it had been a century since she'd been with this man— or a minute. Time ran together in jerky moments, endless and fleeting.

She opened her eyes to find him looking at her, everything he was in his eyes, in the gaze he fastened hungrily on her.

"Lena," he said again, and his fingers tightened on her back. "Lena."

Something inside her burst free, and she knew suddenly and irrevocably that she still loved this man. Nothing mattered, not his history with his lady friend, protection, nothing. Only the fact that she loved him.

He swept her up effortlessly and carried her into the bedroom. His strength held her in thrall—she was not a small woman. The towel fell away, and she was on the bed, naked, reaching up for him, and he leaned over her, his weight on both arms, his clear blue gaze on her face.

"Are you sure of this?" he asked.

Her answer was to unbutton the first button on his shirt, then the next. Her fingers shook, and impatiently he sat on the bed and pulled his shirt off.

He lay next to her, on one elbow. "I never thought I'd do this again," he said.

"Neither did I."

His arm moved in a swift arc, pulling her close, and now she could feel his bare skin. How long it had been, how endlessly long.

They lay together on their sides, mouths and fingers halting wherever they wanted, in a sanctuary of their own making, touching, stroking, murmuring sounds that were not words.

He undressed, dropping his pants on the floor, and returned to her. His mouth was on her skin, trailing exquisite sensations, on her nipple. His hand brushed her wetness, and she gasped, her hips rising, her body twisting.

Time was suspended, reality was suspended, and Lena lost herself in a maelstrom of pure sensation. There was an absence of everything that had marked her life for so long—no haste, no fear, no worry, no ambition, a banishment of all that she'd thought important for so long, of all that mattered in the daylight.

When he entered her, she stopped breathing for a second, then two. It felt so different, so perfect, and she wanted to hold him there, to keep him, to stop time.

But he moved over her, and she felt his hardness growing inside her, and her body wouldn't stop; it was on its own relentless search for fulfillment.

She rose, pressing against him, trying to touch as much of his skin with hers as she could, desperate to pull him into her, more of him. They moved together easily, without hesitation, as if their bodies remembered, despite their stubborn minds. No words were needed, the changes in rhythm understood between them.

She felt her body on the brink of explosion, moving faster, her breath quick, almost desperate, and he thrust into her hard—once, twice—and their mouths found each other, hot and searching, and she shuddered, a cry rising from her to meet his.

They lay silent afterward. Lena was stunned, her mind unable to comprehend what she'd done, but her body seemed to have learned something her brain didn't know. She was afraid to speak, for there was nothing either of them could say, and she didn't want to spoil what had happened between them.

She felt herself drifting into sleep, roused briefly when Mike pulled the covers up over them. Then she drifted again, and she wasn't sure whether she dreamed it or imagined it, but she thought that Mike leaned over to kiss her on the cheek, and said, "I've always loved you, Lena."

KACEY CRAWLEY ALWAYS got to police headquarters before anyone else except the desk sergeant, who was on all night anyway.

"'Morning, Kacey," he said, pressing a buzzer to allow her entry into the enclave. "It's two minutes till seven—you're early."

Kacey tossed her blond ponytail. "Oops. I'd better go out and come in again. You know how they feel about overtime."

"Boy, do I ever," he replied, and then he watched her walk to the elevators. No one looked better in a uniform than Kacey, recently divorced, Crawley, with those blue eyes and those endless long legs.

Kacey took the elevator down to her department, Juvenile Division, and switched on lights as she walked the long corridors. This was her favorite time of day, early morning, when she felt most alive and most efficient.

Switching on more lights, she made her way to her cubbyhole of an office, turned on her computer and stuffed her purse and sweater into the empty drawer of her file cabinet. She sat down, punched her private password into the computer and waited for the screen to read "Good morning, Kacey, code accepted. Have a nice day."

She was anxious to start on a particular search.

It had begun at five that morning. She'd awakened before her alarm rang, something gnawing at her. She'd made coffee, showered and been blow-drying her hair, when the first clue slipped into her brain. It had to do with that cop from L.A., Quinn, who'd punched the FBI agent yesterday afternoon. The story had spread through headquarters like wildfire, everyone snickering, laughing and embellishing the episode until, by the time it had reached the basement, the agent was in the hospital with a broken nose and ribs.

Kacey had asked a fellow juvenile officer what the cop from L.A. was doing in Albuquerque.

"Don't really know," he'd replied. "Something about his kid being missing and doing a search here for a car involved in the abduction."

Then somebody two desks away had called over, "The L.A. cop's looking for one of those old wood-paneled station wagons."

"Interesting," Kacey had said, and she might have recalled the report from Santa Fe she'd read on the computer, except the chatter went back to the big, good-looking city cop who'd decked the fibbie.

"I hear he's a real hunk," one of the women in the office had said.

"Forget it, Flo," another one said. "Guy brought his wife along."

"Ex-wife," someone else had called out.

But at 5 a.m., Kacey had awakened, and the station wagon had nagged at her. A missing kid, an old station wagon.

As a juvenile officer, Kacey read reports of child abusers, kidnappings—mostly by angry ex-spouses—teenage crimes, everything having to do with kids under the age of eighteen on a statewide level.

Each day she cataloged hundreds of reports that poured in from other police departments around the state. It took most of her day. Some reports stuck in her mind; others did not. Why the mention of the station wagon jarred her was a mystery.

"But what day?" she said aloud. "Monday? Tuesday?" It had been recent. She was sure of that.

She began searching the original reports that had come in on Monday. By eight-thirty, when the building was buzzing, she sat back and rubbed her eyes, realizing she didn't really have time for this. Another hour or so, she thought, and she'd give up. The chances of this station wagon thing in her head being connected to the L.A. cop's missing kid were remote at best.

She began searching Tuesday's reports, scrolling through page after page after page.

Waste of time, Kacey thought.

MIKE SAT ACROSS FROM John Hidalgo and frowned. He'd just gotten off the phone with the Malaga cops, having asked them to run Jane Cramm through their local computer records, but they'd never had contact with her—no misdemeanors, no traffic violations, nothing.

He glanced over at Lena, who was working the phone on the last of the station wagon owners. How many times had he promised her they'd get Kimmy back? He'd never tell her, not in a million years, of the doubts that were beginning to assail him.

Lena was speaking to someone on the phone, writing in her notepad at the same time, her long, shining brown hair forming a curtain over one side of her face. He recalled without a bridging thought the way her hair had fallen against his cheek last night and brushed his chest as she'd taken the top position in their lovemaking. He could almost feel the warm, silken flesh of her hips in his hands when he'd guided her, the way she'd unfolded to him like a flower, her back arching. She had the most beautiful hips and breasts, full and womanly, and goose bumps raised on his arms just thinking about the firm roundness of her bosom, the taste of her.

He kept staring, lost in the memory of last night. If anything, it had been even better than during their marriage, when Lena had been younger, more shy. Him, too. But now they fit together like a pair of gloves long separated. He'd never had a night like that. Not with anyone. Not with Jennifer...

Mike tore his gaze away and let out a low breath. Jennifer. Holy cow. He hadn't once thought about her till this very second. Guilt surged through him, then rested hot and burning in his gut. How could he have made love to Lena and not once given Jenn a single thought? And Jenn had suspected that was exactly what was going to happen. How could he have been so naive?

"Ahem." John cleared his throat. "You with me here, Quinn?"

"Ah, yes, sure," Mike said, distracted. "What were you saying?"

"I wasn't. Just wanted to show you these printouts from Records." As he handed Mike the computer sheets, he glanced over at Lena, then back at Mike.

Oh, God, Mike thought. Was it that obvious?

There were three sheets. One was on Jane Cramm, one on Slacks Kerry and another on Daniel Hayden.

He read Cramm's. It was a single line. She'd gotten a driver's license from the Department of Motor Vehicles four years ago. The records didn't even say where, exactly, she'd taken the test. It had an address—in Malaga—which Mike knew was useless. The license had expired last year. There'd been no renewal.

"Dammit," he muttered.

He put aside Cramm's sheet and looked at Slacks Kerry's. Now this dude had an interesting past. In '89 he'd been arrested for possession of a controlled substance, given probation. In '91 he'd been jailed for thirty days in Farmington for auto-parts theft. Then, in '96, he'd spent ninety days in the slammer for failure to stop his vehicle when a state trooper had tried to pull him over for a traffic violation. *A loser,* Mike thought. Maybe a friend of Cramm's? Both real losers. Maybe this Slacks character had been the man in the car at the school. Maybe Jane Cramm had been the woman. There were sure a lot of maybes.

He looked at Daniel Hayden's sheet, and it was even longer. Hayden had been arrested seven times in the past ten years. Of those ten years, he'd spent nearly six in prison. The conviction that had sent Hayden to the state penitentiary was a doozy. The idiot had stolen a car in Santa Fe to make a court appearance on drug charges right here in Albuquerque. Unbelievable. And rather than heisting a nondescript car, the rocket scientist had taken a bright pink VW bug convertible.

"Look at this," Mike said, handing John the printout. "What an idiot."

John read the report and chuckled.

"I wonder," Mike said, "if we could get the mug shots of these two guys faxed to my pop in L.A. He could show them to the little girl who saw the driver of the station wagon. She's a sharp little kid. Who knows? Maybe she can finger one of them."

"If one of them's our perp."

"There is *that,*" Mike said gravely.

"Well," Lena said over Mike's shoulder, "I'm through with the list."

"Anything new?" John asked.

Lena shook her head, but Mike was barely aware of what either of them said after that. All he could see was her: the jut of her chin, the sensuous curve of her mouth, the tilt of those sable-colored eyes. She was standing, and her breasts beneath the oversize dark blue sweater she wore were on a level with his eyes. He could see the firm round curves, and despite all his efforts, he couldn't think about anything but touching her, cupping those breasts, drawing the hard nipples into his mouth.

Mike broke into a sweat sitting there in the middle of the crowded vice squad office. If they'd been alone, he would have swept Hidalgo's desk clean and taken Lena right there and then. He couldn't believe what was happening to him. It was like a mad charade being acted out in his brain despite everything he tried to do to stop it.

He looked up and met Lena's eyes, and he knew that she knew. He felt heat crawl up his neck. Quickly he rose and mumbled something about having to use the bathroom.

"Be, ah, right back," he said, and he got the hell away from her.

When Mike left the men's room, Lena and Hidalgo weren't alone. A woman police officer was with them, uniformed, with pretty, long blond hair in a ponytail, and every eye in the room was fixed on her legs.

"Mike," Hidalgo called, waving him over, "listen to this."

She introduced herself, shaking his hand. "Kacey Crawley, Juvenile Division."

Mike was aware of the smile on John's face and of

Lena—she was biting her lower lip and wringing her hands.

Kacey went on. "If you hadn't hit that fibbie," she said, "I never would have made the connection. Anyway—" she handed Mike a computer sheet "—here's what I've got. A couple of days ago, up in Santa Fe, a lady shopping at a grocery store reported a child-abuse incident to the store manager. Evidently some drunken woman was giving a child—little girl around six or seven years old—a hard time. The woman said she was her aunt, but the lady shopper felt something wasn't ringing true. Anyway, she reported it and the manager called the police. It got put on the statewide network."

Mike drew his sandy brows together. "The shopper didn't happen to notice the car...?"

Kacey grinned. "That's what made me think of you," she said. "The inebriated woman was driving an old wood-paneled station wagon."

It took a moment for that to sink in and then Mike looked at Lena. "Hayden. Daniel Hayden lives in Santa Fe," he said in a harsh whisper.

Lena had tears in her eyes now. "And I'll bet any amount of money that the woman was Jane Cramm."

"Wow," Mike breathed, and he put his hands on Lena's shoulders, a rush of hope and relief flowing between Lena and him.

CHAPTER FOURTEEN

JANE HEARD DANNY'S CAR stop outside the house, and she threw the rest of the drink down as fast as she could, ran water into the glass and rinsed her mouth out with the mouthwash she kept under the kitchen sink.

Danny came in, leading Kimmy by the hand, and Jane was heartened by his expression, which was neutral for a change. She put a smile on her lips and asked, "How'd it go?"

"Okay," Danny said, nodding. "She did good."

"Lucky it didn't rain," Jane observed.

"Yeah, it was okay. All she had to do was run around and pretend to chase butterflies and stuff like that."

"She behaved?"

"Damn right she did. It was hard to make her laugh, though. See, they wanted her to look happy and all."

Jane turned to Kimmy. "I told you to do what the men said, and you promised."

Kimmy looked at her feet and sulked.

"She'll do better this afternoon," Jane assured him.

"Damn right," he growled.

"You'll do what the men say this afternoon," Jane said to the child, "won't you, Kimmy? It's like a game. It's playacting, is all."

Kimmy said nothing.

"I'm hungry," Danny said. "The cheapskates didn't have no food, nothing."

"I'll make you some sandwiches, okay?" Jane hastened to say.

"What kind?"

"Bologna. And cheese."

"Okay, but put plenty of mustard on. I like mustard," he said.

"Okay, Danny."

She even cut the sandwiches diagonally, to make them pretty, and she cut Kimmy's twice, to make little wedges for the girl. Then she opened a beer for Danny and poured a glass of milk for Kimmy.

"Here it is," she said brightly. "Lunch for everybody."

Danny sat and started to eat quickly, his head down, his shoulders hunched. Jane smiled benignly on her daughter and took small, ladylike bites of her own sandwich. Kimmy sat there perfectly quiet, not eating a thing.

"What's the matter?" Jane finally asked.

"I'm 'lergic to bologna," she whispered.

"'Lergic?"

"It makes me, you know, sick," Kimmy said.

"Eat it, kid," Danny said.

"I'm 'lergic."

"Eat the goddamned food."

Kimmy began to whimper.

"Take the bologna out, then," Jane said, reaching over to Kimmy's sandwich.

Danny slapped her hand away. "She can eat it the way it is."

Kimmy was crying for real now.

"Goddammit!" Danny yelled.

Jane got scared then. She always got scared when Danny was mad. And now, with Kimmy, it was worse, because Jane had learned how to placate him, but Kimmy hadn't yet, and it seemed every little thing the kid did aggravated him.

"Be quiet," she murmured to Kimmy.

"I want my mommy!" the child wailed.

"Be quiet now. Shh," Jane said.

"Danny promised. He said if I was g-g-good!" Kimmy cried.

"You did, Danny?" Jane asked. "You promised she could see her mother?"

He shook his head, disgusted. "Yeah, sure, so what?"

"Oh," Jane said, understanding. He'd lied to Kimmy. She wasn't sure whether she was relieved or not.

"Shut up, kid," Danny said.

"I want my mommy!" The little girl's eyes were streaming and her nose was running.

"I said shut up!" Danny stood over her, his hand raised, and Kimmy cowered.

"No," Jane said urgently, "no, Danny, you'll..."

He backed off, obviously realizing he couldn't hit her because she had to look good for the filming that afternoon, and Jane heaved a sigh of relief.

Danny swore and strode out of the kitchen. At the door he turned around and snarled, "Have her ready when I get back." Then he left, slamming the door behind him.

Jane sat there for a minute, feeling the sandwich she'd eaten rebel in her stomach. Then, slowly, shakily, she got up and went to the cupboard, got out the bottle and poured herself a healthy shot, drank it down, then poured another.

She felt better after the second, so she put the bottle back, turned around and said pleasantly to Kimmy, "You need to eat lunch, you know. I'll fix it up for you." Jane went to the table, pulled the bologna out of the sandwich and replaced the bread. "There, now it's a cheese sandwich, see?"

Kimmy sniffed, rubbed her nose with the back of her hand. "I'm not hungry."

"Sure you are." Jane smiled. "Come on, Kimmy, please. Eat just a little bit. A nice cheese sandwich."

Eventually the girl started nibbling at a corner of one of the wedges. She drank some milk.

Jane felt good, as if she'd really accomplished something. She was getting better at this mother thing.

Gosh, she wished this darn movie were over, then she'd find out if Danny meant what he'd said about keeping Kimmy. But it worried her, the way he went and got so darn mad at everything Kimmy did. Maybe he really wouldn't let her keep her daughter. The last kid had just up and run off, after all. But then, that kid hadn't been Jane's flesh and blood, had she?

Jane sat there and watched Kimmy eat, and she nodded and smiled to encourage her. Then she got another of the pills from the bottle and gave it to Kimmy. "Here, take your vitamin pill," she said. "Drink it right down with your milk."

"It sticks in my throat."

"Come on, take it. It'll make you strong and healthy. Danny specially wants you to take it," she wheedled.

"But..."

"Take it, Kimmy. We don't want to make Danny mad, do we?"

LENA, MIKE AND JOHN left for the Santa Fe police station shortly before noon. Hidalgo had called ahead and told the Santa Fe cops the whole story, specifically asking them to do nothing whatsoever until they arrived, especially not to post an unmarked car near Hayden's house.

"The guy's streetwise, got a rap sheet the length of my arm," John had said, "so please sit tight till we get there."

"How far is it?" Lena had asked anxiously.

"Hour. Not far," John had replied.

Lena drove Mike in her car, following John's police cruiser. She was a wreck. She was sure they'd found the man who'd stolen her daughter; at the same time she was terrified she was mistaken or that if it was the man, he would be gone and Kimmy gone with him.

It was about seventy miles north to Santa Fe, and Lena chafed at how slow John was driving, at how long it was taking, at how close she might be.

"Relax," Mike kept telling her.

"I can't. What if this Hayden is leaving Santa Fe this very second, taking Kimmy somewhere else? What if he's hurting her?"

"He has no reason to hurt her."

Lena shot him a look.

"Watch the road," he said, "or let me drive."

The previous night had fled from Lena's mind almost as if it hadn't happened; she was entirely focused on one thing, with no room for considering what she'd done, what *they'd* done, what it meant, what would happen next. She'd think about that later.

"Lena," Mike said, "she's going to be okay." He put a hand on her thigh as she drove, a familiar touch. "Lena...?"

She bit her lip, blinked back panicky tears and shook her head, driving on, keeping Hidalgo's car exactly the correct distance ahead.

The Santa Fe police were ready for them; they'd started organizing a command center, rounded up off-duty policemen, called in their SWAT team. Mrs. Goodfriend, the woman who'd reported the child-abuse incident outside the Santa Fe grocery, was supposedly awaiting their arrival at police headquarters.

"I wish we had a picture of Jane Cramm," Lena said to Mike. "Maybe the woman could identify her."

"Well, we don't," Mike said. "I guess we'll find out soon enough."

"God willing," she whispered.

They met with Captain Bill Hunt at the police station, and John introduced Mike and Lena. He told Hunt that Mike was on the L.A. Hostage Negotiations team, not defining his present status; no sense admitting he was on his own time.

"Mrs. Goodfriend is waiting," Hunt said. "How about I go in with you?" Then he turned to Mike and Lena. "You can watch through the one-way mirror. I think too many people will confuse her."

So John entered the room with Hunt, and Lena stood outside at the window with Mike. Her heart was beating so hard she was afraid everyone in the squad room could hear it.

Selma Goodfriend was a pretty woman, dressed in a fussy, old-fashioned way, with wire-rimmed glasses, her hair permed. She was holding tightly to the strap of a patent-leather purse that rested on her knees.

Bill Hunt introduced himself and Hidalgo and had Mrs. Goodfriend tell in her own words what she'd seen the previous Wednesday afternoon in the parking lot.

"I used to be a teacher," the woman told them, "so I'm very aware of children's behavior. I'm retired now, but I still notice children, and I knew this little girl was not a happy child."

Lena recoiled from the words. What did the woman

mean? Had Kimmy been bruised or hurt or crying? Oh, God.

"And the woman with her, the *aunt*," Mrs. Goodfriend said, "well, she smelled like alcohol something fierce. I thought at the time, when I saw them getting into that old car, that she shouldn't be driving that little girl anywhere. And there probably weren't even seat belts, either."

John Hidalgo pulled out Kimmy's photograph and showed it to Mrs. Goodfriend. "Is this the little girl you saw on that occasion, ma'am?"

The woman peered at the picture for a second, then two. Lena held her breath. Next to her, Mike moved restlessly. He put a hand on her arm, as if to reassure her, and she was grateful for his touch.

Finally the woman nodded. "Yes, that's definitely the little girl I saw."

Lena drew her breath in sharply and felt her knees turn to water. It was Kimmy! This woman had seen her right here in Santa Fe.

Captain Hunt went on to try to get a description of the woman who'd been with Kimmy in the parking lot, but Selma Goodfriend wasn't much help. "She could have been thirty or fifty. She looked...worn, shopworn, if you will. You know, bad hair and skin, ghastly teeth. Trashy looking."

"Uh-huh," Bill said. "If I had a police artist work with you, could you remember enough details to help with a sketch?"

"I could try."

"All right," Hunt said. "We may not need the artist, but just in case, where can you be reached during the day?"

On he went, and all Lena could think was that they

weren't going to need a police artist or anyone else. They could get Kimmy right now. They had Hayden's address; they had all they needed.

"Thank you very much, Mrs. Goodfriend," John was saying on the other side of the glass. "You've been a great help."

"Let's go," Lena said, whirling on Mike. "Let's go now! She's there, Mike. Oh, God, let's get her quick!"

"Not so fast," Mike said. "We can't just rush up to this man's door and tell him to hand her over. Think about it, Lena. He's dangerous. You saw his rap sheet. If we go in without a plan, we could endanger Kimmy's life."

"Mike, she's right here, a few minutes away, and you're telling me I can't go to her?" Lena cried.

John came up to them. "He's right, Lena. We have to make a plan to ensure your daughter's safety. And it's the local police who have to do it. We're only spectators here."

"Oh, my God," Lena breathed. "I'll go. I'll just go by myself and get her. Please..."

"Lena, try to understand," Mike said. "This is for Kimmy's safety."

"I can't just wait here," she said. "I'll go out of my mind!"

"We can't do anything more, Lena. It's out of our hands now," Mike said. "We located her. We confirmed her identity. Our job is done."

"No, I can't..." Lena put her face in her hands.

"Come on, let's get some lunch," John said. "This place'll be a madhouse for at least a couple of hours."

It was the hardest thing Lena had ever been faced with, to know Kimmy was so close, yet be unable to do anything. She had to swallow her wild impatience and go to lunch. She must have eaten something, but she never remembered. She must have made conversation, but she couldn't recall that, either.

Finally they went back to police headquarters, walking the few blocks through scenic Santa Fe, with its square adobe buildings, some ancient, some brand-new, but all conforming to the historical style of the 1600s when Spaniards had built the frontier outpost from native materials. Lena barely noticed, even though John pointed out historical gems on every block.

"This city was here before the Pilgrims landed," he told her proudly.

"Mmm," she said, not hearing him, "that's nice."

The station was in an uproar when they returned. There was a map drawn on a blackboard, the street Daniel—Danny to the local police—Hayden lived on. There were Xs and arrows marked on it. The phones rang constantly. Hunt spoke to a group of detectives in one corner; the SWAT commander was there, dressed in black fatigues, thick boots and a cap, a gun slung over his shoulder. He studied the crude map with his men. Police were on the phones, calling in the troops.

Talk filled the air: parameters, rounds per second, caliber of weapons, unmarked cars, surveillance.

Lena sat on a chair in a corner and hugged herself, trying to keep calm. But the men talked and talked, groups shifted and reformed, and there was more talk. And meanwhile Kimmy was in the hands of that awful, dangerous *criminal*.

Mike and John joined a group, listening, giving an occasional suggestion. Especially Mike, because his experience could be invaluable if this case turned into a hostage situation.

That, of course, was the last thing anyone wanted.

It was two o'clock, then two-thirty, and still Hunt was talking and organizing and phoning. At two forty-five, FBI Special Agents Sabin and Miller walked in.

Lena's heart lurched. Not them! Dear Lord, would they interfere and slow everything down? Would everyone have to start over?

"Well, well, if it isn't the feds," John Hidalgo said.

Mike's face froze, but he didn't open his mouth.

Sabin went right to Hunt. "Agent Miller and I would like to be apprised of the current situation," he said. "We have jurisdiction here."

"For the love of God, Sabin," Mike said through clenched teeth. "No one has time to apprise you of a goddamned thing."

"Excuse me, gentlemen," Hunt said, coming between them, "I really think we can find some common ground here."

It was insane. Jurisdiction! Lena only wanted her little girl back, and she had to sit on her hands and wait while grown men argued and rattled sabers and played games. And what really made her grate her teeth was that the FBI owed her and Mike an apology. They owed Gloria one, too. But they just stood there dickering.

Someone do something! she wanted to scream.

She got up and went outside, unable to sit for another moment. She stalked back and forth in front of the building, not even noticing the clear, bright air or the autumn-hued mountains. Taking deep breaths, she told herself that John and Mike and the other men knew best; they'd handled these situations before and knew how to get the captive person back unharmed. Then she'd remember the many news reports she'd seen about this sort of situation, where there were gunfights and deaths and terrible injuries. Where the cops had blown it and the hostage was killed.

Her nerves were jumping under her skin, and there was a strangling tightness in her chest. *Please,* she prayed, *hurry up and get my baby out of there.*

She saw Mike exit the building and look around, worried.

"Oh, there you are," he said. "I was afraid you'd lost it."

"I have lost it," Lena said.

"Everything's under control. Right now they're checking with a doctor to see how tear gas will affect a child."

"Tear gas?"

"In case it's needed."

"Oh, Mike, this waiting…"

"I know, I know."

"Can't they just *go?*"

"Not until everyone knows exactly what to do."

"Will you be there, Mike? Will they let me come along?"

"Yes, I'll be there. Yes, you will be, too."

"When?"

"Soon."

Mike returned to the interminable plan making, and Lena pulled the cell phone out of her purse, then dialed her home number in California. Gloria answered on the second ring, her voice, as always, anxious.

"Has something happened?"

"Yes and no," Lena said, and she explained about Selma Goodfriend's ID of Kimmy in Santa Fe.

"So you're in Santa Fe now?"

"Uh-huh," Lena said, "but the wheels of justice are grinding awfully slowly. Mom, Kimmy's so close… Every minute we delay… That could be the minute…"

"You just hold on, sweetheart. Don't think about that. I'm sure the police know best. You'll have Kimmy back so soon you'll forget all this. Oh, Lord," Gloria breathed, "I'm so anxious for all of you. I wish I were there."

"I know, Mom."

"You'll call the instant you have Kimmy?"

"Of course."

"Promise?"

"Of course, Mom."

"How's Mike holding up?"

"He's calm, used to this sort of thing. Can you imagine?"

"God, no," Gloria said. "And you two are getting along?"

Lena paused a heartbeat too long. "Sure," she said.

"Mmm," Gloria said. "Am I reading something into this?"

"We'll discuss it later."

"*Lena.*"

"Forget it, Mom. I've got to go back inside now. I'll call you soon."

"My prayers are with you," Gloria said.

When Lena reentered the building the scene seemed unchanged. Groups of men with serious faces, phones ringing, talk, talk, talk.

Then she heard the unmistakable sound of Alan Sabin's voice raised in anger—and Mike answering him.

"I strongly suggest you wait till my team gets here from L.A.," Sabin was saying. "I can't be responsible otherwise."

"You aren't responsible anyway," Mike retorted. "You're out of the goddamned loop on this one!"

"This is a federal case. I have jurisdiction, Officer Quinn!"

"You know what you can do with your jurisdiction, Agent Sabin?" Mike yelled.

It was the last straw, the two of them shouting at each other. Something snapped inside Lena, and she was either going to get hysterical or she had to *act*. What she'd told her mother was true. Every minute they delayed, every second they strutted and postured, might be Kimmy's last.

Unnoticed, she took a good look at the blackboard with its map of Danny Hayden's neighborhood. There was his house, marked with an *X*, the name of his street, the house numbers.

Three-forty-eight Rio Blanco Street. She closed her eyes and committed the address to memory.

Several other cops had joined the argument between Mike and Sabin, and not a soul observed Lena slipping out. It was so very easy, she thought, that she should have done it hours earlier. She simply got into her car and drove out of the parking lot. For the first time in days she felt calm and in control—she was *doing* something.

Stopping at a gas station, she asked directions to 348 Rio Blanco Street and fixed them in her mind. It wasn't very far away, but then, Santa Fe wasn't a huge city like Los Angeles. She drove carefully, watching street signs.

Yes, there was Rio Blanco, running up into a ravine, lined with small, run-down adobe houses. She finally caught a house number and drove on, slowly now, watching like a hawk. Her mouth was dry, her heart beating slowly, heavily in her chest. She wasn't scared, wasn't out of her mind anymore, just ready. Yes, ready.

There it was: 348. Cracked, patched adobe, crooked window frames, a tilted porch. Daniel Hayden's home sweet home. And perhaps Jane Cramm's, too. Could the woman who'd borne Kimmy really harm her own flesh and blood? *No,* Lena's mind said, *no.* Yet Cramm had taken crack during her pregnancy, and Kimmy had suffered.

Lena stared at the house. What kind of people were those two? If the condition of the house was any indication, they were slobs, pigs, mindless human beings.

And Kimmy was with them.

She saw the car then, the wood-sided station wagon, parked around the corner from the house. They were home, then. They were home, and Kimmy was probably in there. A momentary panic squeezed her heart, but it was gone instantly, and deadly anger took its place. They'd stolen her child!

Lena parked across the street. She hadn't made any plans, hadn't thought ahead. She'd been running on autopilot ever since she'd gotten into her car.

She sat there for a time, watching the house, hoping, praying Kimmy really was inside, waiting for a door to open, someone to emerge, a clue to tell her what to do.

But the house squatted there, surrounded by its squalor, utterly silent.

A minute went by, then another, and Lena was no closer to knowing how to approach the house. She'd figured it would be easier than this, and now she wondered if she'd been insane to come here. She told herself sternly not to be a wimp. *Count to ten,* she thought, *then get up and knock on that door.*

She'd gotten to six, when the front door opened. Surprise took her breath away. A man moved into the sunlight, a skinny, homely-looking guy, scruffy, with a short-man's swagger. Danny? Was this the infamous Danny Hayden?

He turned and yelled something to someone inside—Lena couldn't hear the words—then a woman appeared in the doorway. Jane Cramm? She was thin and haggard, much older looking than her real age. Used up. And then, squeezing out from behind the woman, a child, her head ducked, a little girl with long brown hair and...the T-shirt, the blue jeans!

Kimmy! My God, it was her!

That was the last coherent thought Lena had. She didn't remember flying out of her car or racing across the street. She only knew her baby was there, her daughter who'd been stolen from her, and she had to get her back. She ran across the dead brown grass of the yard to where the man was leading Kimmy to the car.

She'd almost reached them, ready to cry out her child's name, when the man sensed something and turned on his heel to face Lena.

"What the hell?" he rasped.

Lena dodged, reaching for her daughter, but Danny yanked Kimmy away.

"Mommy!" Kimmy cried, joyfully, tearfully, glad and scared all at the same time.

The cry wrenched at Lena's heart.

The man stood there in dirty jeans, holding a struggling Kimmy behind him, his skinny legs wide apart.

"You let her go, you son of a bitch," Lena whispered harshly, her hands clenched into fists. *"Let her go."*

IT WAS ALMOST FOUR in the afternoon when Mike realized he hadn't seen Lena in quite some time. A little voice in his head chattered warningly, but he refused to take it seriously.

Excusing himself from the group he'd been talking with, he checked the coffee room, even the ladies' room, embarrassing himself when it wasn't empty.

Hidalgo noticed him and called out, "Getting in the habit of using the girls' room, Quinn?"

"Very funny. I'm looking for Lena. Seen her lately?"

Hidalgo thought. "Not for a while."

"How long?"

"Hmm. Quite a while."

"Shit," Mike said under his breath.

"You think..."

But Mike was striding outside to where he'd found Lena earlier. She'd be there, sure she would, muttering and threatening, as jumpy as a cat.

He walked all the way around the building and didn't find her, then it occurred to him to check the parking lot.

The empty parking space stared back at him like a blind eye. He was filled with a bright explosion of panic.

The GTO was gone.

CHAPTER FIFTEEN

WHEN LENA AWAKENED from the blow Danny had dealt her, she was aware of being in a car, her head lying on a warm lap.

Her eyes flew open despite dizzying pain, and she looked up and realized it was dark out and that it was Kimmy's lap—her own child's little lap—on which she rested.

A rush of emotions surged through her: immense relief and joy, followed by mounting alarm. Whose car...? Where were they?

"Mommy?" said a small voice. "Are you awake, Mommy?"

"Oh, yes, baby," Lena breathed, and she licked dry lips. "Oh, yes, sweetie, Mommy's awake." Tears sprang from her eyes, and her arms went around Kimberly's waist, a waist that had grown smaller. She clung to her child desperately, her brain reeling from both the pain and the release of so many fears. And despite their predicament, which was becoming clearer by the moment, she basked in the relief that her daughter was alive.

Kimmy was clinging to Lena in the dimness just as tightly as she was to her. "Mommy, Mommy," her child kept saying, "I want to go home."

And then the voice from the front seat came, jarring Lena into full reality.

"Shut the hell up, kid."

Daniel Hayden, of course. She and Kimmy were in the car with Hayden, driving somewhere. But where?

Mike, she thought suddenly, where was Mike? But she'd slipped away from the police station, gone to Hayden's by herself. How many hours ago? Did Mike realize what had happened? Oh, God, what had she done?

Lena came to a sitting position, the blood rushing to her head, making pain crash against her skull. She closed her eyes, willing herself not to pass out, and that was when she became aware of the car coming to a stop, the headlights piercing nothing but a vast, empty plain.

Hayden turned to her, resting a gun against the back of his seat, its barrel aimed straight at her.

"'Bout time you woke up," he said.

Lena was instantly disgusted by the figure this man, this *animal* presented. Even in the dimness she could make out his scraggly hair and the unevenness of his front teeth. He had a ferretlike face and his eyes were lifeless holes. He smelled unwashed.

He reached toward Kimmy with his other hand, as if to grab her hair, but Lena drew her more tightly against her side. "Don't you touch her."

Hayden made a grunting sound and swung the gun barrel from Lena's face to Kimmy's and back. "You shut your mouth," he said, "or I'll come back there and shut it real good for you." He turned around in his seat and opened the driver's door. "Get up here now—you're driving," he said, pushing the door all the way open with a booted foot.

Lena tried to think. "I...I can't drive. I'm too dizzy."

"Get up here!"

"I'll...pass out. Really I will."

"You get the hell up here and behind this wheel or I'll beat the tar out of your sniveling brat."

"Mommy," Kimmy sobbed, "I don't want you to leave me!"

In the end, Lena was forced to do as he said. As Hayden warned them, he didn't need two hostages. One would do just fine.

With Kimmy trying to cling to her, Lena had to force herself to open the back door and disengage her child's embrace. She felt as if part of her own body was being torn away. "It'll be okay, sweetie. I'm just going to drive. I'll be right here."

"Shut up!" Danny kept yelling. "Shut the hell up! Haven't you done enough to ruin everything as it is!"

Lena got out and swayed against the side of the car, her head whirling. There was no use arguing, though, because he was right: Hayden did not need to keep them both as hostages.

She got into the driver's seat, while Danny slid in on the passenger side, then slammed the door. "You better know how to drive," he muttered, and he waved the gun in the air.

She tried to ignore him and the sudden nausea that rose in her throat. Her head was pounding and her fingers shook as she found the gearshift and put it in drive. "Where are we?" she breathed.

"Never you mind where we are. Just drive," he grated out.

Wherever they were, Lena realized as she steered onto the two-laned road, there wasn't another car in sight. Not one single car. They might as well have been driving on another planet. *Oh, Mike,* she kept thinking, *why didn't I let you handle it?* She looked in the rearview mirror a hundred times, praying to see lights coming up from behind: Mike, coming to rescue them. How could she have defied him? Stupid, stupid, stupid. And yet she was with Kimmy, her baby. Hadn't she prayed for this moment?

Kimmy huddled in a corner of the back seat, barely visible in the rearview mirror. The headlights stabbed at the blackness ahead, and even when she finally passed a road sign—Route 44—it meant nothing to her. Only the NM below the route number told her they were still in New Mexico.

Danny Hayden eventually leaned his head against the window and muttered something about his not going to sleep. "I was in the army, see," he said, "and I don't need no sleep. Even if I did, I'd hear a dime drop and wake up. So don't try nothin' cute."

Army, Lena thought, *sure*. She'd read his rap sheet. The only time this lowlife had ever done was in prison.

She closed her eyes for a second against a sudden pounding in her temples, then opened them. She had to stay alert. Still, her vision was hazy and she was pretty sure she had a concussion. She glanced again in the mirror at Kimmy, who was so quiet she might have been sleeping, and then she looked over at Hayden, leaning against the window, the gun in his lap aimed at her.

She took a breath. "Where's Jane?" she dared to ask.

He muttered something, and Lena heard the word "bitch." It seemed to be his only adjective to describe a woman.

"Why didn't Jane come along?" Lena asked again.

"None of your goddamn business," he said.

But that was all Lena needed to hear. Jane. Jane Cramm. It really had been her all along.

She passed another road sign. It read Blanco Trading Post—6 miles. Where was that? She looked at the stars, a million bright points of light, but she didn't recognize any of the constellations. Then again, she barely knew them anyway, much less where they were located in the night sky.

Mike. By now he had to know she'd been kidnapped along with Kimmy. Surely he'd found the GTO across from Hayden's house. And maybe, just maybe, he'd found Jane and had learned where Danny was taking them. Maybe Mike was following right now, hot on their trail. He'd spot the station wagon, and somehow she could stop the car and keep Hayden from using the gun. Even if Mike wasn't on the road searching for them, there'd surely be a statewide APB out on this car by now. When it finally got light out, they'd be spotted.

She thought about Jane Cramm, wondering if the woman really did know where Danny was taking them.

Lena cleared her throat. "Why isn't Jane here?" she asked for the third time.

"Shut up," he muttered, stirring against the seat.

"Does she know where we're going? Is she going to meet us or—?"

"One more word," Hayden growled, "and I'll make you sorry. Just drive."

It was no good. He wasn't going to tell her a thing.

She drove through the eye blink of a town called Blanco Trading Post, and that was when she saw the sign, Farmington—28 miles.

Farmington, she thought, the northwestern part of the state. But what lay ahead? Colorado? Arizona? It didn't matter anyway, not if he hadn't told anyone where they were heading. For all she knew, he was taking them deep into the high desert, far, far from civilization. And once he felt safe, once he was certain no one was going to find them, he might turn that gun on them and that would be it. He could dump them here, right out in the open, and no one would find their bodies for years. If ever.

MIKE FIGURED THAT THIS was what it felt like to go stark raving mad. Despite all his training, despite his being used to commotion and confusion during a hostage crisis, he was losing it.

He tried to take a calming breath as he stared at Hayden's house, which was garishly lit up by three spotlights. Around him were no less than fifteen cop cars, blocking the narrow street, parked helter-skelter. Cops and FBI agents stood in groups, some arguing, some just quietly watching the house, others trying to keep the neighbors inside their homes, but to little avail. The one thing Mike knew from experience was that there were a lot of itchy trigger fingers out here.

Then there was the negotiator who'd flown up from Albuquerque in a helicopter. This was his turf, not Mike's, and he'd taken over the bullhorn. They'd tried dozens of times now to phone into the house—they could even hear Hayden's telephone ringing. But no one had answered, which was highly unusual.

"Think they're in there?" John asked at Mike's side.

Mike shook his head. "Frankly, I don't know. Hayden's car is gone. For all we know they could be hundreds of miles from here." He stared at the run-down house with its dirty windows and dusty patch of lawn, and he couldn't help the frustration that surged through his gut. *Was* anyone in there?

The negotiator, Ted Laraby, picked up the bullhorn and tried again. "Danny," he began, his voice friendly, well modulated. "This isn't getting any of us anywhere. You know you can't escape. If you give up peacefully, things will go better for you. You don't want to harm anyone, Danny. I'm going to call on your phone again. Please pick it up this time. We need to talk, and not over this bullhorn, okay?"

Mike knew that Laraby was doing the best he could, trying to keep things calm, peaceful. It was his job. The last thing a hostage negotiator wanted was for things to get out of hand, for violence to erupt. Hell, Mike taught negotiation tactics; he knew the routine as well as anyone. On the other hand, the rest of the cops dealt in violence—they were keyed up, on the edge, getting real tired of the waiting.

To make things worse, the media had begun to arrive en masse. Reporters and their camera crews, satellite vans, pushing in around the cordoned-off perimeter, vying for camera position, making everyone crazy.

John nodded toward a cameraman who'd sneaked in too close and was being escorted out of the area. "What a mess," John said in disgust.

Mike frowned. "I don't know how long things will stay peaceful. Hayden should have responded to the phone calls by now. It's just putting everyone more on edge." He didn't want to step on toes, but Mike finally went over to Laraby and introduced himself, giving the man a rundown of his involvement with the hostages.

"This must be rough on you, Quinn," Ted Laraby said.

Mike nodded. "If Hayden would only respond to the phone calls, we'd get a better read on the situation inside. As it is…"

"I'd sure like this to stay peaceful," Laraby said, "and I know you would, too."

"Damn right," Mike said, and then he looked over at Captain Hunt, who was calling the shots. "I'd like to go in under a white flag," Mike said, "approach the house unarmed. The trouble is, Hunt would never let me."

"No, he wouldn't," Laraby said. "You're the last person he'd let near that house."

Mike locked his jaw. "Well, something's got to give here, and soon. If it doesn't—" he nodded toward the SWAT team "—Hunt will give them the go-ahead to assault the house."

All Laraby could do was agree.

Mike watched eight-thirty come and go. The tension outside the house was palpable. He kept his eye on the eight SWAT team guys in basic black: trousers, shirts, bulletproof vests, knit caps and face paint. Each one held an assault rifle trained on the house. If shooting started, Mike knew they'd tear the walls apart with those high-powered guns and no one inside would be left alive.

Nine o'clock arrived. "There should have been some movement from the house by now," John said.

Mike nodded gravely.

"What do you think?"

"You've asked that sixteen times," Mike snapped, then caught himself. "Hey, sorry. It's really getting to me."

"Understandable," John was saying, when they both noticed Agents Sabin and Miller approaching.

"Quinn," Alan Sabin said. "Pretty unusual situation here."

"Oh? And how's that?" Mike asked.

"Hayden should have responded to the telephone by now. We're starting to believe the house is empty."

"And?" Mike said, knowing what was coming.

"We'll give it a while longer, but then I've got to advise Captain Hunt to go in. Maybe his team can get close enough to—"

Mike swore. "You've got no way of knowing if my wife and child are in there!"

"Ex-wife," Sabin said.

Mike ignored the pointed remark. "Just because the

car isn't here doesn't mean Hayden's not in there. He might be inside and armed to the teeth. If he feels the slightest bit threatened..."

"No one said anything about threatening him."

"*Right*," Mike said sarcastically.

"Look—" Sabin began.

Mike cut him off sharply. "We wait. We wait for days if we have to. Whatever it takes."

Alan Sabin frowned. "Hayden may lose it anyway. There're two schools of thought here, Quinn, and you know it. By waiting we might drive him over the edge, and—"

"Then send in someone under a white flag," Mike said, starting to lose it. "Send just one unarmed man...."

"I can't risk that," Sabin said, "and you know it. Now, I think SWAT can handle—"

"No," Mike said hotly, "you send even one single armed man anywhere near that house and you could start a Waco-style nightmare. If that happens..." But John put a hand on his arm and Mike tried to collect himself. He shut up, turning away from the FBI men, but he knew what he had to do. At 9:31 he made his move. He took two deep breaths and stepped out and away from the patrol car that had been protecting him.

At first no one noticed him because of all the commotion. But when he approached no-man's-land in the middle of the street, voices began to reach him.

"Hey!" "Hold up there!" "What in hell do you think you're doing?" "Quinn, I'm ordering you to stop!"

Mike ignored the protests, and step by slow step he kept going, empty hands held up to show that he was unarmed, entering the bright circles of the light from the spotlights trained on the house. When it was plain he wasn't going to retreat, a hush fell over the crowd, as if all air had suddenly been vacuumed from the scene. He felt as if he couldn't breathe.

Another step. Another.

Mike kept his eyes on the windows. Ever since they'd arrived the curtains had been drawn, and he watched for the slightest movement, feeling the gun he wore concealed under his armpit, cold steel against his flesh.

He stepped onto the curb. Along the sidewalk to the sandy patch of lawn in front of the house.

Had that curtain just moved?

He felt his pulse burst, and goose bumps rippled up his limbs.

Keep going. Slow, slow. He reached the walkway to the tilting front porch. The door was ten, fifteen feet in front of him.

Sweat broke from every pore in his body, and the spotlights felt like spears of heat on his back. He kept moving slowly and breathing. *Keep your cool, Quinn.*

Mike neared the front door. He had no idea what to expect. He knew that door could fly open at any instant and bullets could slam into his body.

He raised his hand to knock, sweat pouring off his brow, blinding him, and he rapped once on the door, twice. Another scenario tore through his brain. They might all be inside and, hours ago, before the cops had even arrived, Danny had panicked and put a bullet in each of them, then stuck the gun in his mouth.

Mike knocked a third time.

ON THE FAR SIDE OF Farmington Danny spotted a dirt road and ordered Lena to pull onto it.

"Is this where we're going?" she asked. Oh, God, she thought, it was exactly what she'd feared most—a dirt

road in the middle of nowhere. "Why are we turning?"
she asked again, her voice quivering.

"Just keep going," he said, "a mile, two. I'll tell you
when to stop."

OhGodohGodohGod. Desperately, Lena stole a sidelong glance at the gun. Could she get to it, fight him for
it? He was a small guy, but wiry. And even if she did
manage to struggle with him, the damn thing might go
off, and Kimmy was right there....

What to do? She wasn't going to let him kill them so
easily; that much she knew. First she'd refuse to get out,
then, if he tried to drag her out, she'd fight tooth and nail.
She'd never go meekly. And maybe she could buy
Kimmy a little time to run and hide. It was dark, no
moon. Surely Kimmy could evade him somehow. She
had to.

"Here," Danny said. "Pull off here behind that boulder." Lena's heart lurched.

"Hey, do what I tell you!" he yelled, and he smashed
the butt of the gun against her shoulder.

Hot searing pain shot down her arm. "It won't work,
you bastard," she said.

"What the hell're you talking about?"

"The cops know you've got us. They'll give you the
chair, Danny, the electric chair. You'll fry. Your best bet
is to let us go. Just leave us right here and drive off.
Maybe you can make it to Mexico or Canada or—"

"Shut the hell up!" he yelled. "I need some rest. I
got gout in my foot and I gotta put it up."

Lena stopped the car. "What?"

"You're gettin' in the back with the kid. I'm gonna
lock the doors, and believe me, I'll hear the locks pop if
you try to open them. I gotta get this foot up. You make

any move toward me and I'll blow your head off. The kid's too.''

"You're not...?'' But she decided not to finish. Why give him any ideas?

Eventually Lena did lie down on the back seat, Kimmy alongside her. She knew Danny had given her child something to knock her out, but she decided not to say anything, not now. But if he tried to give her child anything else, he'd have one helluva battle on his hands, gun or no gun.

She remembered the cell phone then—it was in her purse. She'd put it there after talking to Gloria this afternoon....

It wasn't going to work, though. Even if the battery was still strong enough, how could she make a call without Hayden hearing her? Damn it. But she'd think of something. Eventually there'd be an opening and she'd somehow slip through.

Oh, Mike, she thought, *where are you?*

Against her side Kimmy stirred, her warmth seeping into Lena, the most beautiful warmth.... For a long time she pressed her nose to Kimmy's hair, drinking in her scent, and tears filled her eyes. *We're alive,* she kept thinking, and that was all that mattered right now. Alive and together again.

CHAPTER SIXTEEN

MIKE STARED WEARILY at the woman and realized he almost felt sorry for her. *Almost.* But Jane Cramm had made her own choices. And they'd all been bad.

He glanced at the wall clock in the interrogation room—it read 3:22 a.m.—and he looked over at John Hidalgo, then at Captain Hunt. The captain shrugged.

Mike had found Jane alone in the house in an alcoholic stupor, and since then they'd pumped five cups of coffee into her. Still, after almost six hours, she was scarcely cognizant of her surroundings and her situation. There'd been no activity at Hayden's house despite the host of cops that remained stationed there—just in case Danny Hayden returned. Which wasn't going to happen, Mike was sure.

"Jane," Mike said for the umpteenth time, "we really need your help here. Kimmy needs your help."

She sat slumped in the hard metal chair across the table from the men, arms folded tightly over her thin chest, straight, dirty hair hanging limply in her dull brown eyes.

"Jane?"

"I hear you," she said in a barely audible whisper. "I don't know anything."

Mike sighed. He looked down at her hands; they were white and trembling. She had the shakes.

"She ought to be in the hospital," Hunt said under his breath. "She ought to be in detox."

"Give me a few more minutes," Mike said, not wanting to beg. But, damn it, he would if that's what it took.

They'd been after Jane for hours now, trying to find out where Danny had gone. But thus far the poor woman either didn't know or she was too scared of Danny Hayden to tell.

"Now, Jane," Mike said to her, "everyone realizes Kimmy is your natural daughter. You're not the first mother who wanted her child back. Courts take these things into account."

Jane glanced up, then looked back down at her lap.

"The thing is," Mike said, pressing on, "if Kimmy or Lena is harmed in any way, well, I'm afraid it will be a lot rougher on you. We know that Danny's with them. All we need is a clue, one word as to where he's gone. Jane? Are you listening?"

"Yes." A whimper.

"Danny doesn't have to know. We can always let him believe it was the cops who spotted him. No one will tell."

Jane bit her lower lip.

"Look," Mike said, leaning across the table, "you've got my word. No one will tell Danny. Now, please, Jane, help us. Help your child."

Mike glanced at the clock again. Damn. In a matter of minutes some court-appointed attorney was going to show up—even on Saturday and at this early hour—and advise Jane to keep her mouth shut. It was her right. Mike knew the law and he appreciated it. But in this case...

"Jane? You have my word. Come on, where did Danny go?"

"Don't know."

"Yes, you do. Think of Kimmy all alone and afraid. She's probably missing you right now."

She raised her eyes. "She's got that woman. Lena."

"But she's used to *you* now, isn't she? You've been feeding her and combing her hair and putting her to bed. Jane, she's *your* flesh and blood. I know you couldn't live with yourself if anything happened to your child."

Tears began to ooze from the corners of her eyes.

Gotcha, Mike thought. *Come on, woman, come on.*

"Look," Hunt said, rubbing his face, "I really think—"

But Mike held up a hand. "Come on, Jane, for God's sake help your daughter."

Jane said something. They all sat up and leaned toward her.

"What was that?" Mike asked, his tone calm despite the urgent thumping of his heart. "Jane?"

"Ver...Vernal," she whispered.

Mike pivoted to John and Bill.

John reached out and touched Jane gently on the shoulder. "Was that Vernal?"

She nodded, barely.

"Vernal, Utah?" John asked.

Again, a nod.

"Does Danny know someone there?"

Another nod.

"A friend? A relative?"

"His...brother."

"Is his brother also named Hayden?"

"Uh-huh," Jane said. Then she looked up and met Mike's eyes. "I feel real sick," she said.

"I know," Mike said. "I know you do. And you can go to the hospital now."

Tears rolled down her cheeks and spotted her stained T-shirt. "Thank you," she whispered.

IT WAS BARELY DAWN when Lena pulled into the only open gas station in the Navajo reservation town of Shiprock. She'd seen Danny slip the gun into the back waistband of his jeans, and he'd made it very plain that if she said one single word to the cashier, he'd kill them all on the spot.

They visited the rest room, and Lena used her own money to buy stale sandwiches and a bottle of juice. There was never an opportunity to signal the young Navajo cashier or make solid eye contact. She wondered if the Indian boy would even remember them if asked.

"It's going to be a nice day, huh?" Lena said. "What do you think?"

"Yeah, sure," the youth replied, not looking up.

Lena gathered the juice and sandwiches, aware of Danny standing close now, Kimmy right next to him.

She thought frantically. "Could I have a sack for this stuff, please?"

"Let's go," Danny said behind her.

"I don't want to get the car all messed up," she said, praying the Navajo boy would notice the vintage wreck they were driving. He handed her a plastic bag, never directly looking at her.

Damn, damn, damn, Lena thought as she went back to the car.

Danny was a mess in the morning, in a foul mood, nasty and uncommunicative. Kimmy ate her sandwich in the back seat and remained quiet for the most part, obviously intimidated by Danny's very presence. *I could kill him,* Lena thought, *I really could.*

They left Shiprock, passing the giant slab of rock for which the small town was named, and it did jut up from the high-desert floor like a schooner under sail across the vast, empty spaces of the Four Corners region.

As dawn inched across the land, Lena saw other immense rock formations in the distance, thrusting pinnacles that interrupted the land's arid flatness. They passed canyons whose walls were maroon and ivory in the early light, bands of earth colors against the clearest sky she'd ever seen.

They were in Arizona now, still driving through the huge Navajo reservation. Occasionally she passed a single car or truck, and every once in a while there was a hogan, a round squat Navajo house, off the road, smoke curling up in a question mark from the chimney.

Lifeless, Lena thought. It was like driving on the surface of an uninhabited alien planet. The sun finally rose behind them over a distant chain of mesas, and shadows retreated, crawling across the desert. Lena glanced at the gas gauge. Over half a tank left.

She tried something anyway. "Will we be stopping soon?"

"Shut up," Danny mumbled, his bony knees propped on the dashboard, the gun in his lap.

"I only asked because we'll need gas again unless we're almost where we're going."

"We don't need no gas."

"Then we will be stopping soon? In Arizona?"

"Jeezus," he said. "You never shut up."

"Will we be?"

He uttered a string of oaths that made Kimmy cower, then said, "Utah. We're going to Utah. Now, just drive."

"What's in Utah?"

He sat straight up, leaned over and pushed his face at hers. "One more word and I'm going to climb in the back and give that kid of yours a real licking. You hear?"

Lena subsided, but she thought, *I could kill him with my bare hands.*

For the next hour they drove in silence, Danny lethargically staring out at the empty land, Kimmy resting with her eyes closed in the back, whatever Danny had given her obviously still in her system. Lena drove, biting her lip, thinking about Mike, wishing to God there were a way she could know if he was in pursuit.

Of course he is, her mind would tell her, and then her thoughts would flip-flop. The only way he could know was if Jane Cramm had told him, and only then if *she* knew.

Utah, Jane thought over and over. What lay ahead for them in Utah?

The spurts of anger began at midmorning. It was as if Danny had finally come alive and was shifting into his usual gear.

"Stupid bitch women," he muttered, "ruined everything. Everything!"

Lena gave him a quick, sidelong look. "What's everything?"

"Shut up!"

"Are those the only two words you know?" she taunted boldly.

He waved the gun and grinned wickedly, his yellow, stained teeth showing. "I'll shoot you—you better believe it."

"While I'm doing sixty-five miles per hour?" she fired back, fed up, sickened by the very sight of him.

"Think you're real smart, don't you," he rasped. "Well, you're so smart you let your brat here get snatched."

"What do you mean?"

"Your mother, *stupid.*"

"Gloria?"

"Yeah, that Gloria Torres. Said right in the paper years

ago, right under the picture of you and that cop at the hospital, said her name and where she lived.''

"So you staked out my mother?''

He laughed. "Only took a day. No big deal.''

"Well," Lena said, "that was nice of you, Danny, to try to get Jane's child back for her.''

He took the bait. "You are one dumb bitch," he said.

"Look," Lena broke in, "call me anything you want, but I'm getting real sick of that word.''

"Bitch, bitch, bitch," he said gleefully.

Oh, he was easy, she was learning. Dumb as a post. "So you didn't steal Kimmy for Jane's sake?" she said. "I thought…''

"That's the trouble with women," he sneered. "They oughta give up thinking. No, stupid, the kid was making a movie. A movie, you know? But you had to come along and ruin it. Two big ones. I'm out two big ones.''

A…movie? And then she knew. "You dirty rotten…''

He laughed, and that was when Lena slammed on the brakes and the car skidded halfway across the road and came to rest on a sandy shoulder.

Danny was gripping the dashboard. "What the…?" he cried.

Lena held on to the steering wheel, ignoring Kimmy's, "Mommy?" coming from the back seat. "How far did it go, you bastard?" she demanded, glaring at him. "How far?''

Danny righted himself, looked confused, and then he grinned. "Well, ain't you a real hothead.''

"Tell me!''

"Not far enough" was the answer she got, and he refused to say more.

THERE WAS NO WAY Mike could be positive he was on the right road. He was going solely on the advice of John

Hidalgo, who had a cousin who lived in Salt Lake City.

"Trust me," John had told him back at police head-quarters in Santa Fe, "this is the shortest route. Right through the reservation, buddy. Any other route will take our boy Hayden hundreds of miles out of his way." He'd folded up the map he'd taken from his police cruiser and handed it to Mike.

"Make sure they get that APB out in all four states," Mike had said, opening the door to the GTO. "New Mexico, Arizona, Colorado and Utah."

"I know the drill," John had said patiently.

"And call Vernal. Alert the police. Maybe ask them to put a stakeout on Hayden's brother's house. Okay?"

John had smiled. "I really do know the drill, Mike."

"Right," Mike had said. "Sorry." And then he and John had clasped hands.

"You drive carefully," John had said when Mike was in the car, starting the big engine.

"Like hell I will," Mike had replied, and they'd said goodbye, John promising to look him up when he was in Disneyland that winter with his kids.

"I'll see Lena, too," John had assured him, "and Kimberly."

"God, I hope so," Mike had said, and he left rubber in the street.

Now the immense territory of Four Corners stretched ahead of him, endless country, an ancient geologic battlefield littered with the results of unimaginable violence, eroded by wind-driven sand and severe temperature fluctuations.

Indian country. And somewhere in this immensity were Lena and Kimmy. Were they afraid, intimidated by

Hayden as Jane was? Or was Lena holding on, that temper of hers keeping her going, keeping her sharp?

He drove through the unearthly land of the Apache and Zuni, the Paiute and Hopi, the Ute and Navajo, and he sped by the monuments to their past. He registered only that Lena and Kimmy should be with him, protected and safe, enjoying the scenery, but they weren't. Danny Hayden had them.

He looked at the speedometer. Pushing ninety miles per hour. He knew he was on the Navajo reservation now. If he was stopped by the tribal police, would they listen to him, respect his badge, or would they lock him up and throw away the key? This wasn't like crossing a state line, after all; the Navajo Reservation was a nation unto itself. White-man's law meant little here.

It was outside the Indian town of Shiprock that Mike pulled over to fill up. He pumped the gas—damn car of Lena's took the highest octane—then hurried inside the trading post to grab a sandwich and soda to go. It struck him at the counter that maybe, since gas stops were almost nonexistent, Hayden had stopped here, too.

He looked at the young Navajo clerk, a handsome teen whose face looked as if it were carved out of the rock of the nearby mesa.

"I wonder," Mike began. "You wouldn't have been on duty last night or real early this morning?"

The kid nodded.

"You were?"

"Yep."

"Would you remember a man, a scruffy-looking man in his thirties, who might have been here with a woman and a child... Hey," Mike said, "I've got a picture of the child. It's in the car...."

"Guy in an old station wagon," the boy said.

Mike's heart clutched. "That's right. Wood paneled."

"Sure," the teen said.

"You're positive?"

"My grandpop drives one. A real dog."

"What?" Mike said.

"Car's a real dog."

"Oh," Mike said. "Thanks. Thanks a million."

The boy only shrugged.

Relief surged through Mike as he rushed out to the car—he was so close, so damn close to overtaking them... And then it struck him out of the blue. *Gloria.* No one had told her about Lena. It had been hours and hours, and no one had even bothered to call her.

He stopped in his tracks, pivoted and eyed the pay phone on the wall outside the trading post. Every ounce of his being told him to get back on the road, but hell, this had to be done.

He went to the pay phone, found a quarter in his pocket and shoved it impatiently into the slot, then used his credit card to dial Lena's number. *Come on, come on, come on.*

"Hello?" said Gloria, her voice a nervous croak.

It occurred to Mike that he could lie to her, but then he decided to tell the whole truth. It took him too much time, though, and Gloria had too many questions.

Finally, he said, "Gloria, I know you're a wreck. But I've got to go. Every second I spend on the phone..."

"Go," she said, "go. But for the love of God, Mike, you get my babies back for me."

"I will," he said, "I promise. Safe and sound."

Mike hurried back to the car, frantic to be on the road, knowing every second counted. He started the engine, shoved the gearshift into first, and then it hit him. *Jennifer.* Why hadn't he taken another minute to call Jenn?

He glanced at the pay phone. It would only take a short time to do the right thing and call her. She'd be home. And she'd be up by now, even on a Saturday. *Do it. Call her,* his brain said, but something stopped him cold. No matter the danger Lena and Kimmy were in, Jennifer would still ask him at least one pointed question: had he slept with Lena? He knew in his gut she'd ask. He couldn't lie to her, either.

He looked over at the phone again, and guilt stabbed him. He frowned, exhaled, then, a moment later, he let out the clutch and sped out onto the reservation road, putting the whole situation with Jennifer right out of his mind.

The morning sun painted the land in pastels as Mike crossed the border into Arizona. He was due south of the Four Corners area, where Utah, Colorado, Arizona and New Mexico met in a perfect square, and there was only this single road that ran west into Arizona for a hundred miles before it turned north into Utah. Hayden had to be on it. But how far ahead? He'd snatched Lena sometime after 3 p.m. yesterday. But when had he left Santa Fe? And had he pulled over during the night to sleep? Maybe. Maybe. That old beat-up station wagon wouldn't be doing ninety, either. Maybe they were just ahead, somewhere around the sweep of that mesa.

It occurred to Mike that Jane might have been lying about Vernal. She *might* have been. But he doubted it. She'd been too scared, too out of it to fake her answers. Or had she?

Mike rubbed his face and realized he was running on adrenaline alone. He hadn't slept in what? Over twenty-four hours? He'd gone on little sleep before, especially during a hostage-negotiation crisis. But this was different. This was Lena and Kimmy. He wondered then if he was up to the inevitable confrontation. Was his judgment as sound as it could be? Should he have asked John to come along?

"Ah, hell," Mike said, and he pressed the accelerator to the floor. The GTO sprang forward, and the needle read one hundred mph as he sped off, moving deeper and deeper into the vastness of the reservation.

CHAPTER SEVENTEEN

"TURN HERE," Danny said, pointing at a road sign, but when they got to 191, which cut up into Utah, there was a sign that read Bridge Out.

Lena felt like laughing hysterically. Bridge Out. No detour sign, nothing. And it wasn't as if there were alternate routes out here. They were lucky if they passed a dirt road every fifty miles.

"What now?" she said, slowing.

Danny swore a blue streak, calling the Navajos every name in the book.

"Where to?" Lena said, disgusted with his filthy mouth.

"Just keep going, I guess. There's a road up in Kayenta. Maybe fifty miles."

"Okay," Lena said. "I just hope for your sake there's a gas station there."

"Shut up, will you?" Danny said, and he rubbed at his swollen foot.

As the morning proceeded, exhaustion took its toll on everyone. Kimmy was whiny, antsy, grating on Danny's nerves, and Lena wasn't sure how long she could keep driving these endless miles of eroded red washes and prairies dotted with sagebrush and pinyon trees. To make it worse, there were no fences on the reservation, and what few cattle and sheep there were had the freedom of the roads. The road signs read Open Range. Twice already this morning she'd had to hit the brakes hard to avoid a steer in the road. Her nerves had about had it. Cattle, sheep, coyotes and deer. An occasional car or semi barreling past. That was it.

By midmorning it was getting hot out, too, a dry desert heat that shimmered across the barren land and up the sides of the distant mesas. Danny rolled his window down, and Kimmy whined some more from the back seat.

"It's blowing me," she whimpered. "Mommy, the air's blowing me."

"Shut up!" Danny yelled, then he lifted his gun, stuck it partway out the window and took a few potshots at a road sign indicating a deer crossing.

"That's really adult," Lena said under her breath.

Danny pivoted toward her and pointed the gun. "Bam, bam," he snickered. "You're dead."

God, how she hated this man. She gave him a withering glance. "Why Utah? What's there?"

"A big surprise," he said, still playing with his gun.

"What surprise?"

Danny shrugged. "You'll find out."

"Tell me now. I'm curious."

"Ha!" he said. "But if you must know, my brother's there. He's got real good connections, see."

"Connections?"

"In South America."

"Just what does South America have to do with any of this?"

"He knows some folks who like white women." Then his face lit up. "Of course, you're probably too old. But the kid…"

"Oh, that's a *great* idea," she said sarcastically. "And just how do you plan on getting us out of the country?"

He laughed. "You think it doesn't happen every day? Huh? There're ways."

"Mommy," Kimmy said from the back, "I have to go to the bathroom."

"Just hold it, brat," Danny said, and silence fell over them for a while.

The town sprawled on the flat, reddish desert with red rocks showing through everywhere in big round domes. A hot wind blew dust across the road, and there was a tall water tower with the name Kayenta on it.

Danny told Lena to stop for gas, and no sooner had she pulled up to the pumps at a trading post than a cop car pulled in, too. It was a big white Blazer, and on its side it said Navajo Tribal Police.

Her heart flew into her throat. This was the break she'd been waiting for.

But Danny thought quickly.

Before Lena was even out of the car, he said, "Kid stays here with me. I'm gonna keep the gun trained right on her, see, and if I even *think* you're trying to pull something, I'll kill her. I got nothing to lose. Now, get the gas and pay with that card of yours and don't even look at that cop. Hurry it up."

Lena got out and lifted the gas nozzle off its cradle, her hands shaking so badly she could barely press the correct buttons on the pump to start it up. *Oh, God*, she thought, starting again, trying desperately to concentrate: cash or credit, pay inside or outside. Why couldn't they make these machines easier? And all the while the tribal cop on the other side of the pump was eyeing her, which made her mouth dry and her heart leap sickeningly.

Finally the policeman stepped over the concrete island. "Need some help?" the big man asked. "These things can be pretty confusing."

"Ah...sure," Lena said, her lower lip trembling. "I, ah, want to pay with a credit card, outside."

The policeman helped her, even going so far as to start the gas. He seemed friendly enough, and she thought desperately of some way to signal him, but he did glance twice into the car, making eye contact with Danny.

Oh, God, oh, God, Lena thought.

Then Kimmy, her window in the back now open, piped up with, "I have to go to the bathroom."

"Okay, let's go," Danny said, obviously thinking fast. "I'll walk you over while Mommy finishes pumping the gas. Come on now." Then he was out, opening the back door, taking Kimmy's hand and leading her away. Lena didn't see the gun, but she knew he'd keep it real close. Danny watched her, too. Even while Kimmy was inside the ladies' room, he never once took his eyes off Lena. The policeman finished pumping his own gas, tipped his black Stetson at Lena and disappeared inside to pay. He was still inside when Danny and Kimmy got back. They drove off, Lena at the wheel, without seeing him again.

"Take Route 163," Danny said, nervous himself, "right there." He pointed.

Lena bit her lower lip and wanted to cry. That might have been her last chance.

"I'm thirsty," Kimmy said from the back, and the litany between Danny and her child began anew.

North of Kayenta the distant obelisks and flat-topped mesas and chimneys and lines of cliffs and spires of Monument Valley stood against the horizon like a prehistoric cityscape. Closer, right by the road, the huge sail-shaped rock called El Capitan jutted up. Across from it stood Owl Rock, a perfect stone replica of folded wings and eyes and beak. Lena steered the curves of the two-lane road and realized she'd seen this scenery before—

seen it dozens of times in Westerns. She drove and stared and even in her awful fear and weariness, she saw the beauty of it.

For miles the city of stone went on, and even Danny started looking out his window. They crossed the state line into Utah, the monuments becoming fewer in number, and Lena grew desperate to keep her daughter's mind off her predicament.

"Look, Kimmy," she said, "isn't that a pretty mountain?"

Danny muttered something.

"I'm still thirsty," Kimmy complained, ignoring the spectacular sight. "Mommy..."

Lena turned a little, ready to reassure Kimmy that they'd get something to drink soon, and her eyes went off the road for a split second. The deer bounded out of nowhere, the movement catching Lena's eye, and she hit the brakes in a reflex action. The car swerved, lurched, skidded sideways. It tossed them around as it bounced across the gravel, Lena fighting the wheel, and then stopped abruptly, nose down in a gully, throwing everyone forward, dust rising around the car in the sudden silence.

It had all happened in a heartbeat, and yet to Lena the accident had run before her eyes in slow motion. She lifted her head from the top of the steering wheel and drew in a long, quavering breath, mentally searching her body for injuries.

"Mommy?" Kimmy said.

Lena pivoted.

"Mommy, what happened?"

"Are you all right?" Lena asked in an urgent, rasping voice. "My God, Kimmy, are you okay?"

"Uh-huh," she whimpered, shaken and afraid.

Trying to clear the cobwebs from her own brain, Lena looked over at Danny. He wasn't moving, and there was blood showing on the dashboard where his head rested.

The gun, she thought abruptly. *Where's the gun?* And then she saw it near his feet. Carefully, carefully, she reached down and took hold of it, her eyes never leaving Hayden.

The gun in her hands, Lena became slowly cognizant of two things: there was steam coming up from the radiator and they were nose down in a deep wash. *Have to get out of here,* she thought.

"Kimmy, Mommy's going to climb out and then help you. Okay?"

"Uh-huh," Kimmy said.

Lena glanced again at Danny. She knew she should probably disable him right now—if he was even alive—shoot him in the kneecap, somewhere, anywhere. But she couldn't. She simply couldn't.

Climbing out of the car was a task, and her feet kept slipping on the loose sand and gravel on the steep sides of the gully, but eventually she and Kimmy were scrambling up the bank, gripping rocks and roots, bloodying their hands until they were standing on the flat desert floor.

Kimmy got her breath and clutched Lena's hand. "Is Danny dead?" she asked innocently.

"I don't think so," Lena breathed. "I think he's just unconscious."

"We can get away now," Kimmy said.

Lena suddenly remembered the cell phone. She reached into her purse, felt the gun and then found the phone. *Oh, please work,* she prayed. But it didn't. It was dead as a doornail.

"Can we go, Mommy?"

"Ah, yes, sweetie, we can," she said, and she thought about Danny down there in the wrecked car. They could go; they could actually escape *if* he didn't wake up, she was thinking, and that's when she saw the doe lying on the shoulder of the road at the end of the black skid marks.

Oh, no. "Kimmy, honey," she said, "I want you to stay here for a minute. You sit on this rock and Mommy will be right back. I'm only going over here a couple of feet. Okay?"

Kimmy nodded.

The poor doe was dead, and Lena was thankful at least for that, because the animal never would have survived the injuries and might have limped off to die in some sort of terrible pain.

It was time to go, though. She and Kimmy didn't dare stay around in case Danny woke up. She took her gaze off the deer and searched the road. No one. Not a single car in sight.

She walked back to Kimmy and took her hand. "Sweetie," she said, "we have to leave." Then she stood on the rock where Kimmy had been sitting and searched the land until she spotted something off to the east—a hogan, a Navajo hogan, sitting almost at the foot of a red rock spire. How far could it be? Not even a mile. If they walked on the road, Danny might wake up and be able to spot them. But crossing the desert floor...

"Are you up to a little hike?" Lena asked her child, and Kimmy nodded.

"Okay, let's go, then."

They started off across the dry, uneven land, the squat round top of the hogan just barely visible. But someone would be there, Lena thought, and she could get help. The sun was baking now, rising on hot waves off the sand and rock. A mile or so, Lena thought, that was all they had to go. And they'd be safe. She clutched Kimmy's hand, gave her baby a reassuring smile and put one foot in front of the other. Still every fifty yards or so she couldn't help looking over her shoulder, her heart beating a little too fast.

MIKE HAD his second break when he finally took the time to stop at the Navajo Tribal Police headquarters in Kayenta. He realized he should have stopped back in Shiprock, but he simply hadn't known what kind of reception he'd get. Now, however, he needed help; ever since passing the closed road with the Bridge Out sign, he wasn't at all certain which route to take.

Mike went inside the worn-out trailer that was the Kayenta headquarters and introduced himself, showing his badge and giving the dispatcher at the front desk a thumbnail version of the pursuit he was on.

"I've been following them all night," he began, and that's when a tribal policeman stepped out from the back room.

Mike looked up.

"You say a man in an old station wagon with a woman and child?" he asked, thumbs in his jeans pockets.

"That's right," Mike said, eyeing the big Indian cop. *Wouldn't want to meet him in a dark alley....*

"Well, mister, I think maybe I just helped the lady pump some gas right here in Kayenta."

Mike cocked his head, hardly believing his ears.

"That's right," the cop went on. "Couldn't have been much more than an hour ago."

Mike let out a breath he seemed to have been holding for days. "They were all right?"

"Appeared to be, though the lady was nervous. I didn't

give it much thought.'' Then the Indian grinned. "Too bad you didn't stop when you first drove onto the res. We'd have had your man in custody by now.''

The cop introduced himself as Sergeant Bob Yazzie, and he led Mike into the back room, where he picked up a two-way radio handset. "It's Saturday,'' he said to Mike. "Not many of us on duty. But I'm sure you've noticed by now there aren't many roads, either.'' Then he put the information out over the radio. When he was done, he said he'd take off down Route 160 through the Black Mesa region of the reservation. "You head up 163 toward Utah,'' he said. Then he narrowed his eyes. "That your car out front?''

"Ah, no,'' Mike said, "it's my ex-wife's.''

"Uh-huh. Well, you just keep it under a hundred and don't push your luck. We like to cooperate with outside police, but this isn't L.A. Okay?''

"Sure,'' Mike said.

"And when you get to the Utah border, you find a phone and let us know. Hear?''

"That's a promise,'' Mike said, and he shook the man's hand.

Outside the station, as Mike was getting back into the GTO, Yazzie put a hand on the hood and said, "By the way, you carrying?''

Mike stopped short, feeling the weight of the gun under his armpit. "Yes,'' he said.

"Mmm,'' Bob Yazzie said, then he moved away. "Happy hunting.''

Ten minutes later Mike was heading up 163 toward Utah. He was thinking that Lena and Kimmy were probably exhausted and scared to death. He felt a moment's flash of anger at Lena—what had she been thinking when she went alone to Hayden's?—but then he realized he'd have done the same damn thing. She had courage; he'd sure give her that.

He drove, wondering if he could possibly overtake them in that old station wagon, *if* they were even on this road, when he remembered the other night—Lena sobbing in the shower, the scent and taste and feel of her. He'd wanted her so badly, wanted to hold and protect her and make endless love to her. Had it been just an interlude, the two of them in need of human companionship? He knew he still wanted her; always had. But how did *she* feel?

No time for this, Quinn, he was thinking, driving around a long, sweeping curve in the road, when he saw the skid marks.

Mike downshifted and slowed, and he saw the deer lying by the side of the road. It had been hit recently, too, because the buzzards were just circling overhead.

He downshifted again, into second gear, his eyes following the skid marks that disappeared into the sandy—

"Oh, my God," Mike whispered harshly. There it was, the station wagon, the tail end of it sticking out of a ravine.

He slammed on the brakes and skidded to a stop on the shoulder, then jumped out, his hand under his jacket, reaching for his gun. *No, no, no!* his brain shouted. *Don't let them be dead!*

He scrambled and slid down the side of the wash, his heart pounding against his ribs. The car was empty, completely empty. And then he noticed the blood on the dashboard of the passenger side. Lena's? Kimmy's?

Where in hell were they?

Mike looked up and down the wash but saw nothing. Then he made his way back up to the top of the gully and began to scan the area. He climbed a nearby boulder, shoes sliding on the smooth rock, and stood on top, searching first the road and then the desert, and that was when he thought he could make out a movement near a hogan about a mile away.

Were those people out there?

Binoculars, he thought, but he didn't have any with him. He felt a tightening in his chest—anger, fear, frustration—but he pressed it down and strained his eyes. It had to be people out there. Had to be. But who? All three of them? Or merely some Navajos who lived here?

He made his decision in a flash, jumped off the rock and hurried back to the car, starting it up. He put it into gear and let out the clutch. The GTO lurched forward onto the barren desert, its tires skidding, the chassis bottoming out, and he left a cloud of dust behind him, hanging in the hot dry air, marking his passage.

THE PLACE WAS EMPTY.

Lena looked around and felt her heart sink to her feet. *Empty.*

"Mommy, I'm so thirsty," Kimmy said at her side.

Lena had to force her weary, sun-fried brain to think.

"Okay," she said, standing in the center of the abandoned hogan, "guess we'd better find some water." She smiled down at Kimmy reassuringly.

"There's no water, Mommy," the child said.

Lena felt like laughing—she never could put anything over on Kimmy.

"Maybe out back," she said, "a well or something. Let's look."

There was one, an old wellhead pump sticking up out of the bone-dry ground. Lena licked her parched lips and touched the handle. *Just a cup,* she thought, *just one lousy cup....*

She began to pump. "Go inside and see if you can find a cup, honey, anything to hold water."

"It'll be dirty."

"We'll rinse it out. Now, go on."

She kept pumping, listening for a gurgle, her eyes fixed on the antiquated spigot. *Oh, please,* she thought.

It took ten minutes, but finally, mercifully, a few drops began to trickle onto the sand and then a small stream of dirty water. Kimmy rinsed out the broken plastic cup she'd found, and they filled it and drank greedily. Somewhere in the back of Lena's mind she knew you weren't supposed to gulp water when you were dehydrated, but she simply didn't care. It was probably an old wives' tale, anyway.

"Better?" she asked Kimmy.

Kimmy nodded eagerly, and Lena thought that now all they had to worry about was if the water was okay.

They went back inside, out of the bright sunlight, and Lena put her hands on her hips and frowned. How was she going to get the two of them safely out of here? Then she saw him through the front door: *Hayden.* Terror kicked her senses wide open.

"Oh, my God," she breathed, and she cast around desperately, as if a hole would open up magically and they could somehow hide.

She looked out the door again, gut-wrenching panic seizing her. He was still coming, maybe only a hundred yards away. She could see him limping, and make out the bloodstains on his filthy shirt. But it wasn't stopping him.

Horror swept her, and she had to close her eyes to calm herself. *Think, think.*

She opened her eyes. "Kimmy," she said in as even a voice as she could summon, "Mommy wants you to go out back and find a place to hide. Maybe in that shed.''

''But, Mommy...'' And then Kimmy saw him, too. The little girl froze in fear.

Lena crouched down and took her shoulders firmly, staring her in the eyes. ''Go outside and hide,'' she said sternly. ''I'll be fine. *We'll* be fine. I have the gun, Kimmy.''

''But Mommy...'' Kimmy's lips were trembling.

''Danny is not going to harm us. I won't let him. Now be strong for me and do as I tell you.'' Lena stood up. ''Go,'' she said in the voice she used when she meant business, and finally Kimmy disappeared out the back door.

Lena took a breath and turned toward the entrance. He was there. *Right there.* Shaking, she reached into the waistband of her jeans and pulled the gun out and raised it, holding it in both hands.

Danny stepped inside, shielding his eyes. She saw the wound on his forehead and all the drying blood—so much blood—but he'd made it here, hadn't he?

''You bitch,'' he said, standing there, swaying. ''You left me for dead.'' He took a staggering step toward her.

''Stop right there,'' Lena said, and his eyes seemed to adjust to the dimness. He stared at the gun, which was leveled right on him.

''You ain't gonna shoot me,'' he said, and he licked his cracked lips. ''You'd have done it back at the car.''

''Don't count on it,'' Lena said, and something, something just over Danny's shoulder, caught her eye. It was a cloud of dust, like a rooster tail. She heard it then, the grinding sound of an engine.

A car? *My God,* she thought. *Hurry! Whoever you are, hurry!*

But there was no time. Danny was moving toward her. She could see the car now—hers? she thought in amazement—and she backed up, backed all the way up until the far wall stopped her.

"I'll shoot," she said. "I'll do it."

Danny grinned ferociously. He kept coming, oblivious to the approaching vehicle. "Give me that," he said.

"No."

He kept coming. He was only three feet from her.

Lena lowered the barrel of the gun toward his knees. Surely, surely he'd know she'd do it. "Stop," she commanded, her pulse racing. "Don't make me do this."

"Pull the trigger, bitch," he said, and he reached toward her.

Lena aimed, closed her eyes tightly and pulled the trigger.

The gun went click and her heart stopped. Completely stopped beating.

Her eyes flew open.

"Empty," he sneered, so close his breath was in her face. "Emptied it at the road sign, you stupid..."

And then his hand was at her throat, and she stood there, terror ripping through her.

He shoved her head against the wall and something inside her, some primitive instinct, took over. She started to struggle, fighting his hands, kicking and thrashing, forgetting everything but survival. She never heard the car pull up outside. She never saw the shadow of a man fill the door. She was only aware that if she didn't stop Danny, she and Kimmy were as good as dead.

She sank her teeth into his arm. Danny yelled and swore, and she saw his hand going back, back, forming a fist. *No, no, no!* tore through her brain when, from out of nowhere, something, *someone,* grabbed his fist and

Danny was being spun around like a top. Before she could blink he was sprawled on the earthen floor, a look of utter shock in his pale eyes.

Lena dragged her gaze up from Danny, and it was a long moment before she could fit her mind around what she was seeing. She tried to say something. Tried again. But the sound only echoed silently inside her brain. *Mike?*

SERGEANT BOB YAZZIE turned Hayden's gun over in his hands. "Empty," he mused. "So then it was empty when I saw you at the gas station?"

Lena nodded and shifted Kimmy's weight in her lap, trying not to dislodge the blanket and the teddy bear that Kimmy was clutching. Thank heavens they had still been in Lena's bag in the GTO. "If only I'd known. I kept trying to think of a way to signal you," she told him, and that was when Mike appeared in the doorway of the police trailer.

"You want the good news or the bad news?" he asked Lena.

"How about the good news," she said, although she knew what was coming, really—her car was broken down. Badly. Heck, they'd barely limped back into Kayenta.

"The good news is that the axle can be replaced," he said.

"And the bad news?" she said.

But Bob Yazzie answered. "Let me guess. It's going to take days to replace it."

"Uh-huh," Mike said, and he gave Lena an apologetic shrug.

She looked down at Kimmy and stroked her head, which was resting against her breast. "I don't want to leave the car," she stated emphatically. Then she glanced back up at Mike.

"We'll see."

By midafternoon Tribal Police Headquarters in Kayenta was becoming a hotbed of activity. Lena and Mike heard through another Navajo policeman that Danny Hayden was still being patched up at the local clinic. "Put twenty stitches in his head," one of the cops said in Bob's office. "You should have heard him whine. Just like a baby."

And then, before they could even transport Danny to the jail and lock him up, Special Agent Sabin and his entourage arrived by helicopter to cart him off. It was quite an event in the tiny Indian town, and all the residents stood outside their shops and homes to get a look at the helicopter, which had landed in a cloud of dust in a field behind the police station.

Lena was still sitting in Yazzie's office, Kimmy asleep in her lap, when Special Agent Alan Sabin poked his head in.

"We're all very glad to see you and Kimberly safe and sound," he said as if he were her new best friend.

She looked at him, too weary to be anything but indifferent. All she could say was, "Thanks."

Mike, however, had a lot more to get off his chest, and she could hear his voice outside the office as he spoke to Sabin. "No thanks to you they're safe. If you hadn't spent so much time treating us like suspects, this might have been over a helluva lot sooner."

"Just doing my job," Sabin replied.

There was some talk then about the rights of the Navajo nation versus FBI jurisdiction. Lena heard Bob Yazzie say, "We could keep this Hayden character here if we wanted, but frankly, I'd hate to waste even one jail meal on him.''

The men went on talking, but Lena shut their conversation out—she was through with Hayden and hoped she never heard his name again. She turned away from the open door, carefully shifting Kimmy's weight, and pulled the desk phone over, then dialed her home phone with her credit card number.

She reached Gloria on the first ring. "Oh, my Lord! Oh, my God! Lena, baby! It's really you!''

Lena told her everything, and she even woke Kimmy up to say hello to Grandma. Then, when Kimmy was off the phone, Lena said to her mother, "The axle's shot on the GTO. They say it'll be days before it's fixed.''

"I'll send you plane tickets," Gloria said anxiously.

But Lena wasn't too sure. "Let me think about it, Mom. Maybe Kimmy needs some time away from it all.''

"Mmm," Gloria said. "And will Mike stay, too?''

"No one said I'm staying, Mom. I haven't decided. All this only happened a couple of hours ago. The one thing I do know is that if we return to L.A., the press is going to drive us crazy. I don't think Kimmy can handle it yet. I'll just have to work this all through.''

"Well," Gloria said, "if you stay, then Mike should, too.''

"Oh, really?''

"For Kimmy's sake, honey—that's all I meant.''

"We'll see," Lena said, and she promised to call in the morning after they'd all gotten a real night's sleep.

While Bob Yazzie finished up the paperwork on Danny, Mike rejoined Lena. "You get hold of Gloria all right?" he asked, looking down at Kimmy.

"Oh, yes," she said, "and I had to tell her everything.

Kimmy talked to her, too. Mike, she said she'd send plane tickets...."

But he only shook his head. "Later. We'll figure it out later."

The helicopter lifted off as Mike was on the telephone to his father in L.A. They talked some about everyone who'd want a piece of Daniel Hayden: the LAPD, the state of New Mexico, the FBI. It seemed it was going to take a while to sort it all out. Lena half listened, but the only thing that mattered was for Hayden to be behind bars. And, she hoped, for a very, very long time.

Mike also phoned John Hidalgo, and at one point he signaled Lena to pick up the line. The first thing John said to her was, "That was an A-number-one stupid thing you did, Lena. But congratulations anyway. Now, get some rest."

"I will," she said, "and thanks for everything, really."

"Oh, payback will come. I'm vacationing with the family in L.A. this winter. You could cook us a real meal."

"Done," Lena said. Then she asked, "How's Jane Cramm. Mike told me...?"

"She's under psychological evaluation, not to mention drying out."

"What will happen to her?"

"Depends. A judge will have to decide if she's competent to face charges. It's going to take months."

"I almost feel sorry for her," Lena said. "I think she only wanted Kimmy. It was Danny with the bigger plans."

"You may be right," John said. "Kimberly wasn't his first, either. We're about to tie him into another kidnapping. The child got away. She was older than Kimmy, and she disappeared. We may have a line on her now.''

Lena squeezed her eyes shut. ''Oh, God, I hope you find her. You'll let us know?''

''Of course,'' John said, and Mike took over the conversation from the other phone.

It was a long, long afternoon before Bob gave them a ride to the Holiday Inn—owned and operated by the Navajos—a few blocks down the road.

Lena was exhausted. Still, Kimmy needed dinner and, she guessed, so did she. She and Mike got two adjoining rooms, then met in the dining room.

As they were being seated, Mike mouthed over Kimmy's head, ''Do we tell her who I am?''

''Tomorrow,'' Lena said. ''We'll tell her in the morning.'' She gave him a weak smile.

By nine they were all in their beds. Kimmy had fallen asleep instantly, but Lena lay there, her body thrumming with weariness, overtired. She kept one hand on her sleeping daughter, not quite believing she had her back. She watched the TV for a half hour or so, trying to settle her thoughts, but it was no good. It wasn't Danny or her ordeal that was keeping her up. It was Mike. Just on the other side of that door. The last time she'd put her head on a pillow he'd been there with her. An eternity ago. Or was it only moments? she wondered, and she could almost feel his phantom touch on her skin and the way he'd held her all night; long, long after their desire was quenched, Mike had held her.

CHAPTER EIGHTEEN

IN THE END Mike insisted on staying with them in Kayenta while the car was being repaired.

"But don't you have to get back to work?" Lena asked over breakfast at the Holiday Inn coffee shop.

"Don't worry about it. I've got some time coming."

"What about the basketball team? Surely they're counting on you..."

"Called last night, and I've got it covered."

"But..."

"Lena, I'm staying. You'll need help on the drive home anyway."

She looked at him for a moment and then nodded.

Mike cleared his throat. "There's a more important matter right now." He glanced at Kimmy, who was putting far too much syrup on a waffle, and Lena knew exactly what he was getting at. It was going to be difficult, more than difficult telling her the whole truth. She wondered if Kimmy could handle it all. Were kids that resilient?

She looked at Mike again. "Are you sure?"

"Yes," he said firmly.

Lena had been mentally preparing for this moment for years, ever since they'd adopted Kimmy. She'd read all the books on how to tell adopted children where they came from, and they all agreed on one thing: regardless of the age, never lie to a child.

She let out a breath. "I'll do it. Let me do it, okay? After we eat. Maybe you could... Well, I'll need you there."

"Okay," he said, and he turned his gaze on Kimmy. "Hey, now, aren't you drowning that poor waffle?"

She looked up at him with big brown eyes. "You can't drown a waffle," she said.

"If you're going to pour all that syrup on it, you'd better eat it, sweetie," Lena said.

After breakfast they went outside and sat in chairs in the autumn sun by the side of the empty swimming pool. The day promised to be warm again, but the morning air was cool in the high desert this time of year.

"Come here, Kimberly," Lena said. "I want to talk to you."

Kimmy came, standing between Lena's knees, regarding her mother with great, dark, serious eyes.

"It's about Mike," Lena began, feeling her face grow hot with discomfort.

"Uh-huh," Kimmy said.

Lena looked at Mike, as if for help, then she tried again. "Well, see, sweetie, Mike and I... Mike is..." She faltered, and gave Mike a look that said she needed him.

"Come here, Kimmy," Mike said.

Mike took the girl's hand and tugged her over to stand in front of him. He put his big hands on Kimmy's arms and looked her straight in the eye. "What your mother's trying to say is that I'm your father, Kimmy."

Silence held them all for a moment, then Kimmy asked, "Is he really my daddy, Mommy?"

"Yes," Lena whispered.

Kimmy cocked her head and studied Mike. "You're my daddy?"

"Yes," he said.

Kimmy frowned. "But my daddy is far away. He's sick."

"I'm better now, sweetheart. All better."

Wordlessly Kimmy retreated to the shelter of her mother's embrace. She didn't say anything, but she watched Mike while Lena held her, watched him with a disconcerting child's stare.

Lena kissed the top of Kimmy's head. She hoped this wouldn't backfire—the poor child, so much heaped on her shoulders. "It's okay, Kimmy. I know this is confusing, all this stuff happening."

"I want to go home," Kimmy mumbled against Lena's chest while the two adults locked gazes above her head.

"We will, sweetie. We'll go home as soon as the car's fixed. Grandma's there taking care of everything."

Kimmy peeked at Mike. "Are you my real, real daddy?" she asked.

"Yes," Mike replied, "and I love you very much. Even when I was…sick, I always loved you."

She turned her face into Lena's chest again, and Lena felt her warm little body and worried that Kimmy couldn't take this, that it would damage her. What kind of scar would this leave on the innocent child's psyche so soon after the kidnapping?

Kimmy looked at Mike again. Shyly, still holding on to Lena's shirt with both hands, she asked, "Am I supposed to call you 'Daddy'?"

Mike smiled at her. "You can call me anything you want."

"How come you're my daddy?" she asked.

"Well," Mike said, "see, your mom and I were married."

"You were?"

"We used to be married, and then I got... Well, I was sick, and we got divorced, and that's why you don't remember me. You were a tiny baby when I...went away."

Kimmy thought about that for a time, then she asked Lena, "Why did that lady say she was my real mommy?"

Lena told herself to stay cool. She'd known the time would come. "Oh, Kimmy, it's kind of complicated, but you're a big enough girl to understand." She set her child on her lap and held her very close. "See, it's like this, Kimmy. You know babies grow inside mommies, right? Like when Ally's mother had her baby brother, remember?"

Kimmy nodded.

"So, this lady, Jane, was your birth mother. That means she gave birth to you, sweetie, you understand? But she couldn't keep you—she had lots of problems— so your daddy and I adopted you. You were our own little girl then."

"You 'dopted me," Kimmy repeated.

"Yes, we did. See, that makes you very, very special, because we picked you, we chose you, out of all the babies in the whole wide world."

"Did that lady want me back?"

"I think so," Lena said softly. "She loved you, too. She just... Well, she can't take care of you."

Kimmy didn't seem upset; she appeared to accept the explanation the way children did when they were confronted with clear truths. *Never lie to a child,* Lena told herself again.

Kimmy nodded solemnly. "That lady wasn't pretty like you, Mommy," was all she said.

They took a walk, the three of them, across the street to the shopping center, down the street, then back. Wherever you went in Kayenta you could see the line of striated bluffs on one side and the big red fist of smooth rock that stuck up above town on the other. Eddies of red dust blew across the street, running before the wind.

Kayenta was tiny, and there wasn't much to do, but Lena was still so worn-out by her ordeal that the peace seemed blissful. Just to walk under the vast blue sky without fear was a blessing. She hadn't realized how constant fear had depleted her energy.

Kimmy walked between them, holding her mother's hand. The only sign of her experience was a tendency to stay close to Lena, to hold on to her and to keep her teddy bear and blanket close, although she'd thought herself too old for them at home. She'd cried in her sleep the night before, and she seemed more subdued than usual. But it could have been much, much worse, Lena knew.

"I hope the press doesn't get word of what's going on," Mike said. "I asked everyone to keep quiet about it, but you know the media. They'll figure it out pretty soon. Someone will leak something."

Lena sighed. "I can't face anything like that right now. I really can't."

"You won't have to," Mike assured her.

They strolled farther, stopping to look in a store window at the display of silver-and-turquoise jewelry.

"Let's go in," Mike said.

It was very beautifully crafted stuff, authentic Navajo designs. The owner was named Madeline Begay, and she was glad for someone to chat with.

"Well, the summer crowds are gone now, but there are still a few tourists, so I stay open," she told them. "My family makes the jewelry, and there are a lot of them—my mother's whole clan—so I'm always supplied with plenty of pieces.''

"Mommy, look," Kimmy said, her face glued to a glass display case.

Lena went over to her daughter to see what she was interested in.

"Look, Mommy, see?"

It was a necklace, a fine silver chain holding a tiny silver-and-turquoise bird.

"Oh, it's a bluebird, Kimmy," Lena said. "How beautiful."

Madeline Begay opened the case, took the necklace out and hung it around Kimmy's neck. "There, isn't he a nice bird?"

"Now, Kimmy," Lena started, but Mike interrupted her.

"We'll take it," he said, pulling out his wallet.

"Mike, you don't have to…" Lena began.

"I know I don't, but I want to."

"I can keep it?" Kimmy asked, wide-eyed, her hand on the tiny silver bird.

"Yes," Mike said. "It's yours."

"What do you say?" Lena asked.

"Thank you, thank you very much," Kimmy said shyly, "Daddy."

They walked back to the motel. Kimmy kept her hand on the necklace, and there was a smile on her face. When Lena next glanced down, she saw that her daughter had silently taken Mike's hand, walking between them, occasionally skipping or hopping, holding on to them both, and it seemed as natural as breathing for her.

Tears burned behind Lena's eyelids, but she blinked them back. She stole a sidelong glance at Mike; he was studiously staring straight ahead, but she could see a muscle working in his jaw. Her heart felt full, and she tried to banish any thoughts of the future. This was good enough for now—it was better than good; it was wonderful.

They had lunch, and Lena relaxed into the slow, easy pace. Mike went to his room to make some calls while Lena and Kimmy walked a block to the gas station where they'd towed her car.

"The part's on its way," the mechanic said. "Had to order it from Phoenix. Don't see too many of these around nowadays. Those old 409s were fast. Still runs good, does it?"

"Oh, it runs great," Lena said. And they swapped car stories until Kimmy grew restless.

"So you think it'll be done in a couple of days?" Lena asked while Kimmy tugged at her hand.

"Two or three, depending on how busy I get."

"Well, you know where to reach me," Lena said.

Time stretched out before them, uncluttered. There was absolutely nothing to do. It occurred to Lena that Kimmy would need to be examined by a doctor and a psychologist, but not now, not yet. For now, she just wanted to luxuriate in the peace and quiet of this special little town in the middle of nowhere.

She bought a couple of children's books in the grocery store and a paperback for herself, although she felt as if she'd fall asleep if she tried to read. Her mind and her body had slowed down, recovering from trauma.

Kimmy hadn't slowed down, though. Her natural childish exuberance and energy were reappearing as if by magic. She swung on Lena's hand, dancing, hopping. She sang one of the songs she'd learned at school, then she stopped to hold up her bluebird and admire it.

"He's a nice man," she announced on their way back to their room.

"Do you mean Mike?" Lena asked.

"My daddy," Kimmy said. "I mean my daddy." She looked up at Lena. "Not like that mean man, that Danny."

"Did Danny hurt you?" Lena asked carefully.

"No," Kimmy said, skipping, "but he yelled at me. He yelled bad stuff. At Jane, too."

"He was a very bad man," Lena said.

"I know." Kimmy nodded wisely.

Lena took a breath. Of course she and Mike had discussed when to talk to Kimberly about the movie. It was a difficult subject to bring up, and they'd decided to wait for an opening. She had one now. She only wished Mike were there, too.

She took another breath. "Kimmy, Danny wanted you to be in a movie. Did you understand about that?" *Oh, God,* she thought. How much *had* Kimmy understood?

"Uh-huh," Kimmy said, not the least bit shy or afraid. "I played hide-and-seek outside one day."

"And someone took pictures of that?"

"Uh-huh."

"And that was...all?"

"Uh-huh. I was sleepy, so Danny took me home. He wasn't even mean that day. He got me a candy bar."

"Oh," Lena said, her emotions flying between relief and anger, and she wondered if the FBI could get Danny Hayden to name the other men involved. She prayed that they could.

"Well, listen, Kimmy, if you ever want to talk about Danny and Jane, or if you remember something they did that you didn't like, you tell me, okay?"

"Okay, Mommy."

"You may have to talk to some people when we get home about it. The police, for instance. They may want to know all the things Danny did."

"Okay."

She squeezed her daughter's hand. "That's a good, brave girl, sweetie."

While Kimmy took a bubble bath that afternoon, Lena and Mike sat in her room and talked, Lena telling him that she believed the movie had never gone further than the preliminary stages. "God, I hate that Danny Hayden," she said. "I hope they lock him up and throw away the key. But, Mike, what if he tries to make a deal? You know, by ratting on the other men involved?"

"Oh, he'll probably rat, all right," Mike said. "But it won't get him anywhere on a kidnapping charge."

"You're sure?"

"Absolutely positive."

"Good," she said staunchly.

They made small talk over the sounds of Kimmy's splashing coming from the bath.

"You got all your calls made?" Lena asked.

"Yes."

"To your father and everyone?"

"Yes, Lena."

"Mmm," she said, picking up a brochure from the table and leafing through it idly. "Did you get hold of your friend, Jennifer?"

He was silent for a moment, then said, "Yes, I did."

"Mmm," Lena said again. "I imagine she must be upset. Well, you know, about your being here in Kayenta and all." *Babbling,* Lena thought, *you're babbling.*

Mike didn't reply.

"Of course it's not my business," she went on recklessly, "but I just hope it works out now, you know, what with your marriage plans and all."

Mike looked up sharply. "I never said that."

"Colleen told me."

He swore loudly, then stopped abruptly, remembering Kimmy. "It's not like we set a date or anything, for God's sake. Colleen doesn't know a damn thing about it."

"Mmm," Lena said, and she couldn't help wondering if Mike had told Jennifer everything. If the roles were reversed, would she herself have the guts to confess to a fiancé that she'd slept with her ex?

Lena sneaked a glance at him. Mike would tell all, she suddenly knew. He'd tell the truth no matter what the consequences. So what *had* Jennifer thought?

At an early supper that evening Lena was still wondering, studying him, watching how he interacted with Kimmy. He'd changed; he really had. He'd certainly changed more than *she* had. All those qualities she'd fallen in love with were still there, but the overlay of bad ones were gone. How he must have suffered, she thought. His partner dead, his drinking out of control, his wife gone with his baby daughter. He'd been totally alone, trying to deal with his pain. Oh, sure, he had his family, but the Quinn men lacked the kind of sympathetic touch Mike would have needed. They were all macho, admitting to no weaknesses, and they wouldn't have been much help at all.

It kept coming back to Lena, the feeling of guilt—she should have been there; she should have stayed with him. He'd needed her, she realized now, far too late, but she'd been unable to handle his drinking.

He didn't blame her, it seemed. His anger and his anguish appeared to be washed away, and she was so very glad for him. And she wondered whether she could forgive Mike as completely as he forgave her.

THE NEXT DAY went by as slowly and uneventfully as the first. It rained that day, though, black thunderclouds amassing to the west over the striated mesas and the stark rising remnants of ancient volcanoes. Lena read to Kimmy, sitting in bed, cuddled together. The books she'd found were Navajo stories about clever foxes and mischievous coyotes and ravens and stars in the sky.

Mike knocked on the door at lunchtime and brought them a bag of fast food, so they all ate together.

"Bob Yazzie's gotten several calls from TV stations and papers," he said.

"I knew it," Lena said dejectedly.

"He's instructed all his men to keep quiet. No comment, that sort of thing."

"Maybe the car will be fixed before they inundate the place," she said hopefully.

"How's it coming?"

"The part's here. He'll install it tomorrow. We can probably leave the next day."

"We're going home?" Kimmy asked, jumping on the bed in her stocking feet.

"In a couple of days. Stop that, Kimberly."

"I'm bo-o-ored," Kimmy said, jumping, bouncing.

"Let me take her for a while," Mike suggested.

"It's raining."

"I've got a plastic poncho with me. You get some rest."

"Why—do I look like I need it?" Lena asked.

"No, you look fine. I just thought Kimmy and I could get to know each other."

"You're going to spoil her."

"Yeah, probably." Mike grinned. "It's my pleasure."

"Come on, come on, let's go," Kimmy chanted, running to put on her shoes. "I can tie my laces," she announced proudly. "I learned to a long time ago. Grandma taught me." She sat on the floor, concentrating on the shoelaces, her mouth half-open.

"God, she's cute," Mike said.

"She seems okay, doesn't she?" Lena asked quietly. "No trauma?"

"She seems fine. Remarkably."

"I worry, you know, what something like that can do to a child."

"Sure you do. So do I."

"I'm trying not to be overprotective," she said, "but it's hard."

"Nothing like that will ever happen to her again."

"My brain knows it, but in my gut I'm still terrified. I don't want to let her out of my sight."

"You're going to have to for a little while here," he said. "For starters, anyway."

"I will. I have to. She's got to go back to school, too."

"She'll be fine."

Lena only bit her lower lip, and Mike took her hand and stroked the back of it, holding on to her fingers. "She'll be okay, Lena, and she'll probably get over the whole thing before you do."

"Kids." She gave him an uncertain smile.

"Yeah, kids."

He took Kimmy with him out into the rain, and Lena sat propped up on the bed and read the book she'd bought. The print began to swim before her eyes, and her head nodded, and the next thing she knew, there was knocking at her door and Kimmy was calling, "Mommy, Mommy, let us in!"

Her daughter danced into the room, decked out in a colorful Navajo dress with a silver concho belt and leather moccasins. Someone had even braided her long brown hair.

"My goodness!" Lena exclaimed. "We've got a real live Indian girl here."

"Isn't it pretty, Mommy? And the lady braided my hair, too."

Lena met Mike's gaze. "You're spoiling her rotten."

"I know," he said proudly.

That evening they were invited to Bob Yazzie's house for dinner. He lived within walking distance in a neat bungalow with his wife, Betty.

Lena put on one of the few as-yet-unworn articles of clothes she'd brought, a red V-neck blouse. At least it was colorful. And *clean.*

Mike knocked on the door at six, so they could walk to the Yazzies' house.

"You look fantastic," he said to Lena.

"It's not too loud?" Lena asked.

"It's perfect. You know, you had on a red blouse when I first saw you."

"When you stopped me?" she asked, surprised.

"Uh-huh."

"You remember what I had on all those years ago?" He shrugged.

She smiled, feeling her cheeks flush. "You're embarrassing me."

He met her gaze and held it. "I got you something."

"Oh, Mike…"

He dug in a pocket and took out a small white jewelry box. "Here," he said.

The box held a pair of earrings, silver-and-onyx, an intricate geometric design. Lena drew in her breath.

"I thought they looked like you," he said matter-of-factly.

"Mike," she whispered, and she felt an odd melting sensation, as if her insides were liquefying and flowing, warm and soft and joyful. "You're spoiling both of us."

"I'm enjoying the hell out of it," he said. "Making up for lost time."

A pang of guilt stabbed at Lena again, but she put it aside. This interlude could only be lived in the present, no anxiety about the future, no recriminations from the past. Only *now*. Her daughter, safe and sound, and Mike, her bastion against the outside world. "Thank you," she said, her eyes brimming.

"Put them on," he said, his blue eyes fastened on her, very serious, very intent.

She put the earrings on, looking in the mirror, then turned around. "What do you think?"

"You look pretty, Mommy," Kimmy said.

"Thanks, sweetie."

But Mike was silent, his gaze devouring her, until she had to turn away and make a big fuss putting Kimmy's jacket on over her Navajo dress.

Dinner at the Yazzies' was very pleasant. No exotic Indian food, but meat loaf and mashed potatoes and gravy, with ice cream for dessert.

"This is such a treat," Lena said. "Home cooking after days and days of restaurant food. Thank you so much."

"You sure are looking better than that first time I saw you at the gas station," Bob said bluntly.

"I must have been a sorry sight."

"You sure were."

"Bob, you're insulting our guest," Betty said.

"Oh, no, he's right, and I guess it was a good thing, because he noticed me. He remembered," Lena said.

Kimmy fell asleep on the Yazzies' couch, and Mike carried her all the way back to the motel.

"She's heavy," he said.

"I haven't carried her in years," Lena said. "She got too heavy for me when she was three, I think."

He shifted the sleeping child in his arms. "I kind of enjoy carrying her."

"She likes you, Mike," Lena ventured.

"Yeah, she seems to," he allowed. "She's a great kid. You did a good job with her."

Lena ducked her head. "It would have been better to have had her father around," she murmured.

"Well, she has him around now."

When they reached the motel, Mike came in with Lena and laid Kimmy on her bed.

"Thanks," Lena said.

He seemed reluctant to leave, standing there, so big in the small motel room. "This has been nice," he said finally, "this time together."

She nodded wordlessly.

"It's going to be over soon," he went on, "but I hope you'll let me see Kimmy when we get home."

"Of course I will, Mike."

"That's good. And you, too, Lena. I'll see you, and I don't want... I'd like it to be friendly between us."

Friendly. "I don't see why not."

"Good. Well, see you tomorrow."

BY THE FOLLOWING afternoon, Lena's car was repaired. It was too late to start that day, so they made plans to leave early the next morning. Lena called her mother to tell her, and Mike called his family and Joe Carbone at work. They ate their last dinner in Kayenta in the Holiday Inn dining room, which had become very familiar to them by now. The waitress knew their names and suggested menu items for Kimmy.

Lena was both anxious to get on the road, to get home, to take up the reins of her job again, and at the same time a little afraid of the new route her life was going to take. Not only would she have to deal with any problems her daughter might have, but she'd also have to deal with Mike in her life again.

After dinner they took a walk, said goodbye to Bob Yazzie and his wife, then watched TV in the motel lobby while Kimmy colored in a book on the floor. Peaceful, quiet, relaxing hours and minutes. But these were the last easy hours—tomorrow it would all end.

Lena said good-night to Mike at the door to her room, tucked Kimmy into bed and turned the TV set on low while she changed into her pajamas and brushed her teeth. The whole time her mind was working, though. The one thing that was still a wedge in her newfound friendship with Mike was the apology she truly did owe him. She'd basked in this interlude, this protective cocoon here in Kayenta, and she'd avoided talking to him, coming clean.

She rinsed her mouth and stared at herself in the mirror, painfully aware of Mike next door, painfully aware of the need to bare her soul.

She left the bathroom, and in the dimness of the bedroom she threw on her jeans and a shirt, then pulled open her side of the double doors to Mike's room and stuck the room key in her pocket. She glanced at Kimmy, who was fast asleep, and then let herself out and stood before Mike's door. She lifted her hand and knocked softly. *Crazy,* she thought. *This might be a crazy idea.*

Maybe she should do this another time. *I hope he's asleep*, she was thinking, but he opened the door before she completed the thought.

"Something wrong?" he asked. He was in his boxer shorts, no shirt, his blond hair mussed.

"Oh, I'm sorry. You were asleep," Lena said, backing away. "I'll..."

"Are you okay?"

"Yes, sure, no problem. I just wanted to... I'll, uh, go to bed now."

"Come in," he said, reaching out to draw her into the room.

She was terribly ill at ease, knowing she never should have done this. Good Lord, what had she been thinking?

But Mike was sitting on the edge of his bed and running a hand through his hair. He looked up and said, "What is it, Lena?"

She stood there, in a room that smelled distinctly, uniquely, of this man, feeling lost and frightened and very foolish. "I'm sorry. I shouldn't have—"

He cut her off. "What's on your mind?"

"I...well..." *Oh, God.*

He stared at her, his eyes in shadow, backlit only by a lamp on his night table. "Come on, Lena, I know you. Something's bugging you. Come here." He held a hand out.

She went to him, not knowing what else to do. She sat next to him on the bed, stiff, her hands clasped on her lap, her shoulders tense. "I wanted to apologize, Mike. I was wrong. And it's hard for me to admit that, but I was wrong all these years. I should have let you be part of Kimmy's life. I was selfish and..."

"That's what was bugging you?" he asked.

"Yes." She looked down at her hands, her shoulders hunched.

"Ah, Lena," he said, his voice a low caress.

"It was because of my father, I guess. His drinking...and then he was so sick...and I couldn't face it all over again. I was so scared, Mike."

"I know," he said. He took her hand, stroking the smooth underside of her wrist. "And I owe you an apology, too. For what I did to you, to our marriage."

"But then you changed, Mike, and I didn't. I just went on being..."

"That's all over now," he said. "It's all over, Lena."

"Is it, Mike?"

"Yeah, it is."

He drew her close, and she laid her head on his bare shoulder, drawing in his scent, feeling his warmth and the smooth hardness of him. His heart beat beneath her ear, slow and steady, and she put her hand on his chest to feel it. He kissed her then, a long, slow mingling of their mouths. He pulled back and looked at her. "You know how long I've been wanting this? Every night. I almost knocked on your door every night."

"Maybe you should have."

"I had no right."

She pulled his head down and pressed her lips to his, sipping the sweet nectar of his mouth, and his arms encircled her, crushing her softly. Her heart raced, and a slow heat began to burn inside her. She moaned with her need, and he laid her on the bed, stroking her face, her neck, bending to kiss her, trailing fire with his mouth, unbuttoning her shirt.

Her hands couldn't get enough of touching him, her mouth of tasting him. She felt whole in his closeness. Her jeans kicked off, her shirt trailing off one arm, she ran her hands up his back to the hair at the base of his neck, then down to his buttocks, pushing at the waist of his shorts, feeling his hardness pressing into her belly.

"Now," she whispered. "Please, now." There was no shame, no holding back, nothing but nearness and slick hot skin under her hands as he rose above her and into her, and her breath stopped in her throat for a moment, then caught and she was breathing again.

"Is it good?" he asked, his voice a rasp.

"Yes, yes, yes," she replied, and he rolled, pulling her with him, so that she was on top, raising and lowering herself. She felt ready to explode, but he moved once again, and she was beneath him, and he plunged into her, wild with his own need, again and again.

Something inside her burst, and she felt her body bucking under him, and her voice cried out.

He thrust into her once more, then groaned and convulsed over her, spilling his essence, and then he collapsed onto her, breathing fast, heavy, warm and damp and hard muscled.

Lena lay there, her chest rising and falling under Mike's weight, and nothing mattered just then—not tomorrow and not yesterday. It was, she guessed, just one more moment of her strange interlude. And then she closed her eyes, wallowing in the sensation of his body on hers, and let herself feel her own remorse and relief and love.

CHAPTER NINETEEN

WITHIN HOURS OF returning home, Lena was assailed by the media, with satellite vans in front of her house, reporters with video cameras and microphones at all hours of the day and night, incessant phone calls. The Woodland Hills police finally blocked off the street and tried to keep the vans away. She changed her phone number, never went out without sunglasses and a hat and tried desperately to keep Kimmy insulated from the firestorm of publicity.

Still, she was treated to the sight of herself on the local news, slinking around, or Mike or Gloria or Kimmy caught with a telescopic lens, strangely wavering, disembodied by dancing electronic spots.

"Never talk to strangers" became a mantra that her daughter heard every day.

The furor died a natural death after several weeks and, except for one offer of a TV movie, Lena's world eventually settled down.

Kimmy was back in school, and her teacher had met with Lena. So far Kimmy seemed fine, but they were all keeping a very close eye on her.

Miss Trenholm had asked for parent volunteers to patrol the school playground after school, and the program was so successful that other elementary schools in the district were adopting it. Nevertheless, Gloria picked Kimmy up the minute classes were over. She got there so early that her granddaughter began to complain that she didn't get to play with her friends.

Lena had taken Kimmy to her pediatrician, who'd declared her perfectly healthy, which made Lena heave a giant sigh of relief. The doctor had nonetheless recommended a child psychologist, and Kimmy went once a week, just in case.

"She's an amazingly resilient little girl," the psychologist told Lena. "I don't think there'll be any lasting effects. Just make sure she has the opportunity to talk about her experience without feeling uncomfortable."

They saw Mike quite a bit. He visited; he ate dinner with them a couple of times a week; and sometimes, on weekends, Lena drove to Santa Monica to the salmon-colored apartment building where Mike lived. Kimmy loved it, as it was only a block from the beach.

"She's fine," Mike said one Sunday afternoon, "isn't she?"

They were sitting in the sun by the beach promenade, watching all the in-line skaters, the bicyclers, the teenagers with purple hair and nose rings. Kimmy was watching a juggler, fascinated.

"She seems to be fine," Lena replied.

"I swear she's grown since we got back."

"She needs new shoes already," Lena said, "and I just got her some before school started."

"You want me to take her shopping for them?"

"No, really, I wasn't hinting around, Mike," Lena said, laughing.

"I put money in an account every month for Kimmy, you know," he said. "You wouldn't take anything from me, so I just put it away. It's there, Lena, whenever she needs it."

"Oh, Mike," she breathed. "We're doing okay. You don't have to…"

"She's my daughter, and I should be supporting her."

They'd had this argument many times over the past month. She was distinctly uncomfortable with the notion of Mike supporting Kimmy, and he was getting more and more frustrated at being shut out.

"I told you, save it for her college education," Lena said.

"I'll get her those shoes," Mike growled. "Maybe even two or three pairs."

"Oh, for goodness' sake." Lena sighed.

"Okay, okay, we'll discuss it later."

Lena turned her face up into the warm November sun and thought about the tentative relationship they had. When they'd first gotten home after Kimmy's ordeal it had somehow been easier between them. But then, she knew, that had been before Mike's breakup with Jennifer. He never told her the details, but he had sat at dinner in her house one evening and said, "I saw Jenn last night. We had an honest talk and decided it wasn't going to work."

Lena had looked up. "God, is it my fault? I mean…"

"Absolutely not," he'd said. "It's my fault if anyone's. In retrospect, it would never have worked out anyway. We were oil and water."

He'd left it at that, and a part of Lena had rejoiced, while another part had withdrawn in fear. And since then she simply didn't know how to feel. She was on an emotional tightrope.

Unspoken, but always in the forefront of their thoughts, was their daughter's welfare. Neither, it was understood, would do anything to jeopardize that.

"How's work?" Lena asked, switching to a safer subject.

"It's okay. I'm supposed to go up to San Francisco next month to do a seminar."

"That's good, Mike."

"I'd like you to meet Joe one of these days," he said. "He's been hearing a lot about you lately."

"Anytime." *Oh, Lord,* she thought, it was as if he were asking her to meet his family. *Dangerous.*

"Maybe we can all get together next week. There's a restaurant near here, sort of halfway between your place and his."

"Fine. I'd like to."

"My treat," Mike said.

That night after dinner Lena spoke to her mother.

"Yes, everything's fine," Lena said. "We're getting along fine. Kimmy adores him."

"So what's going to happen next?" Gloria asked.

"Next? The same thing. It's working very nicely. We meet, Kimmy enjoys herself, we go home to separate places, everything's great."

"You two can't go on like this."

"Why not?"

"Because it's not natural, honey."

"Oh, Mom."

"Okay, don't listen to me, but something's got to give sooner or later."

"Don't hold your breath, Mom."

But Lena had to admit that it was becoming harder and harder to keep Mike at arm's length, to stay neutral. It was so natural to want to touch him, to accept his chaste good-night kiss and wish for more, to confide in him. Watching Kimmy climb all over him, pull on his arms, kiss him with big smacks on his cheek, was wonderful, but his face, his whole demeanor, changed when he spoke to Lena. Then he was guarded, and the easy affection was transformed into stiff courtesy. Oh, how Lena would have loved to see him turn his open, boyish grin onto her.

Their last passionate meeting was a taboo subject. Yet it had happened, and just as the psychologist told Lena that Kimmy needed to deal with what happened, Lena knew the time of reckoning would come. The time when they'd both have to deal with the results of their actions.

The only certain things in Lena's life were her daughter and the clear knowledge that her love for Mike was like a delicate spring bud, dormant for so long and yet ripening with each passing day. She was terrified that it might blossom, yet thrilled at the same time. She wondered constantly, too, how he felt. Did he dream of her?

The dinner with Joe Carbone turned out to be a big affair. All the Quinns were there, and Mike had reserved a private room in the restaurant for the crowd. They all ate barbecued spareribs, a messy but cheerful meal, with paper bibs and sticky fingers.

"You're good for Mike," Joe told her after the meal was under way. "He's a happy guy these days."

She liked Joe—he was as bald as a billiard ball, with terrific character lines on his face. "Oh, I don't think it's me. It's Kimmy," she told him.

"Don't be too sure about that, little lady."

She smiled politely but didn't dare believe a word Joe said. It was good to see all the Quinns together, although they drank a lot of beer. But for once she didn't have to worry about Mike—he had plain old soda with a lemon wedge in it.

The only rough spot in the evening came when Colleen arrived just after dessert. Lena's heart clenched—Mike's nosy sister had to realize what had gone on between them. She was, after all, Jennifer's friend. But she said hello to Lena politely, and Lena wondered if Mike had lectured her. It didn't matter, really, because Lena and Mike had every right to be friends. Or so Lena told herself—friends.

Later, as Lena got into her car, Mike was there, leaning down to the open window. "Thanks for coming," he said. "Everyone enjoyed seeing you."

"It was a great evening, Mike. Thanks. And I like Joe a lot."

"Yeah, he's a good guy." He paused, then said, "You drive carefully, hear?"

"Yes, Officer," she replied pertly.

He smiled and raised a brow. "Tell Kimmy," he said, "that we'll do something on Sunday, okay? Saturday's out—got that basketball game with the guys."

"Okay," she said.

He reached in the window then and drew the back of his hand across her cheek. "See you Sunday."

"Uh-huh," she got out, her throat closing.

On Sunday he arrived with a new Barbie doll for Kimmy.

"You've got to stop this," Lena scolded.

"Do I tell you what to do? Let me be, Lena," he said, and the whole afternoon, while he was out with Kimmy at a movie, Lena kept wondering why she was pushing him away. Was she hiding from the truth, in denial?

The following Saturday she had to work. Normally Gloria would have watched Kimmy, but this time Mike was free and offered to take her for the whole day. He had big plans—they were going to Disneyland.

"Is it okay with you," he asked Lena, "if I take my

Adopt-a-Buddy along, too? Jay's a good kid, and he could use some fun.''

"Sure. It'll be good for Kimmy to share you with someone for a change.''

"I'll pick her up early, okay? Around eight.''

"You sure you can handle two kids all day at Disneyland?''

"If I can run a hostage negotiation, I'll bet I can manage two kids.''

Lena only grinned.

That day she got her work done, then did her grocery shopping on the way home. She even cleaned her house, not used to so much time on her hands. She cooked dinner, not sure whether Kimmy would eat out or not—Swedish meatballs and new red potatoes.

She heard Mike's car stop outside at a little past six, then Kimmy burst into the house, full of stories.

"Mommy, we rode all the rides, and we did the Small Small World one twice, and I saw Mickey Mouse, and the spaceship rocked like we were taking off, Mommy.''

"Wow. Sounds like you had a good time.''

Mike came in then, his shoulders sagging. She gave him a glance, then said, "You look beat.''

"I am. They ran me ragged.''

"I warned you.''

"And, Mommy,'' Kimmy went on, "Jay wasn't bad at all. He held my hand when I got scared in the spaceship.''

"That's wonderful,'' Lena said. "Did you guys eat?''

"She ate enough to feed an army,'' Mike said.

"Junk, I suppose.''

"Sure, lots of junk.'' He shrugged tiredly.

"What about you?''

"The cotton candy did me in, but some real food might revive me."

Kimmy nibbled at a meatball, still talking about her adventures. "The jungle ride was so cool, Mommy, and all the animals jumped out at me. Jay thought it was funny." But she was winding down, her eyes getting that glazed look of utter exhaustion.

"She's on overload," Lena said to Mike.

"What's that, Mommy?"

"You're tired," Lena replied. "I can tell."

"I'm not, I'm not."

They put Kimmy to bed early. Mike read her a story while Lena did the dishes, an inadvertent smile on her face as she listened to Mike's voice coming from down the hall.

He emerged from Kimmy's room, shutting the door quietly. "She's out," he said.

"Thanks for taking her. I never got around to it. I kept thinking I was going to, but, you know...."

"Sure, I know. You're busy."

They sat at the kitchen table across from each other. The house was silent. Mike sipped at a cup of coffee, and Lena rubbed at some crumbs she'd missed on the tabletop.

He broke the silence with a surprising suggestion. "I was wondering," he said hesitantly, "if we should consider moving in together. For Kimmy. All this commuting back and forth, well, it must be confusing for her."

Lena's heart gave a lurch, then settled down to beat slowly, turgidly. She couldn't meet his eyes. "I don't know, Mike, I..."

"I thought we could ask Kimmy about it first."

"She's only a little kid. I'm not sure it'd be good to put so much on her head," she fumbled.

"It was a thought."

Silence fell between them again, and Lena still felt her heart beating too heavily. He'd caught her off guard, completely off guard. And yet... Wasn't this the most honest he'd been since Kimmy's abduction?

She could barely face it, barely even begin to examine her feelings. *Don't deny* ran through her brain. *Talk to him. Be truthful.* But what was the truth?

"Well, what do you think?"

Be honest. Don't be a coward.

"I...I'm not sure. Do you think it could work?" She dared to meet his gaze.

"We could make it work," he said softly.

"God, Mike, it scares me to think about it. You know..."

"Sure I know."

"I've made a good life for myself. I've worked so hard. Mike, I can't go through it again and start over. I don't have it in me anymore."

"Believe me, I understand. But sometimes you have to take a risk, Lena, to get something better. Joe taught me that."

She clasped her hands together tightly. "I don't know."

He leaned toward her. "I'd never hurt you or Kimmy. That's a promise."

She looked at him hard, and she knew suddenly that more than anything in the world, she wanted this man. She'd always wanted him. Wanted her family together. Her heart felt as if it had shattered, too fragile to stand up to so much pressure all at once. She bit her lip and could say nothing.

Mike finally leaned back in his chair. "Well, think

about it. There's plenty of time." He pushed the chair back and stood up, stretching. "I'd better go, I guess."

She wanted so much to say, *Stay, hold me, love me, be with me,* but she was held immobile. *Coward,* she thought. *Sniveling coward.*

He came around the table and took her hand. "You'll think about it?"

"Yes, I will," she breathed, and she offered no resistance when he carefully brought her to her feet and held her against him.

"Promise?" he asked, his breath tickling her ear.

"Yes," she whispered.

He tilted her face up and brushed her lips with his. She couldn't fight it. She sighed and opened to him as he kissed her deeply, his tongue searching out the sweetness of her mouth.

He pulled back then, leaving her afloat without a life preserver, alone, chilled. She shivered.

"I'd better not start something I can't finish," he said with a wry smile.

She tried to smile back. "Drive carefully," she said, a sad substitute for the feelings that were locked in her heart.

"Uh-huh."

"Good night."

"Bolt the door after me."

"I will."

"Good night, Lena."

Later, as she drifted into sleep, a realization came to her out of the blue, something she hadn't considered or thought about or paid any attention to in the last month. She was late; she hadn't gotten her period last month.

MIKE QUINN REMEMBERED the day with utter clarity. It was a cool, drizzly November evening; he'd had a tough day, talking down a desperate man who'd lost his job and was holding his family hostage, threatening to kill them and himself. Mike had succeeded, but it had been a long, hard battle, and he'd had to call on every ounce of empathy and training he had in him.

All he wanted was to flop down in front of the TV set, put some food in his mouth to stave off his stomach's growling, then go to bed.

He saw the blinking red eye of his answering machine, and he was tempted to ignore it till morning, but there was always the possibility it was Kimmy—and she couldn't wait.

He pressed the replay button and stood, one shoulder against the wall, his arms folded, while he waited for the message to play.

It was Lena. "Please call me, Mike. It's important." That was all. Not even her name, but of course he knew her voice. And she'd sounded strange, upset maybe—or just tense. Had she made a decision about their living together? If so, her tone of voice did not bode well for him. Or, God forbid, had something happened to Kimmy?

He dialed her number quickly, worried. She answered as if she'd been waiting for the call. "Hello?"

"Lena, it's me. What…?"

"Oh, Mike, I'm so glad you called."

"What is it? Is Kimmy okay?"

"Yes, she's fine. It's not Kimmy. Oh, Mike…"

"For God's sake, what is it?"

There was a moment of absolute silence on the line, and Mike just had time to feel his hand on the receiver growing slick with sweat, when she spoke. Two simple words in a flat tone: "I'm pregnant."

He must have heard her wrong. "What?" he said.

"Mike, I'm pregnant."

This time the meaning sank in. Lena was pregnant. With his child. Lena was...

"Mike, are you there?"

"I...I'm not sure." He took a deep breath, feelings batting around inside his head like a cageful of agitated birds. "Wow."

"What are we going to do? What do you...?"

"I'm coming over," he said in a rush. "I'm not discussing this over the goddamn phone, Lena."

"You're angry. Oh, Mike, I knew you'd be angry. I'm sorry, I...I..."

"I'm not angry, Lena. I'm in shock."

"I didn't know what to do."

"You did the right thing, and I'll be there in half an hour. Don't move."

"Okay."

"Listen, I'll be more coherent by the time I get there—I swear I will."

"You're not upset?"

"Are you kidding?" he asked, then he hung up, his weariness forgotten. He grabbed the sport coat that he'd just thrown on a chair and strode out to his car.

All the way across Los Angeles, his mind churned with the news. It must have been that last night in Kayenta, he figured. He'd never thought, never considered. God, they'd acted like irresponsible teenagers! He should have... But he was fiercely glad it had happened, more than glad. Elated. He realized there was a dumb grin on his face, and it wouldn't go away.

Lena pregnant. A baby. His baby, his and Lena's. A little sister or brother for Kimmy.

It all seemed so simple to him. He loved Lena and she

was having his child—hell, she already had one of his children—and there really wasn't much else he could do about it but marry her. Sure. Marry her *again*. Only this time, it'd stick.

Of course Lena might have other ideas. She was one stubborn, independent lady now, no pushover. His joy faded for a moment. What if she didn't love him and didn't want to marry him?

Well, he'd damn well convince her. Those kids of his needed a father.

Convince Lena? he thought. *Good luck.*

He was a nervous wreck by the time he pulled up in front of her house. She opened the door just as he got to it and stood there looking at him. Her eyes were red. She'd been crying.

He took her arm and steered her inside, closing the door behind him. He'd decided to come on strong right from the first, to brook no dissent. He was the child's *father,* for God's sake.

"We're getting married," he said firmly. "Lena, I've thought about it, and it's the only thing to do, and damn it, I don't want any argument about it."

"Married," she said faintly.

"Yes, married. You know, with a ring, in the church, all the folks there. So your kids have their father."

She looked at him for a breath of time, then whispered, "Okay."

"What?"

"I said okay."

"So, it's a deal?" he said, his gaze on her disbelievingly.

"It's a deal," she breathed.

He held his arms out, and she came to him, nestling there as if they'd never been apart. He kissed away her tears. "I never thought I'd be so lucky a second time," he said softly.

"We have to tell Kimmy. I haven't said a word to her. I was worried you'd... Well, that it wouldn't work out."

"Where is she?"

"In her room coloring. I didn't even tell her I'd called you or that you were coming over."

"We'd better face her, don't you think?"

Lena nodded.

They went to Kimmy's room together, holding hands.

"Hi, Daddy," Kimmy said, looking up from the floor where she knelt amid her crayons.

"Hi, sweetheart. Mommy and I have something to tell you."

Kimmy waited, her big brown eyes on him.

"Well, see, your mother is going to have a baby, and so we thought we'd get married."

Kimmy thought a moment, then she said guilelessly, "I'd like a little sister to play with."

Mike and Lena looked at each other. "Is that all you have to say?" Lena asked.

Kimmy considered the question, her brows coming together. "Well, I guess a brother would be okay."

Mike looked at Lena; she stood there, her hand over her mouth, baffled. Then she gave a little hiccup of laughter and put a hand on his arm, trying to say something, but she was laughing too hard. And then he was laughing, too, and Kimmy was watching them, puzzled, but they couldn't stop, and everything good and worthwhile in the world was right there in that room.

His family.

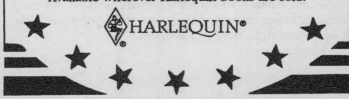

HARLEQUIN SUPERROMANCE®

Welcome back to the Silver Dollar Ranch,
near Tombstone, Arizona. Home of the
Bodine men—and their wives.

She's the Sheriff (#787)
by Anne Marie Duquette

Virgil Bodine. He's the oldest brother. One-time sheriff of
Tombstone and former bodyguard to the stars. He's come
home from California with his reluctant ten-year-old son in
tow.

Desiree Hartlan. She's a member of the extended Bodine
family—his brother Wyatt's sister-in-law. She's also a DA
who's talked herself out of a job…and is looking for a new
one.

The position of sheriff is open. When Desiree decides to
run, Virgil runs against her.

Next thing he knows, he's calling her sheriff. And boss.
And…wife?

Available May 1998 at your favorite retail outlet.

HARLEQUIN SUPERROMANCE®

Bestselling author
Ruth Jean Dale brings back

THE CAMERONS OF COLORADO

Cupid, Colorado...

This is ranch country, cowboy country. Land is important—family and neighbors are, too. And you really get to know your neighbors here. Like the Camerons, for instance...

Jason Cameron—ex-rodeo star and all-around ladies' man—has come home to Cupid. His friends and fellow bachelors aren't pleased because Jason is just too much competition on the romance front, charming all the women in the county, young and old. They figure Jason needs to fall for *one* woman and leave the rest alone.

And he does. He falls for Diana Kennedy and falls hard. She's a newcomer who's just bought the local honky-tonk bar. Sparks might fly between them, but Diana's not sure she wants them setting any fires.

Call it CUPID'S REVENGE! (#788)

Available May 1998 at your favorite retail outlet.

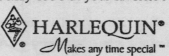

HARLEQUIN SUPERROMANCE®

COMING NEXT MONTH

#786 A FATHER'S HEART • Karen Young
Family Man
Daniel Kendrick wants the one thing he can never have: his
children. Thanks to the testimony of Tessa Hamilton at his
custody hearing, he's a marked man. Now his daughter has
run away to the uneasy streets of the Big Easy. The only
person who can help him find her is...Tessa Hamilton, and
Tessa has begun to have second thoughts about Daniel. Could
she have been wrong all those years ago?

#787 SHE'S THE SHERIFF • Anne Marie Duquette
Home on the Ranch
Virgil Bodine is the onetime sheriff of Tombstone, Arizona,
and a former bodyguard to the stars. Sick of Hollywood life,
he's come home, his reluctant ten-year-old son in tow.
Desiree Harlan is a former Phoenix D.A.—she talked herself
out of one job and is looking for another. Tombstone needs a
new sheriff, and Desiree decides to run. So does Virgil. Next
thing he knows, he's calling her sheriff. And boss. And...
wife?

#788 CUPID'S REVENGE • Ruth Jean Dale
The Camerons of Colorado
Jason Cameron, ex-rodeo champion and all-around ladies'
man, is back in Cupid, Colorado. Jason's friends and fellow
ranchers consider him too much competition on the romance
front; they want him to fall for *one* woman and leave the rest
for them. He does. He falls for newcomer Diana Kennedy
and he falls hard. There are plenty of sparks flying between
them, but Diana's not sure she wants any of them to catch!

#789 THE FAMILY NEXT DOOR • Janice Kay Johnson
Count on a Cop
Judith Kane moves to a small obscure town for one reason—
safety. She's afraid of her ex-husband, afraid for her children.
So she moves to Mud River, Washington—right next door to
a cop. But Chief Ben McKinsey doesn't *want* a family next
door. He doesn't want to get involved with an attractive
woman like Judith—or her kids. But they seem to need help,
and who can you count on if you can't count on a cop?